LAST DAYS
IN
SHANGHAI

LAST DAYS IN SHANGHAI

{A NOVEL}

CASEY WALKER

COUNTERPOINT | BERKELEY, CALIFORNIA

This book is a work of fiction. Names, characters, places, and incidents either are
products of the author's imagination or are used fictitiously. Any resemblance to actual
events or locales or persons, living or dead, is entirely coincidental.

Library of Congress Cataloging-in-Publication Data

Walker, Casey, 1980–
Last Days in Shanghai : a novel / Casey Walker.
pages cm

ISBN 978-1-61902-430-4 (hardback)
1. Americans—China—Fiction. 2. Corruption—Fiction. 3. Political fiction.
4. Suspense fiction. I. Title.
PS3623.A35886L37 2014
813'.6—dc23
2014014419
ISBN 978-1-61902-430-4

Cover design by Jason Snyder
Interior Design by E. J. Strongin, Neuwirth & Associates, Inc.

Counterpoint Press
2560 Ninth Street, Suite 318
Berkeley, CA 94710
www.counterpointpress.com

Printed in the United States of America
Distributed by Publishers Group West

10 9 8 7 6 5 4 3 2 1

To Mom, Dad, Karen & Hazel—

We tend to take the speech of a Chinese for inarticulate gurgling.

Someone who understands Chinese will recognize *language* in what he hears.

Similarly I often cannot discern the *humanity* in a man.

Ludwig Wittgenstein, Culture and Value

DAY 1

BEIJING

WE FLEW BUSINESS class for nearly a day on a packed and pork-smelling China Eastern Airlines jet, chasing back the sunset. Ambien and all the in-flight Harry Potter movies, my companions. When I fell asleep, I was pursued by wizards and schoolchildren with the powers of the devil. Strange how much of life you spend wishing it would only pass, faster, even faster.

Our driver from the Beijing airport wore white gloves and a bellhop's cap. A drifting April haze gave the city a gray tint, with dark and shapeless buildings that blurred out on the horizon even as we approached them. My first city view was from our Buick, at a stoplight: fifteen construction cranes strapped to naked three-quarter buildings, many of which looked too tall already to support themselves. I followed one up as far as I could see until the smog and sunshine swallowed it.

"See it, Luke?" my boss said, pointing. "The national bird of China."

"What's that?" I said.

"The construction crane," he said.

I'd heard him try this joke around the office in the days before we left. I'd heard all his bits. I made a laugh anyway. Congressman Leonard

Fillmore—Republican, California, Fifty-First Congressional District—self-styled Asia hand, now embarked on his first visit to mainland China. He was a presidential hopeful with a familial claim to the office: Leo Fillmore was a distant relation of the thirteenth president of the United States, one of the least distinguished in our history. Nearing sixty, Leo looked to me much older, probably from carrying twice his body weight in grudge and grievance. To his friends he was sometimes known as "Leo the Lion." But the nickname had spread far and wide among his enemies, too—you could hear it whispered up and down the Rayburn Building corridors: "Leo the Lyin."

"Who do we see at the whatever the fuck? Trade people, right?" the congressman said. "I'm fucking starving."

I reached into my messenger bag for our schedule. The bag, the nicest thing I owned, was a beautiful dark leather piece of work my ex-girlfriend Alex had given me on my twenty-third birthday. I never gave her, in our whole relationship, anything half as thoughtful. Two weeks ago, I'd turned twenty-four, but we hadn't spoken. I pulled out every piece of paper, sorting through shape-shifting documents, looking for a schedule I was certain I had. Apparently, no. The congressman turned, as much as he could in his seat belt, to give me a shriveling stare. I didn't acknowledge it. I'd once been more afraid of Leo. I had once been more respectful. Now we just bickered, like he did with his wife—except that she still loved him, possibly.

"You've lost the schedule, Mr. Slade?"

He called me "Mr." only when he was being condescending.

"Everything got scattered when I came through customs," I said. I'd had to dig deep to find my passport, detained for additional questioning while Leo had already scampered to the bathroom.

"Unbelievable," he said.

I pulled out my loaner phone and was alarmed to find it had no working signal. Our phones, like the trip, had been provided to us by a real estate firm called Bund International, a Chinese-American joint venture whose

American face was a benefactor of Leo's named Armand Lightborn. We had a five-day itinerary. The pace would be a horse race, and our ever-changing appointments were basically written in water. To be uncontactable was a piss-poor beginning. I shoved my phone and papers back into my bag and found a handwritten note on stationary someone had filched from the Savoy Hotel in London. When I recognized the scrawl, I felt it in my gums, like a dentist's needle. It belonged to Leo's wife.

> Luke—
> Make sure he takes his meds.
> No booze.
> No whores.
> I'm serious.
>
> xx,
> Theresa
>
> P.S. Daily updates.

MEN IN ORANGE vests—in groups of ten, and there were tens of these groups—were planting weeping willows and begonias by the road. The congressman watched from behind our tinted glass, and at the pivotal moment when workers balanced a hulking tree and began to tilt it into a pit big enough for its roots, I lost his attention. I was spared his annoyance.

"Hardworking," the Congressman said. "It's funny, I don't see Communists. I don't see people expecting the state will do everything for them. You have to give them credit."

I waited to respond. It was a safe bet more was coming.

"Of course, it's all for naught, isn't it?" he said.

The "naught" hit my ear flatly—such a false note, as though to be deliberately antiquated was the lone prerequisite to seriousness.

"China could be a superpower, and who could compete?" he said. "But right now it's all built on sand."

He weighed his words for another second. He could sometimes be caught in the act of thinking, which is a rarer quality among the elected than one hopes. But it was the ruts and certainties where his thinking left him that disappointed me. Leo was a Republican cul-de-sac on which there stood three churches: anti-tax, business-anything, and Jesus Christ.

"It profits little, you know, to gain the world and lose the soul," he said. He reached into a corner of his eye and flicked out an invisible crust.

"Christ," he added. Whether he meant that as an endorsement of the Messiah or a curse, I couldn't say. We spent so much time with each other that he sometimes talked to himself like he was alone. He'd get annoyed when I answered his rhetorical questions, but he'd snap at me, too, if I ignored some pearl of wisdom for which he awaited praise.

"You're absolutely right," I said.

Leo turned his back to me and hunched over, bulging his shoulder blades out into the space of the middle seat between us. I cracked his neck then started kneading my knuckles into his back.

I'd worked for him nearly two years. Leo gave me my first job out of college, my first paid work anywhere, if you didn't count summers at my dad's office reorganizing the law library. My second day in Congress, Leo took a call from a legislator who'd won a few presidential primaries, and for all I knew I was sitting at the center of the world. It stirred all my aspirational feelings. Still, I was under no illusions about my hiring. My father had arranged the interview, only weeks before he'd died.

My father and Leo had been five years apart in school, nodding acquaintances in a small town. The passing years, and their professional lives, had slowly entwined the two men, though my father's political interests always remained strictly bounded. The national squabbles bored him, but he'd staked a tribal claim to our corner of California, the deep southeast where the state turned from coastal cities to lettuce and feedlots. The way our district was drawn, all our previous congressional representatives were from the suburbs of San Diego, so my father had seen Leo in a simple light: a local, and good for our desert town. Every year in the blistering heat of Fourth of July, my father's law firm hosted a huge fundraiser for the congressman. He'd turned out to be right about the benefits. Our town rejoiced in the jobs when Leo steered us prisons and slaughterhouses. Even before I'd worked for our congressman, I'd spent more time around him than I had with some of my cousins and uncles, and I knew him at least as well as I had ever known my grandparents.

I don't know what ends my father envisioned for my nascent political life—we were never able to discuss it—but I did know it was his name that gave me a start. Soon after, he'd been sapped by a cancer that was assumed to be slow and unthreatening but was not. Leo, to his credit, had helped me adjust to the long shadow of loss. To me, it wasn't a question of my emerging from the shadow. What was perhaps possible was adaptation to a life with dampened colors, where every object felt cooler to the touch. More than once, in those first months, Leo had paid for a plane ticket, or arranged work for me in the district office, so I could be closer to home. I owed him that much.

But for a long time now, I'd been creeping toward pessimism about my work. Perhaps it was still just missing my father—a pessimism about the world at large. I'd told Leo it was time for me to move on. I did not tell him his office was a constant reminder of death. In response, Leo promised that if I would stay just one more year, he could find me a position with one of his foundation contacts, something gentle and gloriously funded. "Arts outreach. Or humanitarian shit. Twice the pay," he'd said. "How happy would that make you?" I wasn't sure that happiness was on the table, but I wasn't opposed to the amelioration of suffering.

Among my current duties—unmentioned when I'd been hired—was to loosen up the pinched muscles near Leo's spine and work out the painful bended kink in what the doctor called his "frozen shoulder." When this first started, I'd emailed friends (other assistants, all of us) about this mission creep from legislative aide to part-time masseuse. They had no sympathy. They'd all done worse. One aide had written, uncredited, her boss's entire book on leadership and the importance of integrity in public life. Another was required every morning to prick his boss's finger and run the diabetes blood check, and when it was time for the shot of insulin to be administered, it was an assistant—it was one of us—with untrained hands planted on the furry lower back of the member of Congress. We retrieved enema kits and scheduled colonoscopies. We were next to our bosses when their doctors delivered the results of biopsies. We lied to their wives. We flattered their children. We made airport pickups at Dulles and brought along ice chests stocked with their favorite sodas and snacks. And we had, some of us, driven to Baltimore in Thanksgiving traffic to pick up a senator's granddaughter from Johns Hopkins. We traded these stories, exacting what we could of revenge through exposure of our bosses' privacies. This did not preserve any of our dignity.

I rubbed the knot out of Leo's neck. It occurred to me to strangle him, for a passing second. I noticed the collar on his shirt was looser. He'd been losing weight on doctor's orders.

"You heard the story about Kissinger?" he said.

"His consulting firm? Is Polk talking to them?"

"No, no," Leo waved me off. "Early Kissinger. Kissinger and Nixon. China, in '71."

"'72, I think."

"In '71 they had Kissinger sneak in through Pakistan," Leo said. "Before meeting Mao."

He loved old stories of cloak and dagger, admired the exquisite details like an art historian talking about Vermeer.

"They can't risk blowback in the States before any meeting even happens," Leo said. "So they want Kissinger to get to China undercover. Set it all up with Zhou. You know Zhou?"

"Not personally, no."

"Mao's right hand. Whole burden on Kissinger is to read Zhou close, make sure Mao is really game."

"I guess I hadn't heard this," I said. I was waiting for the part where Leo would claim he was the young pilot flying Kissinger's plane, or the advisor whispering strategy in his ear.

"I love it," Leo said. "They get Kissinger to Pakistan for all the usual bullshit. They've got press around, but they make it look pretty dull. Kissinger goes to a dinner one night, and the next morning his people start passing it around, 'Oh, he's got Delhi belly. He'll have to spend a few days resting up.' They send him to some villa up in the hills."

"They got away with that?" I said.

"Probably harder then than it is now," Leo said. "They didn't have all this Internet shit, but in those days there was still a US foreign press. Anyway, they dress Kissinger up in a big old droopy hat and sunglasses and fly him out of Rawalpindi at three o'clock in the morning. They don't tell the State Department—they don't tell anyone. Kissinger twists the screws, and then, boom, all of a sudden Nixon's going to China. They scare the piss out of the Soviets, push the Chinese on Vietnam. Two guys did it—two fucking guys."

He wagged two fingers in my face.

"Look at me," Leo said. "I'm getting wistful." He laughed. I was happy he'd forgotten about our lost schedule. Only what Leo forgot could be forgiven.

Compared to Kissinger in China, Bund International's plan for Leo, at least what there was of one, sounded prosaic. Boosterish commerce talks bound to be vague because Leo had no power to make them binding or specific; stultifying infrastructure surveys of the latest in agricultural projects or hi-tech districts. Leo would probably be photographed in a hard hat or a lab coat, looking like an asshole. We'd eat dinner with provincial officials inside some newly built business park in the gutted center of an ancient city. I braced for it: Leo sour and glowering, none of the meetings up to the level of his ambitions, and so heaping his frustrations on me, stone after stone. It was Wednesday. I'd suffer him without respite through Sunday. We'd fly home out of Shanghai, but even as I longed for that flight, I knew it wouldn't mean reprieve—just more business-class hours of Leo elbowing me awake to share his ailments. I'd brought two suits in one small suitcase, but I was starting to think that packing light wasn't smart when you were going to be eating all your meals with unfamiliar utensils. On the plane, I'd spilled sauce from gingered pork on the sleeve of one of my dress shirts. The hardened stain already looked permanent.

THE ASIA HOTEL on Workers' Stadium Road had floors of what looked like—though, really, who could tell?—marble. It was polished slick until it was actually dangerous. The lobby wasn't busy, and while Leo checked in I gave my suitcase a kick to see how far it would glide to the elevator. Most of the way, it turned out.

A young man intercepted us. He held a sign: *Congressman Mr. Leonard Filmore.*

"I am CCPIT driver," he said. "For meeting?"

"There are two Ls in 'Fillmore,'" Leo said.

The elevator pinged, and Leo stepped in. He stood with his legs apart in the middle of the tight space and punched at his phone like force would scare it into compliance. He let the doors close onto my shoulder. I pushed in next to Leo, and the driver held his sign out toward us. "Give us ten minutes," I said, as the elevator closed in his face. Leo pounded the lit key for the top floor and groaned when we slowed to let me out five stories below him.

I turned every switch in my hotel room, but the lights never came on. I couldn't get the automated curtains to open, so I changed clothes in the half dark. The room phone rang, and because I was sure it was Leo, and I knew he was angry, I made him wait ten rings.

"Yes?" I said.

"I'm calling to tell you that you're a fucking liar," Leo said.

"Does your room not have electricity, either?"

"I'm on a lobby phone," Leo said. "You're late."

They told me at the front desk, once it was too late to matter, that I had to put my room key into a slot near the door to activate the power.

BEIJING TRAFFIC WAS abysmal, and it took nearly an hour to get to the meeting—a drive that would take fifteen minutes, the driver said, "in middle night." Hundreds of bicycles passed our tinted windows. I took a few pictures through the glass, most of which came out showing Beijingers in mid-pedal with the ghostly reflection of my face superimposed on them. One of our constituents had called the office only last week to complain about an article she'd read alleging China was slaughtering stray dogs by the tens of thousands. I'd thanked her for her concern and promised to look into it. That wasn't enough. She wanted the congressman to introduce an International Bill of Canine Rights. She had drafted one herself. She wouldn't let me off the phone until I promised I would give it "serious time." It arrived two days later, handwritten, on yellow legal paper—so clearly loved and so deeply felt that I had nothing but sadness for the woman's effort. It stunk with amateurism, and no one would give it a moment's thought.

Beijing was so dug up, I imagined rats in swarms. Two townhouses on my block in DC were under renovation—so minor, compared to this— and for weeks now I slept and woke to scratching mice. I'd decided to be ecumenical, thinking the mice had as much right to scramble and thrive as I did. But then I saw their shit in the pan I scrambled eggs in. After that, I set traps—broke their necks, one by one.

"You know what's different about this skyline?" Leo said. "No churches. How long you think they'll last without God?"

"Without our God?"

"Without Jesus."

"I think they'll last awhile," I said.

He grabbed me by the back of the neck and shook me. I think it was meant to be playful.

"You're lukewarm, Luke," Leo said. "Spiritually, there isn't a worse place to be."

Like many latecomers to religion, the congressman had a past that didn't square with this current revival of faith. He said he'd spent years looking for love in a drink—"My genetic affliction," he called it. Sober Leo was supposed to be the new skyline of the man. But where others saw renovation, I saw scurrying rats. I didn't think he'd read much of the Bible outside of some red-letter verses of Matthew, and I could more than match him just from remembered Sunday school. To me, his salvation by Christ sounded scripted. But then again, part of my job was writing his scripts. It was hard to discern where my failures ended and his began.

THE BUND INTERNATIONAL translator who met us at the China Council for the Promotion of International Trade was a young woman— around my age, I imagined—with impeccable, professional English, crisp as the pleat in her skirt. Her name was Li-Li. My first words to her were an apology.

She led us to a conference room set with lidded porcelain teacups. Framed letters of praise from leaders around the world hung six to a wall, including one from a nasty despot whose removal the congressman had very publicly supported. The letters reminded me of schoolchildren's valentines: *To Beijing, in eternal friendship.*

The men we were supposed to meet, though I had lost the papers telling me exactly who they were, kept us waiting. The congressman reached obsessively into his pocket, not because his phone was ringing, but because it wasn't, and it made him feel marooned. I stared at a winding scene of the Yellow River done in a sparkling mosaic on the facing wall. Finally, three men appeared. We stood, they bowed. They were solemn, early forties, ranged from slim to paunchy. Bureaucrats I imagined you could purchase by the pound in an office supply store. Li-Li sat at the distant head of the table, as though translation were a work of umpiring, and she wasn't partial to either side.

My notes from that day reflect a circular conversation of platitudes and vague promises. China and the United States could work together "for mutual benefit"—a "win-win situation." We prepared to sign some nonbinding documents of mutual praise. The pens they gave us were exquisite, worth far more than the pledges.

Leo, who never took a note himself, scribbled something on the back of a receipt. He had me announce that we were taking "a short recess," our code for "emergency bathroom break." I looked at Li-Li and waited for her to filter my English into Mandarin. Leo left the room, walking gingerly.

With Leo gone, the officials began to speak among themselves in staccato bursts, and I waited for them to acknowledge me. Li-Li clicked her fingernails against one another, and their polish shined in the light. I caught her eye and was about to say something to her when I saw her breathe in sharply and redden. Her eyes flicked toward the men, then back to me, and I wondered what kind of insult she'd understood that I hadn't. I took Leo to be the target of the men's mockery, if only because I was too insignificant to be worth denigrating.

When the congressman grumbled back into the room, the trade officials stood.

"This has been most productive," one said, "and now we must adjourn for urgent matters."

Whether this meeting would bring even a single shoelace out of their country and into ours was doubtful, even if we talked for three more hours, but Leo clearly felt that if they'd ended the meeting first, even if he was ready to leave, then he had lost their respect.

"We should have left half an hour ago," he told the officials.

With every man in the room now annoyed or offended, we nevertheless posed for photographs. I took paired grip-and-grin shots and more inclusive group ones. The men who I suspected had just sat mocking the congressman clustered around him. The most important officials stood at the center, and a deteriorating line of nonentities were pushed out to the edges, a ghostly shoulder of the translator hovering barely into the frame. In the two shots where I wasn't taking the pictures myself, Li-Li took them, and I came out half-faced.

AT THE MAIN entrance, a phalanx of suited men stood in a red-roped receiving line. Li-Li hurried us toward a side exit, but not before I saw the guest of honor. "El Presidente," we called him, the latest fist-rattling Latin American head of state to become beatifically popular among the equatorial poor. He was built like a keg of beer, dressed in military epaulets and heavy black boots. Applause for El Presidente—thin-skinned petrotyrant, self-appointed heir to Simón Bolívar—turned to uproar. The congressman's face soured in a way that made me smile. "That motherfucker," Leo said.

Li-Li left us in a side parking lot where we waited for our Buick to come around. Still smog, no breeze. Disappearing at the edge of my sight line were two buildings under construction that looked to be falling into one another.

"I saw him in the bathroom," the congressman said.

"El Presidente?"

"I've never seen a man who needs three bodyguards just to take a piss."

"Just now?"

"I'm at the far pisser, but he pulls up to the middle one. Right fucking next to me," Leo said. "I look over, and of course I know it's him straight off, the fucking faker. Thinks he's been to hell and back because he can put on a goddamn military Halloween costume."

"Do you think he recognized you?" I asked. Leo hadn't been in the military, either, though he had awkward lapses where he seemed to forget that.

"He thinks we were behind that horseshit excuse for a coup last summer," Leo said.

"He thinks it was the CIA."

"White men in suits," my boss said. "We're all alike to him."

"You did sort of suggest you'd like him killed . . ."

"That was taken out of context," he said.

"I'm not sure he reads the corrections in the *Washington Post*."

Leo snorted. "I could feel him looking at me."

"Did you say anything?" I asked.

"Longest piss of my life. He finished first and just stood there at the sink. I was racking my brain for something to say. Needle him, you know?"

"Was he really a general?"

"They don't have an army, they have criminals with Kalashnikovs."

"I didn't know he even spoke English," I said.

"Heavy accent."

"He always uses that translator in interviews."

"Translator. Right. It's a good ploy," Leo said. "What he said to me was, 'You Yankees will never have me swinging by the neck.'"

"He meant us?"

"He didn't mean the baseball team."

"What'd you say?"

"I said, 'Excuse me?' And he said, 'Your government won't hang me by the throat. That's a promise.' I told him not to go thinking his dick was so big, because if the United States wanted him by the balls, he'd squeal just like anyone else."

"You said that?" I said. If some version of this story got out, I wouldn't sleep for weeks from the volume of press phone calls. I'd go hoarse with adamant denials.

"Squirmy motherfucker. He smirks again. Says something in Spanish that I didn't catch. Then he really starts letting it fly, about my mother and all the rest. Not that I understood all of it, but I'm not a fucking idiot. So then his guards hear the yelling and come busting in like I was going to cut him. They all line up and glare at me. I said to them, 'The second we decide to, and this is a promise, we'll have a big dick up your fucking ass.' I gave him a good look at it. Then I zipped up and walked out."

Our car slid up, and I opened the door for Leo. You hear about grown men, in government, behaving like children, but you're never prepared for how much they have at their disposal that a playground kid could never dream of: swinging your dick around really can make embassies close and bombs fall, if you swing it right. I couldn't always protect Leo from himself—my job was only to prevent, as much as I could, full public knowledge of the crooked timber he was made from. That meant I was the voice of the thinker after he spoke without thinking and the face of the family man when his family should have disowned him. I was hired as an adjunct to the congressman's memory, but I found myself cast to play his conscience, too. I knew the next time I saw El Presidente railing from the floor of the United Nations I would think of the old raisiny dick of my American congressman, trying to shake menacingly at a Latin American head of state in a Chinese bathroom.

WE SPENT THE afternoon pawned off on a guide who called himself "Snow." Snow was instructed to show us the entirety of official Beijing in about two hours, before our dinner with men from Bund International. In the Mao Mausoleum in Tiananmen Square, a waxen copy of the chairman lay under glass, his actual body preserved somewhere in the bowels of the building. He'd been pumped so full of formaldehyde at death that he'd swelled to nearly twice his living size.

We entered the Forbidden City. Most of its buildings were under construction, part of the city's facelift for the next year's Olympics. I knew that by the time of the Opening Ceremonies, Leo hoped to be standing tall on his own world stage: at the Republican National Convention, as their next nominee for president. His would be a dark-horse bid—a pitch-fucking-black horse, honestly—but no one had asked my opinion. Leo's intentions were publicly revealed only in the form of an "exploratory committee," an event with press coverage limited to our town's local newspaper.

The Forbidden City was a corpse of its former power, its anatomy forcibly preserved from ruin, like Mao's. The open squares were hot and shadeless, white and blinding. The fresh-red buildings and yellow roof tiles looked brighter still against the background of gray sky. Squint your eyes, and it was all on fire—the tiny bands of blue around the entryway doors like the hottest part of the flame and the concrete walkways the color of ash. It was easy now to walk through the center of an empire, open to anyone, now that there was no longer an emperor. What was truly forbidden, the secrets of power these courtyards once held, was still forbidden of course—it had just been relocated to office buildings and conference rooms.

We crossed marble bridges and walked quickly through gardens built for the recitation of poetry, and Leo told me, as we hurried, that this morning's meeting was just as he suspected: Beijing promised an erratic officialdom, tense and sensitive to slight. He read their wariness as a general trait of "the Chinese." I was willing to trust the research I'd assembled and say that official Beijing's suspicion of foreigners was not paranoid invention—two hundred years of British trading companies and gunboat diplomacy; of French concessions and Portuguese merchant cities; of Japanese adventuring and Western opium; of Chinese coastal cities built for the profit of financial capitals that were oceans away. And the internal distress: In just a hundred years, an empire had fallen, nationalist reign gave way to a Communist insurgency and a civil war; a victorious Mao proclaimed a republic from the back gate of the Forbidden City in which we stood. United States policy for most of Mao's rule was that he didn't exist, that the "real" China was the tiny island one hundred miles off the coast occupied by a defeated army turned political kleptocracy. A quarter century of Mao's rule marked time by peasant starvation and burned temples, with anyone vaguely bookish or otherwise politically suspect sent to rural labor camps to be reeducated by the working peasantry. And Leo complained the officials seemed tense?

The congressman rushed through the Forbidden City as quickly as he had skimmed my briefing book. He showed no interest in the Hall of Supreme Harmony, massed above us on its terrace, with a double-hipped roof that looked like it floated on air. Leo claimed he knew plenty about China already, but I found he was often sloppy with that kind of knowledge, too prone to trust his dimly rendered general picture. He was pleased, though, to have diagnosed our frosty reception as part of some Chinese national personality disorder. He liked ice to crack. There's no charm without resistance.

I lagged behind him. I peeked into closed-off sections of the complex. The side courts were in disrepair and the interior buildings almost entirely off-limits to my prying. Here is where the Empress Dowager Cixi made her extravagant demands. Here is where Puyi took the throne, lost it.

AT DINNER AT Beijing Da Dong Roast Duck restaurant, the congressman got drunk with businessmen from Bund International who slurped their noodles and instructed us to dip our Peking duck skin in the sugar bowl next to each place setting.

I reached out once to stay the hand of the waitress pouring Leo's wine. It was fatal to my boss, what she kept dumping into his glass. The congressman struck my hand out of the way, hard enough that other guests heard the slap. He screwed his face up tight and hung a tough look on me. He was going to sit here with the other men and take his drink, and I had no right to stop him. Leo saw himself as a man of great soul beset, like all great men, by fierce demons—but his only proof of the great soul was the existence of the demons.

I watched him empty his wine. He dissolved into a clutter of symbols. He had an American flag pin he wore on his lapel the way someone superstitious might clutch an amulet. He had hardened hair, thin, combed sideways across his head and screaming insincerity. He was nothing like my own father, but he was a fatherly archetype— big-voiced, impatient, ever vigilant of his status in the room. Whenever he tried to expand his emotive range beyond gloating or annoyance, it was without exception uncomfortable.

Through dinner, the congressman did most of the talking. He was interrupted only when someone thought it necessary to announce the name of a particular delicacy being set before us or to relate a historical fact about our surroundings: "Here is the Cantonese chicken dish that Richard Nixon declared his favorite during the visit in 1972." Something was said about Chairman Mao that I didn't catch. And did we know the restaurant was once a granary for the Forbidden City?

Contrary to the custom of our hosts, who made these pleasantries and discussed nothing else specifically, the more Leo drank, the more eager he became to defend the intricacies of America's global military positioning. He drank himself presidential, as though offering a realpolitik address behind closed doors to reluctant allies. The men from Bund International—with Li-Li along to translate—listened politely.

"Think of it as poker," Leo said. "Saddam was representing aces."

We sat at the table fifteen strong, as though in a well-catered committee meeting. I was served an architecturally plated dish of lotus root and crab. The low light was flattering, the windows at dusk even more inviting as decorative lanterns came lit in the street below. I focused just beyond Leo's head, at the waiter boning out a duck, slivering the meat onto a serving dish.

"Fine, Saddam was bluffing. But it was still the right play, on the percentages," Leo said. Our private dining room invited and prolonged his diatribe. "We made him show."

The men nodded like veterans of Macau poker tables. The highest ranked among them, a vice president of some sort, eventually raised a question. He went by Charles, for our benefit.

"There is always a duty," he said. "To know the tendencies of your opponent. To know how he bets."

Charles was the only man who wore a tie I liked, checkered black and silver, sealed at the collar with an impeccable Windsor knot. He had matted cheeks, among many that glistened red around him, and two tiny eyes in his chinless, oval face.

"Let me tell you a story about our 'opponent,'" Leo said. "Spring, 1990." I stifled a groan. Leo continued: "We had this woman testify before Congress—a girl, really, not even eighteen. She worked in a Kuwaiti hospital. Saddam's army bashed their way into the ward where she worked with newborns. The soldiers ripped three-pound babies out of their incubators, left them to die on the concrete floor of the hospital."

"No one would dispute this is inexcusable . . ." Charles said.

Leo, at the time, had taken the nurse's story personally. He pled for weeks after, to whoever would listen, begged we deploy our vast military for humanity's sake. Pundits joked that the shortest distance between any two points was the straight line between Leo Fillmore and a television camera.

"It was truly awful," Leo said. "And you know what else? None of it was true."

Charles looked to me for clarification. I only scribbled in my small black notebook. On its title page I had written: *The Congressman's Memory*. It started as a joke between Alex and me and afterward turned into a piece of our ritual banter. Once when I was running late in the morning, gathering my things, I asked her, "Have you seen *The Congressman's Memory?*" and she'd said, "No, and I haven't seen his conscience, either."

"She was a setup," Leo went on. "Her father was a Kuwaiti diplomat. They hired a goddamn advertising firm to coach her."

"So what is the reason for this story?" Charles asked. He looked to Li-Li, perplexed, as though there must be context she was omitting.

"My point is this time it was pure calculation," Leo said. "I don't have anymore fucking illusions about saving the world."

He took a pause here to survey his audience. The Gospel of Leo went something like this: "For God so loved the world he said, 'Fuck it, you people aren't worth saving.'"

"This sounds very much like two poor poker players," said a man who hadn't spoken all evening. He'd had the shortest introduction of all the executives and was seated farthest from Charles. His tie was thrown back over his shoulder. He was wildly drunk—a bottle of whiskey that had sprouted lips. He looked like he knew as soon as it was out of his mouth that he'd fucked himself.

"Well Saddam's fucking dead," Leo said. "How's that for a hand?"

Charles directed curt words at the man who'd spoken out of turn. The man stood up, mostly under his own power, and there might have been fire ants crawling up his legs as he marked a curved path to the door. He turned, preparing for a final exchange, and was cut off by three men at once, who ushered him into the hallway. Li-Li translated none of this.

Charles stood for a toast to clear the air, but he looked like a man who knew his operation had just turned from rescue to salvage.

"We look forward to much future cooperation with Congressman Fillmore," he said. Leo glared into his wine glass.

Charles continued: "And now I offer a toast to our mutual friend, Armand Lightborn, for bringing us together tonight."

"To Armand," Leo said, raising a glass to the absent presence. But I didn't write Lightborn's name in my book. I knew better.

MY BOSS FILLED my suit pockets with the business cards he'd collected, expecting me to alphabetize them later.

"They wish to say good night to you now," Li-Li said, indicating the line of men clustered expectantly at the door.

The representatives of Bund International swayed like they were on the deck of a pitching ship. Charles listed right and gave my hand a firm shake, with a sweeping motion to lead me out of the room. He held the congressman back to offer further apologies. I stood in the corridor, and Li-Li was forced to take a few steps toward me as men gathered in tight around Leo. I remembered her red in the face at the morning's meeting, embarrassed by how the men around her spoke, and so I took the risk of saying what came into my head. I had a desire to put a beam of daylight between my boss and me. I leaned to her ear: "You ever get the feeling these guys would rob their own mothers' graves?"

Li-Li worked on what I'd said, visibly untangling it. Before she could respond, Charles pulled her away.

I hung back in the low, gold light at the top of the stairway, and I wanted to crawl into my shadow. It wasn't that I thought I had risked much—it was that her reaction showed me an uncomfortable reflection. Perhaps to Li-Li I didn't appear as different from these men as I wanted to be.

IN THE HOTEL lobby, I started for the elevator, but Leo didn't follow. He collapsed into an armchair.

"Think I'll go for a night swim," he said.

"It's too late. I don't think they'll let you in the pool."

"The hell they won't."

"You don't want to go upstairs?"

"I need some air," he said. Air wasn't going to do it—I don't know what would have sobered him up besides maybe dialysis. The hotel staff, skating by on secret errands, made a good show of not staring at Leo sprawled in the chair.

"Phone," he said, pulling his out.

"They don't work," I said.

He punched his. "Phone," he yelled.

"We can get it fixed tomorrow."

"These people are jerking us around," he said. "Typical."

"Bund International?" I said.

Leo fondled his phone like a baseball, looking for its seams.

"Or you mean Lightborn?" I said.

He made a sharp half rotation of his shoulder, and threw his phone at me, high and tight. I cut it off with my left palm, which spared my face. I had a good chance with my right hand at catching the phone's low rebound, but I let it slip. My reflexes weren't professional-grade to begin with, but a few drinks and my hands were steaks. The phone hit the maybe-marble floor. It wouldn't rise again. A young man from the hotel fell to his knees picking up the pieces.

"You're going to Kaifeng tomorrow," Leo said. "They'll pick you up in the morning."

"To where?"

"I told them you're my chief of staff," he said. "The fuckers."

Our actual chief of staff, John Polk, saw me as a nepotistic hire and barely tolerated me. Chemotherapy had left Polk's head sheen as a missile, but he still kept two cell phones holstered on either side of his cock and would scream at me even from a hospital bed. Fallen sick, Polk wasn't any wiser or more empathetic a person, but much more was forgiven of him. He'd never traveled with us, even before leukemia, because he said it was my job to wash the shit stains out of Leo's underwear in places without reliable plumbing.

The hotel clerk tried to hand the phone fragments back to me, and I refused them.

"What's in Kaifeng?" I asked Leo. He was beyond answering. He held both hands to his forehead like they were the brim of a hat.

"You speak English?" I asked the clerk. He nodded, not enthusiastically.

"If he wants to stay down here, then fine," I said, pointing to Leo, who had slouched until his dress shirt was tight around his belly.

"But you don't let him go anywhere," I said. "And tell them." I pointed to the attendant by the lobby entrance, and the girl behind the front desk. "He stays here."

I fished out two notes with Mao's face—two hundred yuan, what I understood was about twenty dollars. The clerk refused and chewed his lips. I pressed the money on him, and he followed me trying to give it back. I didn't turn toward Leo again until I got to the elevator. The last thing I saw before the doors closed was Leo huddled over a lobby courtesy phone, like it was a toilet he was going to be sick into.

BACK IN MY room, the windows didn't open. Gray night like gray day. I didn't like the bed. I slept on and off—mostly off—in a chair until about five a.m., but then there was the hammering. At the foot of the hotel, a few courtyard houses were being demolished. They were single-story structures with shingled roofs, four buildings set in a square so that each house's central garden was steeled against the wind, against the world—or had been, until now. Narrow alleys threaded between the falling gray walls. Workers pried off tiles, swung sledgehammers.

I thought to call Alex. It was early evening in New York City. My working day was often no more than a fourteen-hour break from my insomniac half dreams of ex-girlfriends, dead relatives, distant friends, and old tormentors. Alex knew something about China—the food anyway. She'd introduced me to hot pot restaurants and soup dumplings. There was a place in the shadow of the Manhattan Bridge we both adored. The staff knew what we were there for and brought out crab and pork dumplings in bamboo steamers and we hardly had to ask.

The whole time we'd dated, whenever I'd told Alex she was pretty, she would always find something. She would say her nose was too sharp at its point or her earlobes too long. I told her no one had ever once looked at her earlobes and her nose was cute, like a little bird's beak. "Words to avoid in reference to a girl's appearance," she had said. "Beak." Plenty of people I worked with would say they didn't take any bullshit, that they "call it like they see it," and what they were really saying is it made them feel important to yell at waiters. Alex would never throw a tantrum and was so polite to people she could come off as stiff, but her resistance to bullshit was a layer hard inside, gem in a rock. It was the thing I missed most about her—that she wanted to set the world straight.

I felt Alex and I were still close. Well, close-distant, near-far—these were relative terms. We didn't hate each other as people who had once had sex often did. Sometimes I imagined trying to explain that idea to a robot, or a child, about two people loving each other very much, or thinking they do, about the awkward grappling in the dark, and then, so much of the time, within a year, wishing that person were never born. You'd get asked why—why is it that way? How does close not stay close? I had nothing to add to the paucity of the world's collected wisdom about love and its disappearance. I did know that despite the odds—which were all in favor of hatred or indifference—Alex and I were better off in our breakup's aftermath than most. I rattled my fingernails on top of the hotel room phone.

We'd met while we were both working on the Hill, though Alex hadn't ever liked DC. There wasn't enough of a city in the shadow of those monuments, she thought, not enough free air: all of it was requisitioned by government business. When the Ohio congressman she'd worked for died in office—physically in office, below his wall of honorary degrees—she took a vague-sounding program coordinator job for a ludicrously named nonprofit in New York City. She had a lot of extra time for email, I noticed, working at Give the World A Hug. They had a tiny office carved between the load-bearing columns of a flat-topped financial district tower, the barest sliver of the Hudson River visible through the hallway window.

For a while after she moved, I spent a lot of hours on the Acela Express. I had the Friday-evening trains memorized and waited all week to be discharged into Penn Station, that horrid, wholly unredeemable hallway. Every week I marveled that I was in the busiest train station in the country, and not once had an architect ever considered how a human would get on or off a train. Invisible entrances, mousehole stairwells. I had, more than once, been walking out of the train station and had a bewildered tourist ask where Penn Station was. I liked to imagine what it might have been like if Alex could have met me in the old Penn Station, the Beaux Arts one built a hundred years ago, with Roman vaulted ceilings and pink-hued travertine marble. We would have had to meet in another time, years before we were ever born, before that old station was demolished. But it would have been a beautiful thing.

I would walk a cross-town block from Penn Station and take the Q train to her out in Brooklyn. I liked to ride over the river, take stock of lower Manhattan, make sure everything was still in its place. My weekend visits never stopped as much as work intervened, and they trickled. Finally, it seemed like we were being realists to cut the official strings. Amtrak talked of cracks in the disk brakes on their Acela trains, and I got stuck in Baltimore about every third trip. Broken-down Baltimore might have been the sourest note—the boarded-up sections of the city you could see from the tracks made visible all the consequences of neglect.

It hadn't been too long since I had seen Alex, probably about four months. No, more—five. She'd switched apartments, taken on roommates, trying to save money. When I imagined men she was dating now, I thought of bankers having affairs. I pictured men of a different infrastructure: a pied-à-terre; the Metro-North; Greenwich, CT. Lonely weekends where Alex's phone rang only when he was sneaking a call from a corner of his property. I was making all this up because it was the worst thing I could imagine for her. The worst proves irresistible at certain times of night, usually between two and four a.m. Now it was nearing six. I have been an insomniac since I don't know when.

I wouldn't sleep anymore, so I walked down to see if Leo had managed to drown himself in the indoor pool. I thought it was smart policy to get away from my room's phone—the easier it is to get in touch with people, the easier it is to forget how often you shouldn't. At the pool, they wouldn't let me in: the young woman was very apologetic, but she pointed emphatically to a sign specifying the seven a.m. opening hour.

I searched, and Leo wasn't sacked out in the lobby, which I took as a good sign. The attractive planters of decorative ferns were no worse for wear—vases of floating cherry blossoms were unspilled and unbroken, so perhaps Leo had just gone quietly to bed. I wished him luck sleeping off Bund's hospitality. In the hotel business center, I found my work email inaccessible, for reasons no one could or would explain, but this felt less like something I needed to correct than like the momentary lifting of a burden. I went out into the Beijing morning, where old limber men stretched at their apartment windows and women unhooked the hanging laundry. It was six thirty, so with twelve hours' time difference, Alex would be just leaving work, maybe as restless as I was.

I was obsessed for a time with how Alex kept my memory, what she told herself about how we'd ended. But now I tried not to think about it. You can't control posterity. When Alex moved away, I felt that all that was left in DC that I cared about were myself and the Jefferson Memorial. But a little sadness at least made the city feel like a more complete place to me: to live there and miss her was evidence that life had transpired, that I was more than my job.

• • •

Out of the breakfast-room speakers, woodwind instruments played an Orientalized rendition of a Simon and Garfunkel song. An erhu accompanied, doleful. I picked at the buffet, dragon fruit and rice congee, espresso and an omelet bar.

"Someone to see you in the lobby," a hotel clerk said, touching my shoulder. I wasn't yet feeling suitable for company.

Thursday morning in a business hotel. The lobby bustled with anxious men hoping to close deals before the weekend. A young woman wandered out from the other side of a pilaster.

"I work for Bund International. My name is Li-Li. You remember?" she said.

There was a mechanical kind of lag as she spoke, as though she pronounced everything to herself in Mandarin, translated it to English, and made sure it was clear before she ventured it out of her mouth.

"I hope your sleep was pleasant?" she said.

"Wonderful," I said. "We are very pleased."

There was nothing to add—and nothing was said—about my misjudgment last night in trying to pull her into my confidence at the roast duck restaurant. I hoped for my own sake that I'd mumbled and she hadn't really heard me.

"And your boss?" she said.

"I'm sorry?"

"The partners in Kaifeng will be very disappointed not to see him," she said.

"This is what was arranged last night," I said, perhaps too severely.

"Did I say something wrong?" Li-Li asked. She went red. "I apologize for my English. Did you receive my phone messages?"

"The phones are another problem," I said. "All of these difficulties are entirely my fault."

"This is not a problem," Li-Li said hurriedly, though I knew she meant the opposite. "The car is waiting. You are ready?"

She certainly was, in defiance of the hour. Her hair swept tightly across the arch of her forehead, held back with pins, the rest short to her chin. She had faint sideburns bleached white and skin one shade toward olive. Nervous and sober, Li-Li wasn't my copy, but she was my counter-part—a fraternal twin in this assistant's life. She held herself together in a way I already envied. Her white blouse was without wrinkle or stain, her skirt and gray jacket right out of a dry-cleaning bag.

"I promise everything will be easier from here," I said.

"I understand," Li-Li said. And maybe she did, if she was as well-trained as I was at telling lies.

DAY 2

KAIFENG

I T WAS EARLY afternoon by the time I landed in Zhengzhou, a coal-fogged city whose glinting towers might have been built a week ago. Two men from Bund collected me from the cavernous airport the moment I disembarked. The teenager carried my suitcase and offered me bottled water. The other man cradled two cell phones in his large hands and reacted to everything quick as a trained falcon. One phone chimed during our introduction, and he answered it while handing me his card and shouting directions toward a driver reclining on a car. The driver became a dervish, rushing to shake my hand then spinning back to open the door. We piled in. More shouting, now directed at a sleepy middle-aged figure standing near a police car, though not dressed in uniform. He pulled an attentive face for the questions, but our car screamed away from him when the man with the falcon's eyes had heard enough of an answer. I finally had a moment to look at the card: *Executive Vice President, Project Manager, Bund International*. His name wasn't translated from its Chinese characters, but he told me to call him "Shoes"—probably because it sounded close enough to his given name for my unrefined American mouth.

Our police escort sped us down avenues of red lights with no cars. We reached an empty toll road. Along the forlorn new highway was farmland—and, eventually, people. The farmers of Henan Province had the Yellow River to keep them in crops and disaster, not so different from the eastern part of California where my family still lived, where fortunes had been similarly lost and found in the cycles of a silty river prone to flood. Except these people had lost more, and lost longer. I saw none of the big-ag machines I knew from growing up rural. This toil was by hand and plow, in the shadow of bulbous-bottomed power plants fed by coal. I watched the smokestacks spout and imagined it was blue sky they were discharging into the already blackened air.

"Kaifeng," Shoes said, "has a history of 2,700 years. It is a birthplace of Chinese civilization. We feel that among the projects of Bund International, the nearest example for Mr. Fillmore's airport project is this Kaifeng achievement."

I hadn't heard of Kaifeng before last night—population, five million. I wasn't sure I'd heard details of a Leo Fillmore "airport project," either.

We neared the outskirts of the city, where deep concrete bathtubs portended future skyscrapers. Loaded cranes swung packets of steel beam thirty stories up in the air, metric tons of movement that looked offhand and casual. Shoes indicated this would be a hi-tech district for drugs and microprocessors, the best in the world. Other Chinese cities had boomed overnight—supplying the consuming earth with socks and cigarette lighters or buttons and toothpaste. But Shoes wanted me to know he was no dealer in cheap textiles and coat clasps. This complex was meant for higher-order exploration: circuits past the limits of human computation, next-generation pharmaceuticals designed to bring contentment and well-being.

Now that he'd turned pitchman, Shoes sounded dutiful, and beneath that, even melancholy. I looked out the window at the workers' housing, cramped outbuildings sitting on the perimeter of the construction site. His abrupt silence, as we passed those trailers, left the impression that

Shoes saw things far beyond what he was willing to describe to me. I felt he was gazing at the coruscating machinery, the denuded landscape, the laborers' small temporary homes, and feeling at least passingly sorry for his role in it.

"You ask Mr. Lightborn," Shoes said. His voice was quiet, his eyes unfocused. "We don't build this all for clean teeth."

The first time I saw Armand Lightborn was from the back, about eighteen months ago. I never got within twenty feet of him. We were at a private party at a restaurant with a boardwalk on the Potomac River and a view of the Kennedy Center. The weather was unseasonably cold; I distinctly remember stepping out when I'd had too many and counting on the air to shock a little speech back into me. I went back inside when I felt sober enough to stand again, or at least was frozen so solid that my legs wouldn't buckle.

The cover band had taken their first break when Lightborn appeared. It was Alex who pointed him out. We were wallflowered in a corner with our drinks, trying to suck them down before the end of the open bar. Lightborn graced our floor only long enough to find the stairs to the mezzanine. We groundlings affected not to watch our betters upstairs, and our bosses affected not to notice they hovered physically above us. We suspected they had the boutique vodka and we had the Popov, but as long as drinks were free, I didn't complain.

Alex spotted Lightborn when he bobbed up again near the rafters. She held two drinks in her hands, both for her, and I had two in mine, and I remember exactly what she said, pointing a full gin and tonic imprecisely in Lightborn's direction: "Check out this motherfucker."

We watched Lightborn talking to Leo's wife, Theresa—I had no idea where my boss was. The opinion around the staff was that you might survive Leo not liking you, but if his flinty wife ever turned on you, it'd be best to start filing unemployment paperwork. Out at the party, an actually smiling Theresa was all pearls and pearly whites. Lightborn was cozy and in close.

"Jesus," Alex said. "I thought it was just congressmen that Lightborn was looking to fuck."

I'm sure I laughed. I bent my head back, looked up at him as closely as I could. The hitched way he held his left shoulder, imperfectly repaired in several surgeries, suggested the pitcher he'd been in college. He was clean-shaven and had a windblown coloring in his face, like he'd spent too much of his youth in the sun, or had just arrived from a ski slope. He apparently possessed clear eyesight—no glasses, no blinking at uncomfortable contacts. There was otherwise not much remarkable about Lightborn's physicality, except that he stood like he was very rich, with firm, never-anxious planted legs and his chest barreled outward. He was top-percentile handsome in DC because he was moneyed, over six-feet, and the correct weight for his frame, and very few men had all three. The hair that Theresa playfully straightened on Lightborn's head was dark and blacker for the products that kept it in place.

We stared at them and at each other, eyes wide, until the sleepy band started up some slow, coercive number. Alex killed one drink, roused by the strains of "My Funny Valentine," and put her free hand around my wrist and tugged. She didn't like that I didn't hold her right, or close enough, or make intimate eyes at her while surrounded by all these people.

"You dance like I'm your little sister," she said.

"I only had a brother," I said. "We didn't slow dance much."

"The slow ones are easy," Alex said.

"We can dance all you want in the dark," I told her.

She laughed, but I'd meant it seriously. I probably looked offended.

"I'm sorry," she said. "You're perfect."

That was a nice moment—as nice as the comical stumble to the taxi must have been, a blacked-out ride that we conjectured only on evidence of a receipt we found the next morning alongside her bra with a broken strap. Lightborn was gone before the song ended, or, at least, I never saw him again that night—and no Theresa, either.

———————

All day, the Bund men and their associates rocketed me from cloistered office to conference room, showing me everything except what I might want to see, the city outside, its brisk market streets. When we finally ventured to their construction site, I poked around for a few curious minutes before they scooped me back into the car. Perhaps I had come too close to the perimeter fence between the work site and the workers' housing. I did the quick math—the number of workers a project this size would require, and the rough number of living quarters on site—and figured they must have ten men to a trailer. What did the workers do there, I asked, with the last of their energy in the evenings? I got a gruff answer about wasting paychecks on games of dice and cards. If you paid them too much money, they all became alcoholics, Shoes said. This was the last word before we left for a welcome dinner with the mayor of Kaifeng.

"This restaurant has a thousand years of history," the mayor of Kaifeng said when we arrived on the fifth floor of the building housing our banquet room. I wondered how that could be true, considering I'd just stepped off the elevator. No answers were forthcoming.

Whenever I returned from one of these trips abroad, other assistants always asked what the place was like, what I thought of where I'd been. I usually said a few obvious things about the quality of the food, or related some allegedly telling cultural attitude regarding punctuality or table etiquette. But the truth is I almost never met people who weren't working for a government, or a Western-directed business, people among the small minority of a country's English speakers—and these made poor, or at least abnormal, examples. So whatever I ended up "thinking" about the country was only some combination of what the host government was hoping I would, divided by whatever skepticism I retained, and helped along minimally by a very few unscripted interactions with people who, by the very fact that they could even converse with me, demonstrated our similarity rather than our difference.

The mayor led me to a private dining room, and twenty men stood to greet me. He presided robustly over the receiving line, and I gave each man one of Leo's business cards. I shook hands with a firm jerk, the way I saw the mayor do it. I watched every face, and none reacted to my English.

After introductions, the staff directed us to our place settings, and the mayor began to address the gathered room in Mandarin. His translator stood mutely alongside, and I understood only "Congressman Fillmore" and the word for "thank you." It was obvious Leo had been expected as the guest of honor.

The mayor turned to me with a gesture of lifted hands. It was my turn to speak. I rose slowly, and my hands tremored until a private joke occurred to me. I huffed a few times and slouched my shoulders, in imitation of Leo's posture, and bowed deeply like an idiot who'd mistaken China for Japan.

"We may not always agree on matters of state," I said, not in my own voice, but in that loud, ponderous one I knew just as well. "But rest assured, honorable men, that America's best interests are also your best interests. We're strategic poker players, not weepy sentimentalists. And together we can all prosper." If I was smirking, and I might have been, I trusted the translator would render the words sincerely.

"To the good people of Henan Province!" I said.

The Henan officials applauded. The premier cru Bordeaux, poured by our waitresses until it nearly topped the glasses, was raised high, and I was implored to chug it to the sediment.

I took my seat, and the man to my left tried to speak to me in English. It was something about how, given my youth, I must be full of talents. As he flailed, Shoes, at my right, offered no help. He dragged his chopsticks like a pen across his empty plate where they left behind no pattern. He closed his eyes tight and held them that way, and when he opened them he did not turn to my neighbor, who was still trying to get his attention. That guest gave up speaking to me and addressed something to the full table that made everyone laugh. I tried to play along and gave them Leo's laugh, from the base of my diaphragm.

The mayor watched me intently. Through his translator, he asked me a question much less pointed than his stare.

"Your ancestry?" he said.

"I'm just your regular American mutt," I said. "Scotch-Irish by way of Texas on my father's side. Southern European on my mother's, which is why you're looking at these thick eyebrows."

"Kaifeng has a history of Jewish traders," the Mayor said. "And it is well known that the Chinese empire under the Khans once stretched all the way to Babylon."

In the time this took to translate, I realized that I'd missed an opportunity to please him. I should have traced my family back to the Arabian Peninsula and the brotherhood of the Khans. Whenever the mayor wasn't looking, Shoes would set his flitting bird's eyes on the man and hold them there.

The waitresses began to serve: duck liver in jelly, shark-fin soup in a hollowed-out orange. Many fingers of the twenty at the table turned the glass lazy Susan. I looked to Shoes for how to avoid faux pas, but he didn't move. His neighbor served dishes onto his plate while Shoes stared mildly at his hands in his lap. The man next to me piled food up for me, too. I didn't see anything I wanted until a chicken dish spun near that looked familiar as Chinese takeout. I was clumsy with chopsticks but reached for a thick piece I could handle. When my catch landed on my plate, I saw I had grabbed the head. Beak and skull—leathern flesh cooked to the color of a mummy's skin. I pushed it to the plate's edge and tried to ignore it. Was it stranger to see the head of the animal I was eating, or stranger not to? I knocked one of my chopsticks to the floor.

The mayor saw it happen and rose to shout at me.

"Chinese custom says that the person who drops a chopstick is the one to pay for dinner," the translator explained. It may have been a joke, but if so the mayor didn't laugh. The waitress brought me a fork.

The croaking translator ferried along the mayor's address to the table about the "modernization" of Henan Province, but several minutes of closing disquisition was rendered in a single English sentence: "Henan Province has the happiest labor force in East Asia," the mayor said.

The waitresses poured baijiu. A glass of it sat in front of me, clear and smelling of kerosene.

"*Gan bei!*" the mayor screamed.

"It means 'dry the glass,'" Shoes whispered.

I took the baijiu down. They compared baijiu to vodka, but vodka's virtue is neutrality. Henan baijiu was a militant grain.

"It's good you don't flinch," the mayor said to me. "You see? He drinks without flinching!"

With this endorsement, five enthusiastic officials of Kaifeng's government raised their glasses to me from several seats away. They expected me to stand, toast, and light a wildfire down my throat. I did, and they did, and we were all good friends.

The teenaged waitresses watched us like judges. Finally there was a lag between talk and toasts where people began to eat. The chicken head remained, its eyes on me like it might address me with recriminations. I wanted to mush it up into a ball and toss it under the table, but my napkin was cloth, and its top corner was tucked under my plate. Dumplings arrived in wooden steamers, and I speared two with my fork and built a small fortress around the head. The chicken eyes still poked above the dumpling wall. I looked so long into them—their hundred-yard stare—that I imagined a banquet of animals, with my own head spinning on the table's center.

The mayor stood—arm extended, palm facedown, fingers wagging. He pivoted toward me and toasted to the congressman. I stood, shakily, as Leo's earthly representative. A waitress in a qipao dress crawled out of the wallpaper to pour me one step closer to death. I was goaded to speak again, so I repeated something I'd heard Shoes say earlier that day.

"The sky is high," I said. "And the emperor is far away!"

The mayor grinned. His associates raised glasses. When I thought no one was looking, I spit my baijiu into my water. It was the only trick I could think of to avoid heaving later in the bathroom.

"Thank you for that, Mr. Congressman!" my neighbor exclaimed in English. I turned to see myself beheld in glassy eyes. Only then did the depth of their misapprehension become clear. A shiver ran through me that I was afraid must be visible. Shoes might have been meditating, mouth and eyes closed, inhaling deeply through his nose. I looked into my lap, trying unsuccessfully to focus my eyes.

Before I could think of how I might begin correcting these men, the mayor made two fists with his hands and started swiveling his arms in a machine gun motion, with a stuttering *ch-ch-ch-pop* noise. You didn't have to know a single Mandarin tone to understand the shouts of "Rambo, Rambo!" that intercut the mayor mimicking heavy gunfire.

"The mayor now describes a very famous battle," the translator said. "The Chinese fighters were outnumbered by the Japanese. But all of the Chinese fought like Rambos. The Japanese were cowards."

At "cowards"—he apparently knew the English word—the mayor stood up on his chair. His porcelain eyes tried to lock onto his nearby deputies. They stared into their hands as their boss, arms exultant, searched the room for any object as vital as his beating heart. For the first time all night, the room was silent enough to hear footsteps in the outside hallway. I excused myself from the table. Twenty men could testify that an American congressman had born witness to it all.

• • •

SHOES FOUND ME steadying my elbows on the restroom sink top.

"The drinking is custom," he said. "You are a good guest to accept it. I know it does not always make for nice memories. Or nice mornings."

He took my arm to stop my swaying.

"I have a feeling they are very impressed by you," he said softly.

"You told them I was a congressman?" I said.

The tile floor echoed our voices.

"Do you feel unwell?" Shoes asked. He took a bottle of water from a row near the sink and tried to hand it to me.

"They think I'm Leo?" I said, holding my stomach in.

"The mayor has been very honored to have this meeting with Congressman Fillmore," he said. "I can only say that certain of my superiors see the mayor as a useful ally. My duty is to facilitate the wishes of my superiors and assist an introduction. I have done no more than this."

"So who told everyone I was Leo?" I said. I'd delivered a mocking speech, tossed off a few toasts for private amusement in a distant place, but I couldn't accept that as sufficient reason for such a vast mischaracterization of who I was.

"You gave to everyone the business card of your boss," Shoes said.

"Not because I was claiming to be him," I said.

"Consider it from the other perspective," Shoes said. He tapped two fingers on his open palm, and it made me think of an old telegraph machine. "The mayor expects a powerful guest. He invites his associates to a banquet. But the powerful guest does not arrive."

The baijiu climbed back up my throat, and I closed my eyes and imagined a cork in my esophagus.

Shoes continued: "If the mayor wishes not to lose face, and if he sees you rise and speak as an authority, he would quite reasonably believe that you understand the necessity of what he has done." He sighed like he was talking to a recalcitrant employee. "He might believe that you agree it is more beneficial."

"Beneficial to whom?" I said.

"It has seemed you were a willing participant," Shoes said.

"That's a misunderstanding," I said.

He took my arm, and I jerked it out of his hand.

"It is not so consequential," Shoes said. "The dinner is finished."

"What happens when his guests find out I'm not really a congressman?" I said.

Shoes shifted his weight and looked past me to the dragon-embossed doors of the toilet stalls. "The mayor did not have to tell any of these men anything they were not already prepared to believe. Nor did you appear to decline assistance."

"Fucking hell," I said.

"Please," Shoes said. "If we do not return to say good night to everyone, they will believe you have been made sick."

Faintly through the bathroom doors, I heard the liquored camaraderie in the banquet room. Shoes was considerably taller than me, and his movements became a mirror of mine—fallen shoulders, shimmering eyes. He anticipated my next objection.

"Who knows Mr. Fillmore's beliefs and habits better than you?" he said, crossing his hands and leaning forward, speaking close to my ear. "And please consider: how would any of these men benefit by exposing as false what their benefactor has suggested to them is true?"

WE DROVE, AFTER dinner—a night tour for my benefit. The Yellow River had long ago claimed what was left of the city of the Northern Song, the last dynasty to have made Kaifeng its capital. Somewhere, under the silt, were its palaces. Now the city was the rising steam of pork buns, the smoke of open-air fires, the whine and whistle of pasted-together motorcycles. Mao had Beijing's walls torn down—veneration of old things was an impediment to revolutionary progress—but here the city walls remained, saved by Kaifeng's irrelevance. The sky was high, the emperor far away.

The mayor sat in the front passenger seat of our Buick, and I sat in back next to Shoes, who seemed lost in the caves of his own consciousness. On the other side of Shoes was a thin man in a bulky-fitting suit that made his head look small. I recognized him as our police escort from the airport this morning. Shoes introduced him as a captain, and the man, unsmiling, showed me an identification card. I gave it a glance and handed it back, but then he shoved it at me. He seemed to think I didn't believe his rank or title, but it's not like the quality of his ID helped: an American teenager couldn't buy beer with that kind of flimsy laminate. The captain looked to be wearing the same suit in the picture as he was in the car.

"My grandfather was a police officer," I said to him in English.

I could have tried Mandarin, I suppose. I hadn't told Leo this, because he would have overestimated my grasp and sent me on hopeless errands, but I took a year of Mandarin my first year of college to fulfill a language requirement. It had proven no help in China, but it's true I might have attempted a little basic politeness. The police captain looked to Shoes, and I heard Shoes say the Mandarin word for grandfather, one of the few I still recognized. The captain was unimpressed. He went on clearing his throat and spitting out the window.

My dinner drinks bit deeper, and I tried to grab and hold a last connection to my sentient self. Lights hung across the water of a small lake, and I concentrated on a few men fishing, even at this hour of the night. "Peasants" was the first word that came to mind, doing work that could have been performed the same way a hundred years ago—old men with wooden fishing poles, young boys delivering watermelons by handcart, women up in the middle of the night making five-spice bread under lean-tos of tarpaper and scrap wood. A man balanced his bicycle with a load of twined cardboard, easily six feet high, and I watched the herky-jerky way he pedaled, always a second from toppling.

We arrived at a square at the end of Imperial Street, where stores rebuilt in the style of the vanished dynasty were decorated in strings of white lights. The square ended at a lagoon, where a bright causeway led through the haze. The mayor, with choppy movements and half bows, wanted me to follow him into the street. He had me pose with him for a picture in front of the Dragon Pavilion—a magisterial structure on the far side of the lagoon brightly illuminated in green and yellow.

A small crowd of shrunken saleswomen watched, selling Buddhist prayer beads and collecting stray bottles. Standing side by side with him, the mayor was my height, and I saw black circles flecking his white teeth. His smile looked like a row of dominos.

"We are not just business," he said in English. "We are friends."

It struck me as a question, so I answered it as one. "Yes," I said. "Friends."

None of the mayor's associates remained for us to lie to, and I thought it was time to say good night.

The mayor spoke to Shoes, who then said to me: "He wishes you good health, rejuvenation. He says he has a remedy for your weariness."

I'm not sure how I looked when this was said to me, but I must have appeared concerned, because the mayor, who had been stiff and formal, gave me an awkward back slap that turned into a half hug. He might have thought this was American custom. I tried to say I preferred to go back to my hotel, but our conversation felt like an endlessly recessed set of mirrors, multiplying under the burdens of translations and mistranslations. The mayor smiled his black-and-white teeth, and Shoes looked at the ground, and I became preoccupied with another problem: when two people are talking through a third, then whom do you make eye contact with?

WE WOUND THROUGH common streets of little distinction—committee-planned buildings thrown up as quickly as possible, each like the last, spanning a long block. Then the next street would be salvage-heap structures and houses with odd additions, each one unique to its family's limitations. We stopped in front of a glass-fronted three-story building with a sign that read *Foot Health Massage*.

"You have?" the mayor asked.

"I'm sorry?"

"You have had massage?" the mayor said. "A specialty of this region. Better than Swedish. You know Swedish? Great experience!" His English was better, I thought, than he had been letting on.

Once upstairs, I started to feel sick—baijiu sick, discomfort sick. The building was a converted hotel. Girls carried buckets of steaming water down the long corridors. Uniformly young, these girls, in uniform, too, white blouses and black pants. But how young, exactly? I worried for them—burdensome young girls from the country, fast-used-up pack animals. Like there might be a glue factory ahead for them, or maybe this was already the glue factory. The mayor took his suit jacket off and yelled in angry bursts at small girls who were so obedient to the yelling they never looked him in the face.

I relaxed slightly when they led me down the hall and I saw three beds to a room. Shoes vanished around a corner. The mayor waved me in, flicking his hands and curling his lips. He entered the room directly behind mine.

The light overhead was harsh and clinical, and I sat down on the middle bed. An attendant brought green tea in a paper cup, and a plate of sliced watermelon. But only one cup, and only one plate. A scurrying tuft of black hair, with no eyes that I could see, came in and closed the door behind her. She took my shoes and socks off, fingered the blisters, and shoved my feet into saltwater so hot I almost screamed. My feet stippled white around the toes. I put myself through mental paces. In my stomach I could feel the one inadvisable bite I'd taken of a lobster that tasted like it had been on land as long as your average cow. I envied the real Congressman Fillmore. He was no doubt comfortable in Beijing, stripping to his underwear and counting out pills that would ease him through the night.

I already knew I wouldn't share details of this massage parlor visit with Leo. By his lights, it was fine to let Armand Lightborn pay for our trip—the House Travel Disclosure, if we ever bothered to file it, would be a fiction by exclusion—but Leo would still think it suspect for me to be behind closed doors with the local women. Your average voter's eyes might glaze over at ethical lapses of the fiscal sort—in fact, these were basically expected—but a tabloid would see no difference between a Kaifeng foot massage and a Bangkok brothel.

The girl dried my feet and tapped my foot with a pair of nail clippers. I looked down at my scraggly, tormented toenails. She wanted to cut them. It was a strange sensation. No one had cut my toenails for me since my mother, when I was too little to do it myself. The girl worked skillfully, and it felt very kind. She had a flat face, wider than you would expect for her thin body. She was tall, relatively, and not, I thought, pretty.

Soon she was using her weight to push her palms to either side of my heart. I didn't want to draw the comparison, but there was Alex anyway. I felt her body conjured from the masseuse's hands. For a moment, succumbing to myopia, I imagined Alex had been the last girl I'd slept with. I would have liked to claim I had been faithful to her memory, so I could feel sorry for myself. But it wasn't true. There was one woman— one night—after Alex. It still haunted me, what I had wanted, and the reasons I had wanted it. I asked an older woman in pearls to fix me one more Negroni and allowed her to hand me the drink as though I didn't know exactly what I was doing or why I had come so far, and so late, to see her. She was my boss's wife.

I tried to brush all these thoughts away—Alex, and Leo's disapproval, and Theresa in pearls—and to think of this masseuse like a dentist or an internist: dispassionate, palliative people for whom a human body was just a work site. No more sexual charge than a mason feels for bricks. My muscles were plastic and dead in her hands. According to the wall chart, there were color-coded energies in the body, and she was busy realigning the coursing of my spirit through my flesh. I tried to ignore my rising desire.

Above us, a television played some kind of Chinese opera, where a plaintive emperor with a Genghis Khan haircut wailed over the loss of a beloved concubine. Or perhaps he'd lost his entire empire. The music became very beautiful to me, as though I could understand it, some contact from a world where our deepest feelings of loss were transformed into consolations. But the feeling couldn't survive the desperation of the place.

At a lull, I heard a man's voice through the wall behind me. I recognized the distinct rhythm and high volume. It was the mayor. When he stopped speaking, I heard a muffled series of groans, an unmistakable animal satisfaction. Three sharp grunts, before the last and loudest one. I tried to believe I was mishearing. It was terrible to me, the thought of him, more baijiu than blood, with his domino teeth, making whatever use he wanted of one of these whipped little girls. More terrible, in fact, to find my position was just the same.

The girl tugged at my belt. She made a motion for me to undo it, and I hesitated. I looked down at her through the bottom of my eyelids.

"Why?" I asked. It was the first thing I'd said to her in Mandarin.

"*Ni hui hanyu ma?*" she said.

"*Bu hui,*" I said. "I don't speak it well."

We felt our way around in our own instant creole, putting the screws to both languages. Her minimal English, my tiny Mandarin. She repeated a phrase several times that I only heard as "lost babies."

"Las Vegas?" I said.

She smiled, clapped her hands. "I want to go," she said.

"What do you know about Las Vegas?"

"From a movie."

"Don't believe the movies," I said.

"You know it's in . . ." I stuttered. I didn't know how to say "desert." "You know it's very far away."

{ 48 }

She waved her arms in a semicircle, like drawing a rainbow.

"Big lights," she said.

"Somewhere else," I said, "might be better."

"A friend of mine goes to New York," she said. "So beautiful, I hear. Not like Chinese cities. So clean. So much trees and fresh air! The TV from America," she said. "*Friends*?"

"Yes."

"*Friends* is New York?"

I didn't know what to tell her.

"You look like the one called Ross," she said.

"You think so?" I said. She appeared to have forgotten about my belt.

"He is not handsome," she said.

I lay back on my pillow.

"But he is very educated," she said.

I didn't actually remember Ross's job on the show—to the extent anyone in a sitcom could be said to have a job.

"New York might be okay for you," I said. "I don't think you should move to Las Vegas."

She looked hurt.

"There's a huge Chinatown in New York City," I said.

"I do not want to go to America to see Chinese people," she said.

She started to undo the belt again.

"What are you doing?" I asked.

She jerked her hands back and held them defensively at her chest.

"Yes?" she said.

"I don't understand," I said.

"Yes?" she said, reaching back to my pants.

"Is this what happens?" I asked.

Her face curdled to a scowl that she took pains to hide. She didn't speak anymore, and she yanked my belt loose and I let her. She opened my pants and took me in her hand and stared off deep into the wall like she could see through it. I was afraid that my body wouldn't respond, as though somehow that would be worse. But it did. Whatever was going on in my head was unimportant. And it was fast, which was a relief. The least embarrassing thing was for it to be wordless and over. She cleaned me up with a warm cloth. I had a vision of her cold round mirror of a face looking out from the Las Vegas Strip with the lights in her eyes.

"Do you really think you'll go to America?" I asked. She didn't respond. She unfolded a fresh towel, wrapped it around her hand, and used it to pick up the soiled one crumpled at my side. She left holding the entire bundle at arm's length, her face turned away from both me and the mess I'd made. I scratched at the drying white stain on my zipper flap and hoped it could be mistaken for toothpaste.

I WAITED ON the lobby couch of the Foot Health Center for the mayor and Shoes. I never saw the girl again.

"Yes?" the mayor said in English. "Good?"

"Yes," I said. The spirit of my body had fled, but the machinery still ran. We helped each other into the car, arms over one another's buckling shoulders.

Bright white lanterns lit a wide street with poplars planted in the median.

"Your hotel," Shoes said, pointing out a set of buildings I could faintly see through a gateway in a high stucco wall. A vast red banner hung across the arch, with white lettering in two languages, welcoming the congressman to Kaifeng.

"The most grand hotel in our city," the mayor added. "The former President Jiang Zemin has stayed."

"It looks perfect," I said. I heard the relief in my voice, which otherwise sounded like I'd been gripped by flu.

We passed the hotel, and the car never slowed from its clip. I looked to Shoes for an explanation. I could find no trace of the quick, efficient man I'd met at the airport only this morning. He'd been replaced by a weeping willow, drooping over its reflection. Up front, the mayor looked pallid and slumping, his suit askew, the once-careful part of his hair now limp and stringy. I thought he wouldn't get much further in Communist Party politics without a more presidential coif.

Soon, we were at the mayor's house. In fact, we were inside his house. It wasn't clear to me how it happened. This absent whir of the body when the mind isn't in residence: I was a heart-lung machine.

The mayor's residence was decorated in the exact palatial style I thought of as Saddam-chic—glinting chandeliers, baroque flourishes in the hand-carved moldings, gold or faux-gold fixtures, right down to the doorknobs. Our present placement, in central China rather than a Baathist palace, was suggested by silk wall hangings with flying phoenixes and embroidered rugs with tongue-wagging dragons. I became absorbed in a ten-foot-long scroll painting I was told depicted the city of Kaifeng a thousand years ago. It was filled with people in spring, and the spring of their lives—dozing in sedan chairs, wandering in straw hats. Scholars talked under trees, women ate noodles. I could say I was drunk, but something in the old city scene haunted me, something beyond the easy sadness of its being past. When I looked up, all I could think was that I was far from home, that I didn't understand this country, but that I knew these men absolutely, to their guts, and I didn't want to.

The centerpiece of the mayor's residence was an interior courtyard open to the sky. Beneath a stand of trees were two overstuffed chairs flanked by three couches. My companions sat, while I excused myself to a nearby bathroom. Under a gilt-plated mirror, I wretched up my dinner and the baijiu sitting on top of it. It didn't make me feel any better. I rinsed my mouth in a sink with a gold drain stop.

When I returned to the courtyard, the mayor and Shoes were arguing. They were standing partly obstructed by a latticework screen, beyond which I could see their cutouts in motion—flailing arms, pointing fingers. I moved closer to them, but when they became aware of me, they fell silent. The mayor offered me the chair next to his. Shoes took the couch to our right.

"He says you are a literate man," Shoes said to me. Small mounds of gray skin swelled up under his eyes. It was beyond me why the mayor would find me impressive, so I understood it as flattery.

"The mayor is the real scholar," I said. "He had us all in rapt attention at dinner."

"Rapt?" Shoes asked.

"I just mean we were listening to him very closely," I said.

The mayor spoke to Shoes.

"The mayor is curious about your position on the people," Shoes said.

"How do you mean?" I asked.

"People of China," the mayor said in serviceable English.

"It was the first thing Congressman Fillmore noticed when we arrived," I said. I watched the way the mayor might react to a direct mention of my boss, but his face reflected only blank inebriation. I continued, "Mr. Fillmore says the people of China seem to be very hard workers."

I didn't have the clearest mind, at the moment, for policy. But I realized it wasn't difficult to repeat the congressman's platitudes—like riding a bike, which I could also do drunk.

"'Serve the people,'" I added. "Isn't that the saying?"

The mayor laughed.

"You have read Chairman Mao," he said.

I hadn't, but I liked that he thought so.

"Chairman Mao was a most gifted leader," the mayor continued. "Still, even the Great Helmsman is only 70 percent correct in what he did for China. This gives to everyone humility."

I was unsure what precisely he was trying convey to me with this Mao talk, until I realized the mayor believed this 70-30 split indicated fair-mindedness. Forget Mao, I thought: I worked in the US Congress. There was no way the ratio of truth to fuck-up in human affairs was anything but the reverse.

An attendant brought a new bottle of baijiu. "The mayor would like to know what you think of the Kaifeng New Zone," Shoes said.

"You mean Bund's project?" I said.

"Bund and partners," Shoes said.

"Well I'm certainly impressed with the scale," I said.

The mayor smiled: "We expect no more than eighteen months this will take."

"Even more remarkable," I said.

"Is this possible in the United States?" the mayor said. His English was getting unaccountably better as the night wore on.

"Not that quickly," I said. "You could never get everyone to agree."

"But in China we all agree!" the mayor said. I let it go. It wasn't a fight to have deep in the night and half in the bag. The mayor drank like a dead poet. Except after eighteen whiskeys, even Dylan Thomas left the White Horse Tavern to go ungently into that good night.

"The mayor hopes that showcasing Kaifeng's development will demonstrate that he could be an effective partner with the airport project in your district," Shoes said carefully. He watched my face.

I bluffed—the first firm mention I'd heard of an airport project was this morning.

"An airport would be a huge undertaking," I said. "Though I imagine if anybody could manage those complications, it would be Mr. Lightborn."

I felt servile and on display.

"I do not wish to leave you a false impression," Shoes said in fast, low English. "This discussion between Bund and the mayor about investment and construction abroad is only in the very early stages. 'Feasibility'? Is that your word? My personal interest is still to discover if your airport project could even be done."

"He is so modest," the mayor said. "It is this man who has already built entire cities."

"Have you?" I asked Shoes.

Shoes's look was the plea you might give on behalf of your rambling grandfather. The mayor was undeterred.

"The new capital is his work. All from his head," the mayor said.

"Beijing?" I asked.

"The mayor is flattering me," Shoes said.

"What is Bund building in Beijing?" I asked.

"Not in Beijing," Shoes said. "He's referring to a project I consulted on. A very small matter and quite some time ago."

"He built Naypyidaw," the mayor said. "Much better than Yangon!"

"In Myanmar?" I said to Shoes.

"A limited partnership in which I am no longer involved," Shoes said with some hesitation.

"A master project," the mayor said in English. "They have a zoo. Penguins."

Shoes set his jaw. "I have never heard of penguins."

"One million people," the Mayor said. "Very pleasing. Each ministry of the government with its own neighborhood. Each neighborhood with its special color. You know who a man works for by the color of his house!"

"Our involvement was very minimal," Shoes said. "A little consulting on technical matters."

"They didn't consult you about the penguins?" I asked.

"It is not necessary to agree with every position of a partner just to do business," Shoes said.

He turned to the mayor and fired several sharp rounds of Mandarin. My guess was Shoes was conveying that it wasn't the best American public relations to advertise his involvement with the grandiose construction projects of a paranoid military junta. I fidgeted and played with the keys in my pocket. I carried them even though the locks they fit were an ocean away.

"The congressman has long desired to come to China to see the economic progress for himself," I said. "But I'm sure he would be concerned that an American project proceed in the right way."

Political fluff—like spun sugar. The mayor asked Shoes a question in Mandarin and received a long response.

"In China we know we are not modern," the mayor said. "But every person will contribute to make a great nation. This is what will make China great, just as it is what has made America great."

He'd stopped talking about Myanmar, to Shoes's evident relief. We'd returned to platitudes. I talked this sort of empty politics all the time and found it easy to follow along. Bullshit has its function. I grew up in farm country, I sometimes told people, and you can't knock manure if you want a harvest.

The mayor switched back to Mandarin.

"A thousand years ago, Kaifeng was one of the most important cities in the world," Shoes said, translating. "Sophisticated. Educated. There were a million and a half people living in Kaifeng while in the West you were still in what you call, if I am not mistaken, 'the Dark Ages.'" He paused while the mayor shouted at him. Then Shoes added, unhappily ventriloquizing: "The mayor believes Kaifeng can be great in such fashion again. He has been very forward-looking with private investments and wishes to grow Kaifeng's economy with partnerships across the world."

"The Dark Ages," I repeated. Phrases like "forward-looking" and "private investment" made me wonder how much currency the mayor had plastered into the walls and which Swiss schools his children attended.

"Is 'Dark Ages' not a correct term?" Shoes said.

"There's a little darkness in every age, don't you think?" I said. I mumbled toward a line of ants on the arm of my chair. "Look at me: I'm twenty-four, and right now things look dark as hell."

"I'm sorry?" Shoes said. "I don't believe I understand."

The mayor wasn't listening to us: "To win-win situation," he said in English. He toasted us all around.

All-day wear had made Shoes's white shirt turn brown at the neck. His baggy, raccoonish eyes stood out even in low light. If he was supposed to show me Bund's Kaifeng project from the most flattering angle possible, it seemed Shoes couldn't even make himself believe this shaky, blood-vessel-burst mayor was a respectable steward of his responsibilities. He saw the mayor as I did—a man who spent more hours of his day drunk than sober, not a partner, but a liability. In better circumstances, both of us off the clock, Shoes might have simply taken me out late and asked me a thousand questions about what Americans thought of China, about Hollywood stars and pornography. Instead, he took another of his deep, nasal breaths and excused himself from the courtyard. It would be the last time I saw him that night.

The mayor gripped my right hand in both of his.

"It has been a pleasure to meet you, and I hope you take good tidings back to your boss, the Congressman Fillmore."

The mayor released me and wagged his hands in that way of his—shaking his fingers like he was casting a spell. An attendant appeared, this time holding a brown leather briefcase with two clasps and a lock. My eyes swam to see it placed at my feet. The mayor twitched with a smile he was trying to conceal from his face, as though I was his only son about to receive his first car. When I didn't grab the briefcase myself, the attendant lifted it onto the arm of the chair and unlocked it. He pulled back the velvet cover over the contents. On top was a manila envelope marked in Mandarin with an English translation that read: *Documentation.* Beneath the envelope lay stacks of American money, side by side, deep as the case, an emerald sea.

"Congressmen Fillmore should understand," the mayor said, pulling his gravest face. "There is greatest potential for Kaifeng as a partner. Win-win situation."

Somewhere far away, Leo attended to less incriminating matters of his own rest and comfort. I wondered if he knew—if this was expected. I wanted to turn this night over to see the stitching on the backside, the threads that composed it. I felt painfully what it said about me that I'd stood here, flattering this man all night while offering not a word of protest. I was a barbarian of a very special kind. Not the mere violent nomads of bad reputation who lingered outside the city walls. No, I was one of the barbarians inside, in some quiet council chamber, working up the official pocket-lining plans, running things luxuriously into the ground. I heard a voice calling to me, admonishing me from a great distance. It reached me, my conscience, as a quiet echo. It said just what the poet did: you must change your life.

I closed the briefcase and stood up and met the mayor's eyes. And as to what happened next: Let me blame my drinking. Let me curse the jet lag and the late yawning night. Let me say that I didn't want to cause offense to my host or that many other people would do the same. Let me point to my confusion and the inadequacy of Leo's instructions as mitigating circumstances. Let me sliver the hard truth into something smaller. Let me say anything but what actually happened: I carried the money off.

AT THE VIP section of the hotel, the night clerk showed me to a room. Chairs covered in soiled plush and picture frames with chipped gold paint. The carpets were mismeasured and didn't reach the walls. Mentally unkempt, too wild to sleep, I tried to draw a bath in the Jacuzzi tub. The hot water came out tepid, at a pace so slow that it would be cold completely by the time the tub filled. The in-bathroom sauna wasn't even hooked into the cracked pipes jutting from the wall. The phone rang.

"Yes," I said.

I heard Chinese I couldn't understand and street noise in the background. I hung up, and the phone rang again. The voice was female, speaking heavily accented English.

"You lonely?"

"Yes," I said.

"I come to your room?" she asked.

"No," I said. "No, thank you."

"Massage?" she said.

I hung up, and when the caller tried a third time, I let it ring and rattle the night table. When I was hired, the congressman had stressed that nothing was innocent or free—"Be suspicious of good treatment," he'd said. I'd tried to look askance at the men who came calling on our office, but Lightborn was the richest of these men, and Leo, as far as I could tell, didn't evince any suspicions of him. Perhaps he believed he was above the petty suasions that would tempt his staff.

I opened the briefcase on the bed, and using a pillowcase as a glove, I dug out the stacks and saw they went all the way down to the stitching. I fumbled the packets around and saw only hundred-dollar bills—dead weight whose worth must reach into the hundreds of thousands. After a painful few minutes of sprawled, spinning nausea, I fell into nervous reflection. Insomnia was my worst friend, who came knocking at night to spew out every dark thing on his mind.

One day last April, Alex's boss had come into the office seeing double and died of a massive seizure, right there on the taxpayers' leather loveseat. We'd stayed at my apartment that night, the parlor floor of a HUD-subsidized town house, part of the government reconstruction of a once-boarded-up and burned-out area near the Capitol. She butchered open some wine and drank most of the bottle without my help, cork debris buoyant in a juice cup.

"He was so erratic," she said. We sat cross-legged on my mattress. "So maybe that was a sign? Of whatever was happening in his brain?"

"Do those things have warnings?" I said. "It sounds, you know, more like a stray bullet."

"He complained for months that he was exhausted. Was that a sign?"

"Stop saying 'sign,'" I said. "You're not a doctor."

"One of us should have known," she said. "He screamed at the whole staff. Flung anything he could get his hands on. He hadn't done any real work in months."

"Alex," I put a hand on her thigh. "There are five hundred men in the building who fit that description."

She stared at my blank walls, painted slate gray by the last tenant. It was like waking to a perpetually overcast day. I traveled so often with the congressman that I didn't have much investment in my DC place except to be the simplest, barest thing—I called it minimal, but even I knew it was bereft of warmth. My mattress was on the floor, and my books were piled high without shelves. Alex said that I was trying to live like a poet without being a poet. I liked the books as furnishings: stacked in odd towers, they reminded me of sand castles. The few days a week I was in town, I usually slept at her place. I stole from her a sense of home.

"So is it bad that maybe I find this liberating?" Alex said. "The man's dead. Just like that: dead."

She seemed to catch herself here. "I'm sorry," she said, touching my elbow. My father had only been dead eight months then.

"It's not like you're happy about it," I said. It wasn't clear anymore who was supposed to be consoling whom.

"Don't say 'happy,'" she said.

She looked at my open suitcase. It lived on my floor, halfway packed or unpacked.

"It's just a junket," I explained. "Apparently Lightborn's got this place in Venice."

"Venice?" she said. "Who can Leo even pretend to meet with in Venice?"

"I said I should skip it. I told him I should be around to help you get things sorted out."

"You don't have to do that."

"You want to know Leo's answer?" I said.

"I don't know," she said. "Do I?"

"He says you should just come."

She cocked her head at me. "Go to Venice with you?" she said. "It'll look like I'm dancing on a man's grave."

"It's basically a long weekend."

"And I pay for that how?" she said. "With severance?"

"Are you being funny?" I said. Maybe the wine had hit her too hard.

"It hasn't been a funny day," she said.

"It's all Lightborn," I said. "No one's paying for anything."

No moonlight and lanterns and teeming night now, just sun, and Kaifeng in empty morning daylight seemed at the furthest possible remove from any place I had known in my life. People screamed calisthenics outside, limbering their sleep-tightened muscles all in unison.

At seven, the hotel rang to say a driver was downstairs. He was a lean man, chewing a toothpick. On our way out of town, he helped me buy two cheap phones from a street-side electronics bazaar, negotiating the price down to a quarter of what was initially offered to my white smiling face. I saved one phone for Leo and used the other to leave a message at our office with my new number. My call to Leo's room in Beijing went unanswered.

In the airport security line, sweat streaks ran from my armpits to my elbows. I received a skeptical once-over from a woman with the brisk movements of a drill-team dancer, and the briefcase cycled through the X-ray scanner and rolled to the end of the conveyer belt. The woman traced her hands over my bags and called over two dreary officials. I stared straight ahead. The recklessness staggered me—I was angry at myself for accepting the cash, but also at the mayor for lacking the sophistication to offer his gift in some subtler way. The officials looked at the briefcase, then at me, and made me follow them to a windowless room.

Minor officials the world over sat behind such desks: pedantic two-somes, heartbeats of the bureaucratic will. I sat stiffly and tried not to look like some itchy heroin runner. The older woman pawed my passport open to the travel visa, which featured an elaborate illustration of a red, bursting sunrise and the Great Wall loping over hillsides. I worried about my puffy, pale face. If it was a crime to board a plane with this much cash, I didn't know it. If there was a penalty, I hoped the contents of the briefcase would suffice to pay. She unlocked it and scanned the envelope containing the mayor's "documentation." She showed the document to her partner, who leaned forward in his chair, scrutinizing the mayor's letter. He looked on the verge of asking me some further question. Instead, he repackaged the envelope with care.

The woman pointed dismissively for me to collect my things, and I'd hardly stood before she was looking at me as though she'd never seen me before. I lifted the briefcase. Did I drop this in Leo's room without a word? Did I try to explain? Would he be pleased or upset?

THE FIRST-CLASS BATHROOM housed a sick woman embarked on a long occupation, so I squeezed down to the two in the back. I was reluctant to leave the briefcase for even a moment. The load was heavy and sharp-cornered, and I knocked into a man's knee hanging out into the aisle. In the tiny bathroom, I set the case between my feet, flattened my hair, rinsed my stale mouth, removed the mister from my cologne, and spilled it into my palms to mask the baijiu leaking from my skin.

Elbowed back halfway to my seat, I paused in turbulence. I saw a man who had been concealed by his newspaper on my walk down. The gaunt face, the blunt nose—mostly what I think I recognized was that incorrect ratio of neck size to suit size. This man with the tiny head—or, not tiny, but made to appear so by inartful tailoring. I turned from him as I passed. Back in first class, behind the rough curtain, I peeked through the slit. I was sure I had just seen the police captain from Kaifeng, escorting me with the mayor's gift back to Beijing. Or, that's the problem of it: it was a half glimpse and I became very afraid, which, when you put them together, feels very much like being sure.

BEIJING

DESCENT INTO BEIJING, through no-visibility smog, left me dizzy and distressed. Business class meant first off the plane, and I waited near the choke point of the boarding gate for a second look at the police captain. I wanted to run flush into him, to reintroduce myself. I wanted to mention all of last night's associates by their proper titles—to say his name as to a fairy being, and thereby break the spell. The next flight's passengers snaked and elbowed around the gate like they were witnesses to an accident. Something was happening with canceled flights or over-booked ones, or sandstorms were grounding planes, or the Beijing air-port was an airlift and these the refugees. Or this was everyday life. I couldn't tell. My arms were pinned to my sides by nearby bodies. People tried to push onto the gangway before the plane was empty. I never saw the Kaifeng captain disembark through the commotion—no man that was him for certain, nor whichever man I might have mistaken.

Outside, the bright mix of smog and sun—call it smogshine—made my eyes swell and itch. My taxi driver loitered in standstill traffic. Long ago, Beijing had been laid out on an orthogonal grid, a Ming-era design of concentric squares and ring roads that concealed the Forbidden City in the center. But the Ming pattern was now so swallowed by opportunistic sprawl, the pattern makers would have been lost instantly in the city they'd made.

"Last five years only," the driver said, enunciating every syllable, pausing at the end of every word. He nodded happily to himself when he finished the sentence.

"What's that?" I felt guilty asking him to clarify.

"Everything," he said. He took both hands from the steering wheel and swept them across the length of the windshield, horizon to city horizon. Ordinarily this would have been a frightening maneuver to watch, but since we were basically parked, the car didn't demand much of his attention.

"Next year people see," he said. "Olympics."

This last word was a hurdle for him, but he spoke proudly. I wanted to join him in his enthusiasm, but my thoughts were full to bursting.

We nudged like worms into Beijing's dirt. Off the freeway, the city chaos felt like the objective form of my personal circumstances, entirely continuous with a glimpsed police captain on my plane and the gifted briefcase at my arm. A boy on the side of the road tried to fix the bent wheel frame of his bike, and his friend pumped air into the back tire, and above them, a team of workers adjusted the wirings of a leaning power post, while off in the farther distance a line of men as small as a row of pigeons stood at the roofline of an unfinished apartment tower. In all that flatness of Beijing before me, girls cut hair and blind men busked folk songs on erhus and attendants cleaned public restrooms. Life teemed out to the northern mountains, invisible today in the sandy wind. An old woman replaced yesterday's paper with today's at a display stand where people read as they waited for the bus. Beijing had the traffic of a city being evacuated. Cars and motorcycle rickshaws were piled into the road like all these buildings were in flames and every one of us fled a column of fire.

. . .

BACK IN MY hotel, I barred the deadbolt against my thoughts of the Kaifeng captain and sat on the bed. I kept turning over the matters it fell to me to broach with Leo, and my worst suppositions about him couldn't be whisked away. I pulled the case into my lap and opened it, hoping it would contain something different this time, a magician's box with rabbits or pigeons. Under the lamp, the money shone with its emerald light. I felt already like "Congressional Staffer #1" in the affidavits.

One dinner in particular came to mind, from back when I first started working for Leo. I had to know then, I suppose, that I'd cast my lot. I was sitting right off Pennsylvania Avenue, halfway between the White House and the Capitol, and they never handed us a bill. I don't know what we racked up, a dinner for eight, all rib eyes and Cabernet, but I know the check never came around, and Leo showed no surprise. I knew then that he was a man who'd learned how to take what was being offered, who knew not to hesitate, or make a show, but to offer a quick suture of pandering conversation. The owner, who had a tidy, barely there beard, like a shadow on his face, came over to shake Leo's hand. Leo rubbed his stomach, boomed out, "Everything was wonderful!" and changed the subject to the Washington Nationals bullpen, how they'd lose 120 games if they kept running out this waiver-wire rotation in front of a Double-A relief corps guaranteed to get torched in the late innings.

That dinner wasn't the most important, perhaps just the earliest, of the times I'd kept my mouth shut. I had eaten my share, and drank more than that, and I didn't want to look ungrateful. On my salary, if you priced out the bottles ordered up from the cellar, I couldn't afford my own wine. They were idly talking House seats that night— how they'd recruited this millionaire to run for a California seat with favorable demographics but which Republicans hadn't held in twenty-five years. The Democratic incumbent, a guy everyone liked personally, had just about fondled and groped his way out of office.

They talked about what the recruit could spend, how even without fundraising he'd be up on the incumbent three-to-one because he could finance from his own bank account. I remembered thinking: why would someone spend three million dollars of their own money to get elected to a position that pays under $170,000 a year? I should have walked out right then, once I solved that elementary problem of arithmetic. But I doubt anyone has ever quit a job while full of a fifty-eight-dollar steak they didn't pay for. What you start to do is convince yourself you can handle integrity personally, as a matter of feeling. You accept what's on offer, but you say you're different—because you didn't ask or because you're skeptical in your heart or because you're not the worst. As though these leave you still free. You decline to ask who is paying for what. Really, you might prefer not to know. Knowledge becomes culpability.

I woke up hungry, and the sun was fading and my new phone was ringing. Leo's voice was always instantly recognizable for its annoyance, and he usually began talking before he even dialed the phone, so when the male voice on the other end said "hello" and waited for a response, I knew, even swimming from sleep, that I wasn't speaking with my boss.

"How's Shanghai?" the voice asked.

"I hope it's fine without us," I said. I managed to choose pronouns with care. "We're still in Beijing."

"Beijing?" The voice cracked, and I placed it. An intern Leo had brought in, Glenn, a recent college graduate who Polk had turned into his personal secretary during his rounds of debilitating treatments. I heard papers shuffling, unless it was a crackling connection.

"Mr. Polk's schedule says you're in Shanghai today," Glenn said, hesitant.

"What's the date on that schedule?"

"April 19."

"There's a newer one," I said. I was sure that was true. Bund had emailed a new itinerary twice daily in the final run-up to the trip. It was my job to manage the circus of changes, and I had failed at it.

"You didn't let Mr. Polk know?"

"How come I'm talking to you? Polk can call when he's in."

"Mr. Polk is out sick."

"He's out sick?" I said. "He worked through chemo."

Glenn had a suit he'd bought new for the internship, but he didn't know to cut the jacket vents or the pockets, so he walked in it stiffly, with no place to put things. I never clued him in. He was eager enough, sometimes even helpful, but I could also see he was prone to red power ties and a creeping fascism.

"How's the boss?" he asked.

"I can't really tell," I said.

"Moody?"

"Go home," I said. "Go back to bed." I'd fallen asleep in my suit. I sat up and fumbled at the knot of my tie, yanking it hard and only tightening the knot. I steadied my fingers and went back like a surgeon and got the tie undone and popped the top buttons of my shirt.

"While I've got you," Glenn rattled out, sensing I was about to hang up on him, "I'm trying to square up some of Congressman Fillmore's committee coverage. They dropped reams of stuff on us at like five o'clock yesterday."

"So read it," I said. "Summarize. Use big fonts." Sightings of Leo actually reading a briefing book were apocryphal, like encounters with Bigfoot—no matter, he still demanded them.

"I promise I'm not being difficult," Glenn said. "Just one more thing."

I checked my impulse to throw the phone across the room. I turned on the television to newscasters on BBC World, all of whom had the same indeterminate international look—khaki-brown skin, but never too dark, English with a global lilt. The woman who reported the time in Singapore, London, and Dubai could be from Lahore, Athens, or

Buenos Aires. I pulled off my sweat-through socks, barely listening to Glenn in my ear. I undid my belt and scratched at the yowling red welts left by my waistband. They looked like stretch marks. I needed a haircut and to see a dentist, both of which I had been traveling too often to commit to. My slouch in the mirror reminded me of Leo's.

"What's that schedule say about Shanghai?" I interrupted.

"Shanghai?"

"Yes, Glenn" I said. I was standing on a narrow ledge, which was my patience. I was going to jump.

He paused. "Most of today and tomorrow says 'Cultural Excursion' or 'TBD.' The only firm commitment I see is tomorrow night. Dinner with Armand Lightborn and . . . I can't read this first name. Mr. Hu? Is that pretty much what you have?"

"Pretty much," I said.

"Theresa's been calling," Glenn said like it was all one word.

I hung up on him and tossed out my messenger bag. In my nest of envelopes were two plane tickets, booked weeks ago, for a China Eastern Airlines flight that left Beijing for Shanghai tomorrow morning. Beyond that, I had two tickets home: Sunday morning, Shanghai to New York City.

Calls to Leo's room buzzed without answer. I was routed back to the front desk.

"Has Mr. Fillmore checked out of the hotel?" I said.

"I'm sorry," the clerk said. "This is a reservation marked confidential."

I sagged into the bed in my undershirt. I stared at the ceiling, then at the briefcase, feeling the change all at once. I had come all this way, but where had I gone? Alex, I remembered, had left DC saying she'd reached her limit of complicity: lying for your boss, saving face for your boss, covering for your boss. The force of her example sat on me. And yet, the longer I'd worked for Leo, the harder it became to walk away from the down payment of my sufferings—months I remembered as nothing more than dirt-caked windows and saccharine energy drinks and prescription sleeping pills pilfered from Leo's stash. I felt Leo owed me consideration for my sacrifices, which was just the same sunk-cost fallacy that kept most everyone at the job they had, when we had equal cause to riot in the streets.

I packed my things for the morning flight, an optimistic gesture that I half-believed might have the power to make Leo appear by boarding time. I unsnapped the briefcase again, thinking I might tally the amount just to have a number. I didn't get far before I started to think there might be barriers between tonight and tomorrow, unthought-of eventualities—stiff airport guards who might need bending, or minor security officials who could make trouble while Leo was gone and this briefcase was in transit. I slid a band of hundred-dollar bills out from among the firm stacks and split it up between my wallet and my jacket pockets, stuffing myself like a scarecrow.

THE NIGHT CLERK shambled after me to the congressman's room, where we knocked without reply. A hundred-dollar bill talked him into letting me peek inside, with the caveat of his continued presence.

The suite was twice the size of my own, with an L-shaped executive desk and a king-sized bed. The bed didn't look touched since the maids were in this morning. No messy suitcase lay on the floor, and none of Leo's pill bottles cluttered the bathroom vanity. The unabated pounding from the neighborhood construction was just as loud as it was in my room, but the congressman's floor had a better view of the wreckage and the city beyond.

My phone vibrated against my thigh. I grabbed for it.

"I wanted daily updates," Theresa shouted. On the cheap phone, bass drained, her voice reached me as a high-register whistle.

"Schedule is hectic," I said. "I apologize."

I looked across Beijing into a particulate sunset of Gobi dust and pollution.

"The toilet in the guest bathroom," she said, "the tank won't refill."

"I'll call the plumber when I'm back Monday," I said. I rocked in the executive chair and heard the boom of walls collapsing somewhere below the visible skyline.

"My mother is coming this weekend," she said. "You want me to have her walk downstairs in the middle of the night? She's eighty-five years old!"

"Call Glenn," I said.

"Glenn makes my teeth hurt," she said.

Her natural timbre was actually quite sweet, oddly matched to what usually poured from her mouth. I pictured Theresa on the other end of the line, with that glare that could break a bone in your face. She was attractive in a severely wound, pursed-lips way that made her look more Parisian than American, though she had some spare midsection she spent mornings trying to shrink on the elliptical. I always wondered if Leo knew what people whispered about the fidelity of his wife. Perhaps he did, and he was satisfied none of it was true. Or perhaps he and Theresa had some other accommodation that was none of my business.

"Well," she said, leaving the plumbing aside. "How is he?"

She and Leo rarely spoke to each other by phone, leaving me to play go-between. But I would not tell her that the last time I had seen Leo was two days earlier, that he'd been spectacularly drunk, that he'd leveled a phone at my head, and that after I blocked the projectile, I left him unattended in the hotel lobby, half in love with an image of his choking death.

"Booze?" she asked.

"He hasn't had a drop."

"Bullshit," she said. "If Armand doesn't send him home smelling like gin and whores, then I'll pay your salary for a year."

Theresa's background was in finance, where she'd elbowed into the boys club. I was convinced she'd have made a better member of

Congress than her husband, except retail politics didn't suit her. She had a sharp sense of personal dignity that wouldn't allow her to dress down and flip pancakes next to a costumed chicken at the county fair.

Suddenly her end of the line was drowned out by public-address speakers squealing a station stop.

"Sorry," she said. "I'm on the train to New York. Apartment hunting."

The night clerk tapped me on the shoulder.

"I can't get into this right now, Theresa," I said.

"I want every detail when you're back," she said.

"I promise."

"Remind me that drink you liked?"

Talking to Theresa was like standing at the opening of a trench whose bottom I couldn't see. At ground level, a bulldozer hit its last wall of the day, and a slow centipede of helmeted workers filed from the construction site.

"Negroni, right?" she said. "I remember. Nothing to soften the blow there."

"I'll call you tomorrow," I said. "Leo's fine."

"Leo is Leo," she said.

We hung up. I put my hands on the desk to help me to my feet. I'd spent just one night with her, but I obsessed over the memory. I'd gone to the house because Theresa said the upstairs fireplace was blowing smoke into the bedroom. Leo had been away fundraising. Alex and I had finally decided our distance was hurtful, and the best means of preserving whatever good feelings remained was to end our relationship. Theresa and I had four cocktails before we were wrapped together on the living room couch. At first, I felt what I thought I might: a private satisfaction that I had somehow paid Leo back for how he belittled me. But that feeling proved fickle. Theresa took the real spoils. When she visited the office, she gave me conspiratorial winks, and I eventually understood that these were not come-ons as much as signals that she held something over me. The intractable question, that I have never

answered to my satisfaction, is whether you regret more those tempta-
tions you resist, or suffer more from what you have done.

I FOLLOWED A bend of rubble piles and cranes and found a noodle
shop on a side street, behind the hotel. I'd hoped the night air would be
calming. I found nothing consoling in it.

Long ropes of noodles were pulled and cut into a steaming pot. They
had the look of threads in a loom. I ordered by pointing, more to have a
seat than anything. I held the bowl up to my mouth, twirled the chopsticks between the weave of noodles, and slurped small bites. I sipped
the broth, salty enough to sting the lips. I wished I had any appetite at
all—dangling, I felt, between Leo's recklessness and my own. As well
as I knew him, it was hard to imagine where he'd gone. The restaurant filled with a late rush of shouted orders, the noodles loomed and
un-looming, and Beijingers crowded around my seat. Their mutterings
eventually drove me away. I left my bowl of noodles nearly full, and two
workers stared in my direction, disbelieving—the *laowai*, the foreigner.
One of them, caked in plaster, picked my bowl up and finished the left-
overs himself.

I walked toward the back face of the hotel, rising sheer like an obe-
lisk. To all appearances, every guest was out. I could see where I had left
the light on in my room—the one lone light. The curtains were drawn.
I was pulling my room card out of my wallet when it occurred to me
that you needed to have the key to turn on the room's lights. I took two
steps back and recounted the floors: ten stories up, corner room. It was
too late for housekeeping. I was almost sure I'd left the curtains open.
Then the light went out.

I ran in the side entrance of the hotel and took the service stairs
two at a time, ten flights. I spent a long moment kneeling on the top
landing, winded. The face in my imagination was a composite of the
Kaifeng police captain as I remembered him last night and in the

blurred uncertainty of this morning. I looped my head around the stairwell door. The corridor was empty. I wanted someone else to discover who was in my room, and from a phone near the elevator, I called the front desk and asked for housekeeping to leave me fresh towels.

I snatched a *China Daily* off another guest's floor mat and held it open at the far end of the hall and waited until the elevator pinged. An attendant emerged, balancing a stack of linens up to her eyes. When she began knocking at my door, I followed. She keyed in, the lights blinked on. A pneumatic spring kept the door from slamming. I had more tension in my arms than I realized, and I shoved the door open and smashed into someone coming the other way. I fell into the switch, and the light snapped out. Behind me the door hit the deadbolt. It was dark save for a vertical band of light from the hallway. Fabric brushed on fabric. An interior door closed in the dark—the bathroom, or the single closet.

When I'd put the lights back on, I took the room in. I couldn't see who I'd struck. The girl with the linens had vanished. I raised my fists and walked with trepidation to the far side of the bed, finding nothing but the armchair I'd passed my first night in. The briefcase lay on its side near the desk, and I couldn't recall if that's how I had left it. I cracked it open, and the only thing missing were the bills I'd taken myself. I heard a murmur, and I spun around nervously and announced to the empty room that hotel security was on its way up. I lifted the bedskirt carefully with my foot, and I met two black eyes glaring back at me. I was face-to-face not with the suspicious police captain of my worst imaginings, but with the housekeeping girl, so badly shaken she'd scurried out of sight.

Embarrassed, but relieved, I said everything I could to get her to come out. I tried to explain I'd had a teeth-rattling few days and had managed to convince myself someone had broken into my room, when in all likelihood I'd miscounted the floors. I kept talking to the poor girl until she crawled into view. She looked about fourteen in her black button-up shirt and a black skirt. They were street clothes, not housekeeping ones, as though she'd been halfway to freedom before being sent on a last, undesired errand. I continued to offer apologies, unsure if she understood me.

It occurred to me that she could complain—call her manager, call the police, say I'd assaulted her. I unfolded a hundred-dollar bill from my jacket pocket. I creased it into a tent and set it on the bed and pointed so her eyes would follow.

She fingered an eyebrow as I pled with her. The bed was a buffer between us. She took a step around the foot, toward me, and then lost her composure, twisting her wrist in front of her eyes and mine, shaking her hands at me like she wanted me to acknowledge and bless her pain. She spit out angry words I didn't understand. I sat down in the armchair thinking this looked unthreatening. She grabbed the bill and ran out.

I wanted to run cold water into the sink, dump a bucket of ice into it, hold my face under until my corneas froze. When I tried the bathroom door, it was locked—slammed shut in the commotion. I jiggled a credit card in the door latch, futilely, before calling the front desk. I hoped they would send a different worker than the trembling one who'd just sprinted out the door.

I was relieved when an employee I'd never seen before appeared with a master key. He sprang the lock and what we found inside, to my surprise and his, was another cowering girl—this one woeful and tearful, with a growing red knot on her forehead. She was dressed in the hotel's black uniform, which had a much bulkier, institutional fit than what the girl under the bed had worn. A stack of fresh towels on the bathroom vanity made me understand I'd made a grave mistake.

"There was a girl hiding in my room," I said to the boy with the key. "Tell her there was someone else here."

I left him ministering in a serious whisper to the crying maid. I grabbed the briefcase and went chasing after some other girl who I was positive was already far gone.

• • •

"SHE WAS ABOUT this tall," I said, hovering my hand at my breastbone, talking to one of the bellboys. "Black skirt. Young."

The bellboy tried to help, but I could tell I only worried him. With the help of his shift partner, whose English was slightly more advanced, they conveyed to me that I'd circled the hotel for a girl who'd left behind no impression.

I stalked away from the hotel into a night that blew a cool diesel breeze. Not knowing Beijing, every direction was as good as any other. I felt the impossibility of my situation. Corruption filled my sight without shape or contour—a gray wall. I held tight to the hopeless compromise of the briefcase and could make no sufficient account of Leo's invisibility. I wanted time to parse the piling confusions of search and surveillance, but Beijing seemed to possess no quiet or private space. The city's explicit inhospitality to the uninitiated was as choking as its smog. I was twenty-four years old and felt every short day of it.

Beijing's daylight was like sunlight through smudged glass, and the night, with artificial lights by the millions, a perpetual dusk. I walked with the briefcase until I arrived at a park. I wound my way inside, around tiled pavilions, faint and gray, under a canopy of green leaves that grew purple as I strayed from the streetlights. I came to a vast lake. My skin perked, and I shivered like I was some hairless little house dog.

I sat on a bench and nestled the case between my feet where the nubs of my ankles held either side. I stared across the dark water. I'd been with Leo in places where we were as sure that we couldn't drink the tap water as we were that our hotel rooms were bugged. Only I'd never been in those places alone. I hoped I was right that Leo had simply gone to Shanghai ahead of me, to enjoy the kind of stunning entertainments Armand Lightborn could provide, but my speculation also felt like it wasn't worth much—if it was a currency, you'd need a wheelbarrow full of it just to buy a bowl of noodles.

Finding movement best for my nervous thoughts, I left the park and wandered. I walked through a hutong alley of the sort I'd seen near my hotel, with an air of having stood for centuries, even as I knew they took only a morning to demolish. In stray conversations, the Bund men made it sound like the residents uprooted by this spectacular development, the people in these courtyard houses, were the very people moving into the apartment towers replacing their homes. I had a hard time believing that could be true. The location was too central, too valuable—if it wasn't, the old houses would still be standing, and the people in them would have been left alone. I paused at one crooked lane to see two ceremonial lions perched on either side of an arch that framed an empty space beyond. I felt strange—maybe burdened is the better word—to be in possession of one of the last pair of eyes to see houses that had been built long before the Constitution of the government I worked for had been signed. Above the dust of falling walls was a picture of what would replace them: towers not more than a few years old, already scuffed and worn. It seemed almost deliberate, a ruin aesthetic—the new Beijing so poorly built that it counterfeited the age of the hutongs being destroyed.

I took a pedestrian walkway under a major road whose name I would never know. In the underpass, people camped next to bursting canvas bags. Men who looked just-arrived from the provinces were dressed in long sleeves and long pants in this windless walkway on a windy night, looked nervous and beaten. A boy stood guard over a rusted bike as though this crowd was nothing more than a parade of jealous eyes. He seemed unable to imagine that what he so prized wasn't something everyone else coveted, too. I pressed through until I got back above ground, in front of a train station that looked like one of the old Paris gares. I walked aimlessly for a very long time. Finally I met peddlers selling ten-pack postcards of Tiananmen Square. I turned to find the square behind me, the empty concrete center of the city. It was haunting, so barren. I set down the briefcase to rest my arm.

As exhausted as I was, weighted with concern and a growing paranoia, I continued to imagine I could lift the mystery of surveillance and rob it of its power by confronting the spectral Kaifeng captain to say, "You are following me and having me followed. You sent a girl to search my room." And I thought that if I could only say this, and make him agree, then his agreement would turn him to dust or smoke. I was positive I could explain that I wanted, just as much as the captain and the mayor did, to deliver this money to my boss without further delay— that my lips were sewn shut and my real longing was only to get home.

I flagged a taxi and mimed "drink" to the driver, like I was throwing one back. He puzzled at my charades, then hit the steering wheel with a satisfied smack. He kept telling me where he was taking me, and I never understood. At a stoplight, he pointed: "Sanlitun Lu," he said with a sweeping wave of his arm up and down the street, like it was impossible it would not contain everything I could ask for.

I found no bars I liked—all crowded and clubby—until I turned off the main street. I climbed narrow stairs, and it seemed like a dream to walk through an entryway of hanging beads and be the only person in the place, where the beer was Carlsberg and no European dance track roared from the jukebox. The bartender, who also seemed to be named Li-Li, spoke almost no English, and her Mandarin was in a dialect that I couldn't even identify, let alone understand. She ran the least popular dive in Beijing. It was the sort of hideaway I thought would compel the morning to come without further incident. I put the briefcase between the stool and the bar, and Li-Li seemed to be asking me about it, and I was glad that I could act like I didn't understand her.

After I'd had a few drinks, she tried to teach me a game. We each shook clusters of dice under our cups and then peeked. She flashed numbers on her fingers. And then I wasn't sure what. She got fed up and finally just looked at my dice each time and pronounced a winner. Sometimes I won, sometimes I lost. I took my camera out and showed her my pictures of Beijing and Kaifeng. I skipped quickly over the official ones, like I wasn't here for anything in particular, was just some lonesome traveler. I kept touching her arm, she kept bringing me

Carlsberg. I took her hand and brought her to the karaoke machine with me. We chose together. I wanted Johnny Cash, and she wanted Michael Jackson, so we played them both. She handed me the microphone, and after mumbling my way through "A Boy Named Sue," which I don't think she'd ever heard, the Michael Jackson came on. We belted out "P.Y.T." together—I knocked over one of her barstools and pulled her close to the microphone. Her sweat was acidic and sour. She sang loudly through crooked teeth. Her voice broke, and mine was too deep, but both of us tore our hearts out running up to the chorus: *I want to love you—PYT!—pretty young thing.*

The song ended, and my ears rang in the silence. We went back to the bar, and I lifted the briefcase onto a stool, and she pretended she was going to open it, and I pretended I was going to stop her because it held a bomb. She thought that was funny. We wrestled over it until I held her close. My burdens were in no way lessened, but they seemed to be. She had a bony body, with some surprising paunch in her belly. The course of my life's errands did not become any clearer. Leo's whereabouts were not revealed, and the Kaifeng police officer had disappeared from my sight, but not from the world, and the girl I'd caught in my room still pattered her secret little steps over some part of Beijing unknown to me. But my thoughts contracted to the bartender's cotton shirt in my hands, and we kissed for a long time. I got the sense we were equally puzzled, having no language to speak to the person in our arms. She gave me her home number and a cell number and an email address, and I made her an awful lot of promises I meant sincerely, as I said them, but would not keep.

FROM FOUR TO eight a.m., I slept curled on my side on a massage table in the Asia Hotel's gym, hugging the briefcase to my chest. I got probably fifteen minutes of hard sleep, ended when two vigorous Swedes came in to use the treadmills and shook me so hard they must have feared I was dead. I apologized to them and stumbled to the shower in the pool house. When I finally had the courage to peek into my room, two maids were stripping the sheets. I collected my bags and discovered, upon checkout, that there was no bill to pay.

I called Polk on his home phone.

"I should be happy to hear from you," he said. He ran out of breath. He wheezed hard. "And yet I'm not. So explain this to me. Because you're fucking impossible to find."

"Who?" I said. "Me?"

"Why don't you answer your fucking phone?"

"Leo broke my phone," I said. "Inside fastball. I gave Glenn this number."

"Glenn never gave me shit," Polk said. "He said you were evasive."

"Glenn's going to have a long and successful career," I said. It hadn't occurred to me that I would have been roughly as difficult to reach in the last forty-eight hours as was Leo.

"Put Leo on," Polk said. "Your voice is like listening to someone shit."

I didn't know what to say to him. Leo's disappearance was a flat horizon, a blue fading beyond reach. But I wanted to stack it on Polk's shiny head, because it should have been his unwinding as much as mine. I told him, to the best of my knowledge, it seemed Leo had gone to Shanghai without me. Polk went hoarse with frustrated screams, phlegm in his throat. I heard his nurse's voice, a Jamaican accent trying to calm him.

"So what do you want me to do?" I asked.

"What do you do? Is anything you're saying serious? Do you have a goddamn time machine? Get one of those. Set it for last Tuesday before you fucked everything up."

I told him I'd be reunited with Leo by this evening, an assertion that landed somewhere between a hope and a lie. I said I'd call again. I thought from the silence the line had gone dead until faintly I heard Polk's wheezing.

· · ·

I DRAGGED MYSELF up the jetway and boarded to flight-attendant scowls just before they barred the door. As we ascended, I watched Beijing recede. Leaving the city offered me one small relief: the image of the police captain grew minute to me, like the shrinking towers.

I had never thought much, or long, about what might come after this life, but that morning I was so out of sorts, so dubious about whether I would find Leo in Shanghai, and what state he would be in if I did, that I had the strangest vision. I suddenly felt in sympathetic contact with a world of bygone things, a world of ghosts. With the lone exception of the Forbidden City, what I saw in Beijing below was the manic destruction of every brick of the architectural past. It was like getting rid of the past tense of a language. The present tense was supermalls with eight lucky floors and big-box convention centers and starry hotels for people like me. Residents evicted in favor of those just passing through. It made me think that if the spirit world was anything like our own, their desires must tend toward what they lack. They would spend all their time thinking of the beloved objects they could never touch again. So how the ghosts must wail as we bulldozed ourselves a present—tore their walls out of joint and pulled down their *pai-lous* and leveled the gardens where they had once found peace.

SHANGHAI

I.

RECOGNIZED A WOMAN standing at the end of a tired receiving line of taxi drivers and errand boys just outside baggage claim. She smoothed her skirt with her hands, and in the process wrinkled it, so that she had to set to work again, smoothing. She lifted her head to scan the terminal and found me standing in front of her. She was startled but smiled in a bolder, toothier way than she seemed capable.

"Mr. Slade. I am Li-Li," she said, offering me her business card with both hands. "From Bund International. You remember?"

Each time we met, she was convinced I would have forgotten her. I felt in a hurry but looked her card over politely. These formal graces needed renewal each day.

I explained that my boss's arrival in Shanghai had preceded me.

"Very good," she said. "This is no problem."

"Maybe not for you," I said.

"I'm sorry?" She concentrated on my face.

"I don't mean to rush you," I said. "But I feel like a donkey lugging these bags."

Li-Li panicked and reached out to take the mayor's briefcase off my hands. I yanked it back in a reflex.

"I don't want to burden you," I said. I hoisted the case and grimaced like a weightlifter. She turned her face a quarter ways, angling me from the corner of her eye. I thought all the while about an accidental conjunction—how, long ago, Leo and my father were born under the same desert sky, and how that first coincidence had now, through a thousand permutations and bad decisions, brought his son groping into Shanghai with a suitcase and a messenger bag and probably half a million dollars embezzled from the taxes of Chinese peasants.

WE TOOK THE Maglev train out of Pudong Airport—bullet speed through gray flatlands, the train barely swaying despite the ground it covered. Li-Li's presence didn't dull my apprehensions about Leo's drinking, or ease my worry that I might have trouble corralling him, but it did comfort me, at least, to have arrived in the city from which our flight home would depart tomorrow. Wherever he was, he didn't want to stay in China forever.

Shanghai was dripping, gloomy. Skyscrapers pushed into view, a cloud city rising to life out of some old illustration of the future. From the Maglev stop at Luoyang Road, Li-Li found a taxi, and we crossed the Huangpu River in halting traffic, under global financial towers that crept up and groped the sky. Nothing in my imagination of the world's possibilities—the hands that built it, the lives it contained—could help me account for Shanghai's over-awing presence, its high-rises multiplying from the soil into a miasma of soot and acidic rain.

We sputtered through a commercial district of wide boulevards emptying onto eight-story shopping malls. Li-Li's version of the congressman's appointments listed only what pertained to her direct boss, whom she called Mr. Hu. In some paper universe, Mr. Hu awaited the pleasure of Mr. Lightborn's and Mr. Fillmore's company at dinner this evening. This confirmed what Glenn had told me, but I was desperate to see how ragged a state Leo was in, to gauge if I could speak to him about the Kaifeng money and the girl I'd found searching my room. I felt like I'd been sewn into my clothes.

Li-Li followed me into the Hua Ting Hotel. I checked in and asked the young desk clerk if Leo Fillmore had arrived, but the girl would neither confirm nor deny. Li-Li waited while I dropped my bags in my suite. The briefcase I kept with me.

"It's chaos, I know," I said, by way of apology. "Our trips usually run more smoothly."

Li-Li considered this, then looked back to her phone, which scrolled blue light along her face. She said she'd called to reconfirm dinner, but Armand Lightborn's layers of assistantry told her Lightborn was shuttling between meetings and couldn't be reached. If the point of secretarial work was to insulate Lightborn from people like us, his staff performed their work superlatively.

"Don't let me keep you," I told her.

"My work is to see that you and the congressman are arrived to dinner," Li-Li said. One knee was buckled, and her other leg shook. I didn't like the concern that darkened her face with my every sentence, like she was solving algebra problems without scratch paper. We were both of us like this, I suppose: squirrelly assistants with endless worries.

I found two chairs that sat in a facing pair, far from the bellhops and check-in counter. I hoped to settle myself before the dinner. The waitress came by shortly and she didn't understand "Negroni," so I took a beer instead.

"So where are you from, Li-Li?" I asked. I liked her for sitting with me. It soothed my nerves to keep up appearances, and talking with her gave me something else to occupy my head.

"Where are you from?" she said.

"You go first," I said.

"Anhui Province," she said. She would have been happy to leave it at that.

"And what's there?" I pressed.

"One of the most beautiful mountains in China," she said. She flushed at the word "beautiful." "It looks like a painting."

When the waitress came back with my drink, Li-Li changed her mind and ordered a glass of white wine.

"And you grew up there?" I said. "On the mountain?"

"No," she said. "Two hours away. Where did you grow up?" She looked relieved whenever she lobbed back a question.

I told her where I was from, and to my surprise, she was familiar with my corner of the Fifty-First Congressional District of California—its skin-peeling sunlight and cattle feedlots, our ranch-style, white stucco houses roofed in Spanish red tile. She said that she'd visited our district with her boss to survey a potential airport site in the desert north of town.

"The project is very early," she said. "It was not so interesting."

Her first try at the wine was a gulp, like she was thirsty. She made a sour face. I left aside the matter of the airport for a moment and asked Li-Li to describe her impressions of my hometown.

"The people in your town," she said. "They live a very simple life."

"Simple is good?" I asked.

"California is not what I imagined," she said. "I thought I would see mansions everywhere."

"Not there, you won't," I said.

She lifted her hands from her lap, gestured like she was pulling a length of string.

"Your streets were long," she said. "Clean. The buildings were interesting to me. Everyone was very kind. They took me to American buffet. They took me to Mexican food. They even took me to eat Chinese foods. I could accept this . . ."

"But you missed Shanghai," I said.

"I did not like driving."

"Do you drive here?"

"Never," she said. "In America I learned. In two weeks. My boss said I should drive anyway, it does not matter. Californians are very 'laid back,' he said. You understand?"

"I know the phrase," I said.

"It was not even the heat," she said. "It was the isolation."

Li-Li described the toll it took on her boss as they surveyed the desert, and I felt deeply sympathetic. At the end of nearly every workday, she said, he would get screaming drunk on a bottle of the closest liquor to hand. She shook her head as she related this nightly wallowing. I wanted to tell her, in Mr. Hu's defense, that as far as my hometown went, he was basically honoring a local custom.

"Two times a week he made me drive him to a casino built by Indians," Li-Li said. "I did not know that the Indians of America were such big gamblers."

I started to correct her but felt the history was too complicated to explain.

"There's a lot of empty desert between you and that casino," I said. On bad nights, she told me, Mr. Hu would lose her whole year's salary at the craps and roulette tables. She would sit in plush chairs near the entrance, reading simple books in English.

"My favorite to read was Ernest Hemingway," she said. "I always understand him."

Three strong gulps made short work of her wine. She started to lose her formal bearing, slouching in her chair like a teenager. She told me how she'd finished *The Old Man and the Sea* one evening while Mr. Hu was at the roulette wheel chasing his money down the deep hole it had disappeared into hours and hours back. She fed her nickels into the slots and won ten dollars and quit. At the end of each night, her boss threw his arms around her, less from lust than from drunkenness. Her candor surprised me. She told me she'd help her boss lurch to the car where they'd blow back through the desert, Mr. Hu demanding all the time that she drive faster, placing a hand on her thigh to force down the pedal. Along the way he had to get out of the car several times, because he was sick or because of his bladder, and once Li-Li sat at the side of the road near tears, too petrified to move, feeling the car shudder at the big rigs passing a few feet away. In his looser moments, with Li-Li behind the wheel ranging across these sand-strewn highways, Mr. Hu despaired at what he was so hard at work on—what he was killing himself for, in exile, in this wasteland, happy only when he was drunk and dreaming, or the moment before the ball on the roulette wheel stopped.

"I make it sound terrible," Li-Li said. She brought her hand to her mouth and sat up straight again. She'd startled herself by talking so long. "It is good to have a job."

"This probably isn't what you dreamed of doing with your life."

"Did you say 'dreams'?" she said.

"Goals," I said. "Ambitions."

"I have been saving," she said quietly. "To leave this work and start a business of my own."

"In real estate?"

"Skin cream," she said, breathing her words over her empty glass, "to keep girls pale. To keep them young. I see tiny bottles women buy for hundreds of yuan."

She tapped her fingernail on the wine glass. The passing waitress heard the tinkling and brought her another.

"What has been your feeling of this development project for your town?" she asked.

"If Leo thinks he can get us an airport, I suppose I can see the benefits," I said. "It'd bring jobs. A flood of government money. It's not impossible."

"The vision is very large. Airport. Shopping. Hotels," she said. "But Mr. Hu is not optimistic. His experience tells him America will soon fall far behind. Projects are impossible there. He said every problem is easier to deal with in China. Problems with permits. Problems with workers."

"Or problems with officials," I offered. She didn't react, but I felt a confidence had begun to develop between us.

"Do you know Mr. Lightborn?" Li-Li asked.

"I've met him," I said. "I wouldn't say I know him. His wife probably didn't know him, back when he had a wife."

"What is he like?"

"In what way?" I said. "In the cocktail-party sense, he's a charming guy."

I wondered what else I could tell her. I could point to a few magazine profiles, but they were all toothless. Lightborn's lawyers would descend like creatures of hell on articles that ventured into why he didn't speak to his father, why he'd been thrown out of boarding school, why his first wife had filed a restraining order against him.

"I am only curious because Mr. Hu feels so much stress about any meeting with Mr. Lightborn," Li-Li said.

"Leo turns into a teenage boy around Lightborn," I said. Our customary currency, as assistants, were these stories about the fears and failings of the people who controlled us like marionettes.

"Mr. Hu says Mr. Lightborn is very excited about the potential of this project with your boss," she said.

"Well, this is what I would say about Mr. Lightborn," I said. "He has a habit of knowing the future."

"What does he know?" Li-Li asked. She handled her second glass of wine like the first, a full mouthful to start.

I realized I wanted to hear this out loud for myself—three days in China had forced me to face up to more about Leo and Lightborn than two years of work in Leo's office had. The tentacular structure of Lightborn's projects was foremost in my mind—the link between the airport plans and Bund's grandiose construction in Kaifeng and the briefcase nestled near my unpolished wingtips. Lightborn had Chinese partners with limitless visions, Leo's district had empty land a few hours from Pacific ports and cities, and I had the briefcase that forged another link in that chain. A congressman runs on money the way a power plant runs on coal.

I leaned forward to Li-Li. "I'll put it this way. Lightborn is one of those guys who can buy an abandoned farm property for pennies right before the state just happens to need that land to run a highway extension."

"A good businessman?" Li-Li said.

"Lightborn's more than good," I said. "And much more than lucky."

I leaned back, and what I felt, to my own surprise, was pride—like I had untied myself by explaining what I knew, or could surmise. It occurred to me that all I had to do at dinner was tell Leo I quit, and I could be flying free to New York City the very next morning. I waited for Li-Li to see what I was seeing, new vistas of sunlight with no glare of shame.

She looked me up and down carefully. "You seem to have stress. Does your head hurt? I have medicine."

I told her my bulging head was just lack of sleep, and anyway I had spent two miserable years like this.

Loosened from the beer, I asked her a favor I'd had on my mind for an hour. I'd been too ashamed to voice it. I held out the mayor's brief-case between us.

"Would you mind taking this home with you?" I said. "I have papers in here that I don't trust in a hotel. I'll arrange to get it tomorrow before our flight."

Li-Li returned to her officious posture, happy to be of assistance. I told myself that in the best version of events, simple logistics would force Leo to leave the mayor's gift behind. Li-Li would have it all to herself. She could use it to start her dreamed-of business, expensive creams for pale faces. But mostly I was relieved to be rid of a burden, even at the cost of deceiving her.

A TAXI DROPPED me at the Shanghai riverfront for which Lightborn's venture was named—the Bund. I stood in front of a looming Beaux

Arts building that occupied an entire corner, with arched windows mounting to a cupola. It wouldn't have been out of place in a better-preserved part of New York City, a formerly public or municipal building turned into luxury apartments. Standing in front of it gave me a sense that it was detached from a more romantic time, though even I knew the architectural legacy of Old Shanghai was pretty only if you were capable of forgetting the colonial depredations it rested on.

I'd pulled out my last unworn shirt, French-cuffed, trying to look less obviously discomposed. A pair of my father's silver cuff links poked out from under my rumpled blazer. I felt ready to offer Leo my resignation.

On the fourth floor, in a lantern-lit entryway, I mentioned Mr. Hu's name to the restaurant hostess, and she led me to his table. As I approached, with his face in silhouette, I saw a gaunt man who had enormous hands. I started to introduce myself, only to find that I had already met with those birdlike eyes.

"You're Mr. Hu?"

"A pleasure again," Shoes said.

It was Bund's project manager from Kaifeng. "You're Li-Li's boss?" I said. Another encounter with melancholy Shoes wasn't what I had prayed for in my private moments. I was dragging all of Kaifeng behind me.

"She is very formal, that one. Even away from the office," Mr. Hu said. "Please sit?"

In contrast to the banquet seating of my other formal meals in China, we faced each other across a table for four. The intimacy of it made me long for the enormity of the glass lazy Susan and the dispersal of eye contact that comes with a table of twenty. I pumped my legs under the table. We sat together waiting for our superiors to arrive.

"You enjoyed Kaifeng?" Shoes said. "So much to learn there. China has a very long history."

"I've studied some of it," I said weakly.

"So you know the Tang dynasty? The Song? The Ming? The Qing?" he said. "You know Qin Shi Huang?"

"He's the one who built the Terracotta Army," I said. "He ordered it built, I mean."

He grunted and looked toward the ceiling. I preferred talking history to calculating what to say to him about the mayor's money or Bund or the shaky state of my boss.

"And so the Kaifeng Hi-Tech project," Shoes said, ducking his head nearer to mine. "Do you believe in the success of a business venture with Kaifeng? For example, now that Bund is interested to take their Chinese success to partners in the United States?"

He was so eager to hear what I would say that his lips started forming words, like he was trying to kiss them over to me. One fact about my job in Washington: I didn't speak until I'd first learned what people wanted to hear. With Mr. Hu, I couldn't establish the ground beneath us.

"What is most important in business is to be absolutely forthright," Shoes said.

"I'm happy for us to be as honest as possible," I said.

He scratched at a lemon wedge on a small plate near his water glass. The waiters stood off at a distance, in black tuxedos, against the flower-print walls, straight as the bright orange columns that separated diners from one another. Wine glasses reflected on every table like a deconstructed chandelier, and our conversation was accompanied by the xylophonic tinkle of bused water glasses and heavy silver forks tapping stoneware plates. I affected not to notice the drawn silence between us. I stared above Mr. Hu's head trying to make Leo and Lightborn materialize behind him. My breath was high and shallow in my chest.

"Perhaps it is best we order a dinner?" he said.

He was less manic than the hopeless man Li-Li had described, but when he hung his head, I could see all the worry burrowed under his conversation.

"I'm fine to wait," I said.

"Why is that?"

"For Mr. Fillmore and Mr. Lightborn."

Shoes shook his head. Never had stiff manners seemed to conceal more despondency.

"Mr. Lightborn will not be with us this evening, I'm sorry to say to you," he said. "I have word that his meetings continue in Hong Kong. About your boss, you can say better than I."

"Are you sure about that?" I asked. I tried not to show him he'd knocked the wind out of me.

"Order yourself a dinner," he said. "This is, as you might say, 'my treat.'"

I stretched my napkin with numb hands.

"Is there any way you could put me in touch with Mr. Lightborn?" I said.

"We can talk, you and I."

"I appreciate that, Shoes," I said. "But it's more of a personal matter, if you don't mind."

My spastic movements, shoulders shaking, and my voice rising a tone, drew askance looks from neighboring tables. The double take of two businessmen eating soup, ties tucked neatly into crevices between their shirt buttons, made me counsel myself to keep my nerves down.

"Let's be honest now, please," he said. "Where is Mr. Fillmore?"

It was like he'd reached across the table and slapped me in the face. With his long arms, he could stay seated and knock me to the floor.

"Mr. Fillmore is here in Shanghai," I said. "That's the best of my knowledge."

He grimaced.

"I cannot be any help," Shoes said, like it pained him to be told such obvious lies, "without knowing the truth of the situation I am asked to assist."

"Leo must be with Mr. Lightborn," I said. I rolled my shoulders, though it felt like even the smallest adjustment would rip my jacket in two.

"This is not true as I know it," Shoes said. "As I say, Mr. Lightborn is yet to return from Hong Kong."

"You know that for sure?" I asked.

"I do not know anything for sure," Shoes said.

The waiter buzzed near, and Shoes flicked his wrist to wave him away and never took his eyes away from mine.

I leaned in hard on the edge of the table.

"My boss started drinking again, okay? With your people, in Beijing," I said. "He got drunk, and he's probably kept on drinking. So maybe Lightborn got held up with other business, but that means Leo's alone. That's not good for anyone. He's done this before. He's a wandering goddamn soul. Eventually what's going to happen is someone is going to find him."

"Where would you find such a man?" Shoes asked.

"How do I know where?" I came close to shouting. Shoes raised his hand and lowered it slowly like settling a lid on a pot.

"Maybe he found a nice hotel," I said, more steadily. "Maybe he's in a whorehouse. Maybe he's out of his mind and dancing in a cabaret calling himself 'Louise' . . . I wouldn't rule much out. The point is he needs to be on a plane to New York City tomorrow morning."

Beyond the stress and fear, what I felt was resentful—like many whose fortunes have depended entirely on a benefactor's heartbeat.

"Let me ask you." I put one finger on the table, like I was about to trace a route. "If the police were to pick him up before tomorrow, then what?"

"The circumstances will depend. I know people in public security. They can be reasonable men."

"I'm afraid of someone getting the idea that they can score points if Leo turns up somewhere he shouldn't be. And the optics won't be good for Bund or Mr. Lightborn, either. Nothing about your project will be helped by Leo being caught in some scandal."

"Optics?" he said, confused. "Points?"

"Political points," I said.

I was holding fists and punching the air between us for emphasis. Sometime between the beginning and the end, I had let fury suppressed for days flood out to my limbs.

"Let me make some calls," Shoes said. "It is as important to me to speak with him as it must be to you."

"Call who?" I asked, lowering my voice so far that it barely registered as a question.

"There is not anything you can do," Shoes said. "What will you do?"

"I have to think of how it looks," I said. "Attention is the worst thing possible."

I watched two young men flip through a legal pad between them while a waiter bussed their plates. It seemed darkly possible a negotiation like mine was happening at every table.

Shoes held his thought for a second. "You're sure of this. His drinking?"

"It's happened before," I said.

He took this under advisement. His next question was unexpectedly gentle.

"Can I ask you details of your business here?" Shoes said. "Your knowledge of your visit?"

I tried to face him. But what was I willing to admit? It was clear that Lightborn, with Chinese partners, was angling for Leo's assistance building a vast new project in our district. And I understood that the mayor of Kaifeng wanted to partner with Bund in the effort, though Mr. Hu despised him. Where Leo actually stood, what he might have promised or overpromised to Lightborn and Bund, I could only guess, but we were here, after all, and there was money. I held the first of it. Beyond that, I thought any further explanation I could get for the events of the last few days would only reflect the interests of the person I asked to cut the knot. Shoes waited on an answer I never gave him.

"I have a classmate from university," Shoes said. He spoke as though musing sadly to himself. "An excellent friend. Very smart. A good athlete, too. A very all-around man. He rose to the head of a ministry quickly—State Food and Drug Administration. I was always envious of him, during our friendship. He was a very flexible man, I would say. I studied him very closely. Flexibility is a necessity. He knew which way to bend, do you understand?"

I had a hard time making myself nod.

"This country changes with a great pace," Shoes said. "It is too rapid to be just one person. The problem with my excellent friend was that he became too flexible. He started to be flexible all the time, without judgment. He will soon go on trial. I am less envious of his station now."

I started to speak, but Shoes held me off. "When Deng Xiaoping led China toward reform and opening, he said, 'It doesn't matter if the cat is black or white, as long as it catches mice.' Many people, I believe, took this to mean the rules disappear. This is an error. One part of what is necessary is the rule. And the second part is to know when the rule itself is not necessary. I have been doing business in China many years now. The cat must still be a cat and must remember it is after the mouse. My friend needed to be a lion. And the lion is not happy catching mice, you see?"

All I saw was a faint, yellow glow out the windows, behind the terrace tables. When I looked closer, it was the bright reflection of the Oriental Pearl Tower across the river. A table near us held a group of Dutch tourists. A serious woman documented every plate of food put in front of her. Her camera flash caught my eyes.

"The Party will wish to make an example of my friend," Shoes said. "I am certain that what he will receive for his flexibility is a bullet in the back of the head."

I chewed the fat middle of my upper lip. He folded his large hands on the table.

"My question has to do with what your boss is looking for," Shoes said. "And to ask if he has disappeared for any reason you are not accounting."

He stared at me now with a widow's eyes. I could see him poised over a roulette wheel. I could see his sticky hand pressed onto Li-Li's leg. I could see him sick at the side of a desert highway. This one-time technical consultant to the Myanmar junta wasn't a picture of rectitude, no matter how he wanted to present himself. I assumed he was at least as complicit as I was with the mayor's "gift." He stared at me until my composure waned.

"I did not mean to cause you any offense," he said. "Would you like a cigarette?"

"I need to leave, so smoke all you want."

Two waiters rushed in as they saw me stand, one to pull out my chair, another to refold my napkin.

"If you do locate my boss," I said. "I have to know before anyone else." I flicked out a pen and wrote my phone number on the back of Leo's business card. I hoped I sounded capable and not like an abandoned child.

Shoes accepted my card with both hands, but his obsessions ran tangential to mine. "You might have observed that the mayor and I did not see eye to eye," he said. "For some time, his position has been to have me removed from this airport project before it proceeds. My position has been the mayor's involvement must be avoided. That man would bring only complications. And yet, he feels he has prevailed in our dispute."

He was insistent that I hear this, and yet all of Mr. Hu's affect was odd to me, like his statements undermined themselves, or his assertions were self-canceling.

"I am certain that the mayor overestimates his standing," Shoes said. He voiced it with resignation rather than triumph. His manner turned strangely deferential.

"You understand it is necessary for me to explain this situation to your boss," he said. "But please permit me to say I sympathize with your personal complications. It is clear to me your boss has behaved in such a way that he has lost your esteem. I have found in my experience that many other things can be rebuilt, but once you have lost faith in a man, there is nothing that will restore that."

I turned so quickly to leave that I collided with a waiter snatching away my napkin. The waiter fell backward into his trailing partner. The partner bumped hard against one of the restaurant columns. I wondered that the column didn't fall, too, onto the row of tables, that the tables didn't flip and shatter the waterfront windows, that the beams that held the outdoor terrace didn't also dislodge and slide down four stories to the street, dragging us all into the waiting river.

In front of an old bank building on the Bund, I called Polk. I confessed: I'd lost Leo. I waited for the words to register. As far as I knew, there was only one congressman in all the history of the US Congress who'd left on a foreign visit and never returned. He'd been murdered in Guyana, at Jonestown. He was also named Leo.

Polk rasped back at me, his voice small even at its peak exertion: "How did you fuck this up?"

On the Huangpu River, ferry boats and yachts cut the water. I was lost somewhere within myself trying to find the words that would guide me out.

"Should I call the embassy?" I said.

Polk sounded physically unwound and went momentarily quiet. "Those assholes?" he said. "Tell me you didn't."

"Maybe Leo's fucking dead," I said. "Are you considering that?"

"You suck dick at your job. Are you considering that?" Polk said. "You suck toothy shitty dick."

I looked up at green and gold towers, their spires piercing the clouds. I was one small person among Shanghai's twenty million, all of us scurrying under construction skeletons on former swampland. Maybe this skyline was progress, the best work to make of our limited human days—building cities, building nations. But I wanted to close my eyes, or slow it down. I wanted to pause for one still moment of consideration. Neon characters flashed ads that were nonsense to me. Mirrored windows hung over the anonymous crowd. Friends met on the sidewalk, took one another by the hand, let go to let others pass, and then linked hands again. I wished I could become any one of these people streaming past and vanishing from my sight.

"You don't know what position he's put me in," I said.

"Don't start talking like his fucking wife," Polk said. "Neither one of you are in positions you didn't choose your goddamn selves. I'll call Lightborn. I want you to do nothing. You're a plant until I talk to you again."

"I'm going to be on that plane home tomorrow morning," I said. "With or without him."

This threat felt difficult to carry through, even as I said it. But I offered it so Polk didn't think he had me on a leash.

"Get cancer," Polk said. He hung up.

The other Leo, in Guyana: he'd been shot on the tarmac next to his plane. An assistant was shot alongside him—a woman, about the same age then as I was now. She'd played possum for the better part of a day, bleeding on the runway until help arrived. Decades later, she ran for and won her old boss's seat. I knew staffers in her office. They kept a wary eye on their idioms: "drinking the Kool-Aid" was off limits; so were "pulling the trigger," "under the gun," "left for dead." She must, from time to time, still think of her old boss, and I always wondered what she thought of him—if she'd made that Leo a hero, or if she'd decided prying into Jonestown hadn't at all been worth it, that

Jim Jones would have continued his paranoid apotheosis among the believers, but done it without killing anyone, had he just been left the hell alone. I felt suddenly unaware of the buried capabilities of the men we were involved with. And my fear was that these men were equally unknown to Leo Fillmore—that his corruption was not even accompanied by understanding.

II.

I N THE HOTEL lobby two teenaged girls took turns at the piano. The morning was a far-off destination. I ordered a drink—more than a few, actually, but just Tsingtaos, sitting as near as I could to the entrance. I preferred the commotion while waiting on Polk's instructions. Three women in pink pillbox hats greeted travelers circling through the gold revolving doors.

The scattered armchairs filled with other weary guests. I wasn't the type to strike up conversations, though I often attracted them. Cab drivers, lonely businessmen, married women—they saw me, and they saw someone who never missed a day shaving, who wasn't physically imposing, who was neither fashionably dressed enough to be intimidating nor shabby enough to be suspect. I was blessed with the wise words of sad, adrift people who'd had too many cocktails after the conference. Women pressed stories of personal dissatisfaction, and men more often had some unfunded dream. I did not interrupt: Leo liked that about me, I think. I seldom knew how to end a conversation, unless I was trying to prolong it. The way I got to know Alex was by working late in the Rayburn Building, planning my exit to coincide with the sound of her heels clicking down the hallway. I could stretch my day out an extra hour to bump into her and then manage to fumble the conversation closed as soon as it began.

A man sat in a chair across from mine without asking if it was occupied. I knew I looked alone, reeked of it. He had two inches on me, so he was an actual six feet, not my liar's six feet. His suit was slim-fit and his shirt tailored. I looked him over and guessed finance, New York City. He was too put together for DC.

"American, yeah?" he said. He had the faint accent of a stifled Midwesterner who'd gone east for college and stayed.

"Good guess," I said.

"What business?" he asked.

I considered lying to him.

"Government," I said.

"The big thief, huh?" he said. "Which part?"

"The Hill," I said. "Congress."

He laughed.

"Is that funny?" I asked.

"Isn't it?" he said. "Sorry. No offense."

"Some taken," I said.

"Long day?" he said.

"You know bosses," I said.

"I don't miss them," he said. He wasn't much older than me—five years, tops. He looked like he worked out, but the muscle was for show, a little bulge of bicep and scrawny legs. I couldn't guarantee he spent his weekends playing touch football in the park, but he'd definitely be the one you'd think to call if your team was short a guy.

We seemed to both be staring at the lobby fountain, like it was important to take it seriously.

"So you've seen some shit, huh?" he said after a minute.

"Nothing special."

"Come on," he said. "Congress?"

"You know," I said, leaning in. "It's nothing but briefcases of cash. I don't even know what to do with all the leftover briefcases. They're starting to clutter my apartment."

He smiled and settled himself into his chair, draping a leg over the corner of a low table in front of us.

"So it's as fucked as it looks?" he said.

"Even more fucked than that."

"You work for anybody I'd know?"

I took a breath, said the name sighing, blowing it away from me to lose it in the night: "Congressman Leonard Fillmore."

"I've heard that name," he said. "Had that money thing a couple years back, yeah?"

"That was paperwork," I said. "People made too big a deal of it."

"Leo the Lyin', right?" he said. "I remember."

"Headline writers," I said.

He was referring to a campaign-finance fuckup from before my time, the kind of thing opposition research scatters into the media winds from time to time. Nothing had come of it.

"Hey, no judgments," he said. "People want to give him money, he should be able to take it. You're going to run the world on three-dollar checks from old-folks homes? Come on. Everybody knows how it works."

"They think they do," I said.

"So? What's your angle?" he asked.

"Obtuse."

"I see," he said. "You think you're the clever one."

"I wouldn't say that."

"You're the one who's so smart he can't even see he's getting screwed," he said. "I bet you don't even clear 60K. Get screamed at all day? Might wind up in jail at the end of it?"

"I get a free Metro pass," I said.

"You should be getting Super Bowl tickets."

"That's a little above my weight class."

"C'mon, don't be a sucker," he said. He thought I was that college roommate still stupid enough to study for an exam whose answer key could be had for a couple dollars. He didn't realize I'd bought the answers, too.

"I got a World Series ticket once," I said. I was angry with myself once it was out of my mouth. "Box seats."

"Whose box?" he asked.

"Armand Lightborn."

"Lightborn?" he said, and he whistled. "Risky business."

The revolving door spun like a pinwheel and reflected lights off every polished surface. Was that Liszt on the piano or Chopin? I never knew anything.

"What'd you say you do again?" I asked.

"I didn't tell you yet," he said. "I own a company. We've got our manufacturers in China."

"What do you manufacture?"

"Mesh."

"Huh."

"That nylon mesh you find on backpacks—the netting stuff. A million uses for it. If you stop to think about it, the whole world runs on mesh. To me it does."

"How'd you get into that line of work?"

"It's a convoluted story," he said. "But it's paying now."

"Really."

"Billion-dollar industry," he said. "And I'm the king."

"Any openings in that business?" I said. "I could use some billions."

"Yeah," he said, "what would you do with it?"

"Fly to the moon. Buy a DeLorean." I tried to consider what I might actually want from a windfall of money. "Who the fuck knows?" I said.

"Have you met the girls here?" he said, leaning close, dropping his voice a tone.

"Not really my thing," I said.

"You a fag? No judgments."

"You got me," I said.

He looked at me and was laughing again: "Man, if you're not into whores and free shit, then what exactly do you do in Congress?"

I tried to pivot. I thought I might learn something from this King of Mesh. "I've always heard China was a difficult place for an American to do business," I said.

"Less than you might think," he said. "You need Chinese partners. And people are scared of the corruption. But Washington's corrupt, too."

"You really think those are the same thing?"

"Am I hurting your feelings?"

"No," I said. "But you understand why I ask."

I could smell scallions frying in the hotel restaurant behind us, and it reminded me I had walked away from Shoes before eating dinner.

"Let me tell you the difference between you and them," the King of Mesh said.

I distrusted all sentences that began, "Let me tell you . . ." It was always men who insisted they had the world all figured out and were about to hold it before you, dangling on a string. He continued: "It's that the corruption here is manageable, rather than stupid and wasteful and at eternal cross-purposes. The thing is, you could throw money around Washington all you want and your shit still might not get done. You people are corrupt without even being dependable."

"You're right," I said. "Bribery is really a matter of decency."

"Bribery is a lawyer's word."

"Lawyers have excellent vocabularies," I said. "Collusion, conspiracy. Misappropriation of public funds."

"Put it this way," he said. "In China, they might pass a law that says you can't make people work when it's over 105 degrees, but then the official temperature will never be over 104."

"You ever been outside when it's 105?" I asked.

"I only mean that to be illustrative," he said.

"So everyone wins, then."

"I'm just saying at least this way some works gets done," the King of Mesh said. "That FCPA and Sarbanes-Oxley horseshit ties you up like a fucking roasting chicken. What you people don't understand is that what the United States calls 'bribery' is what half the world calls 'doing business.' If you don't pay, someone else will—there's no addition or subtraction."

"You know," I said, "It might not be smart for you to be telling me this."

"You're pretty harmless, buddy," he said, pounding down the rest of his beer and looking to order two more. "Am I wrong?"

He paused, like he was holding me up under a light. A petite Chinese woman walked in on the arm of a sallow-faced man three times her age, and the King of Mesh gave me an exaggerated eyebrow.

"The girls here are phenomenal," he said. "Particularly in Shanghai."

He'd decided I had the usual weaknesses. That was fine. I couldn't disagree. He handed me a card.

"These are the girls you want," he said. "Not the scummy ones who'll leave your junk infected and rob you. These ones come to you discreet. They love Americans. Anything's better than these Chinese millionaires. They're psychotic."

I rubbed my finger across the thick card stock. It had the same cotton feel as money.

"That code on the back," he said, "that's my account."

"That's generous," I said. I flipped it over. The back was blank.

"I'm fucking with you," the King of Mesh said. "Pay for your own whores."

"That's how my mother taught me," I said. I put the card in my wallet.

"I say whores, that's not right," he said. "They're lovely ladies."

"I'm sure they appreciate that."

"So satisfy my curiosity: Armand Lightborn," the King of Mesh said. "I hear he shows off this house in Venice that's like a fucking palace. Like he thinks he's a count."

A party emptied out of two cabs and came into the lobby, screeching to the ceiling. I couldn't hear him well.

"I'm sorry," I repeated. "Did you say 'his account'?"

The King of Mesh slapped me on the thigh. He couldn't hear me, either. He leaned in, "You're exactly right: he's a cunt."

He paused. "But you reap what you sow, right?"

"That's never been my experience."

"Government work make you a cynic?"

"I don't know," I said. "Chicken or the egg?"

I didn't share with him that not only had I heard of Lightborn's Venetian palazzo, I'd once been a guest. I'd enjoyed it without reservation, maybe the three best days of my life. It takes long enough, sometimes years, to confess. Even then it might only be to ourselves—we who are the most forgiving of our transgressions.

"You're one of these serious types," the King of Mesh said. "I got a brother like you. Spends all day dressed in black, writing sad things about the moon."

"I've just had a long couple days," I said.

I felt my phone buzzing in my pocket—Polk, I assumed. I pulled it out and held it up for the King of Mesh to see, like the call was a nuisance, though I would have paid the waitress a thousand dollars of the mayor's money to ring me out of this conversation.

"You're back on duty," he said. I told him it had been good talking to him, even shook his hand. He said he'd clear our tab.

"Tell the fucking fraud 'hello' from me," the King of Mesh called out.

"You're going to have to be more specific," I said.

· · ·

It wasn't Polk calling, but Li-Li.

"I apologize for Mr. Hu," she said. Her voice was patchy and somber. "I did not know when I sent you to dinner that he would be so rude."

"He wasn't rude," I said, evenly, though several drinks with the King of Mesh hadn't chipped away at Mr. Hu's disquisition about lost faith, flexible men, and the bullet-in-the-head ends of corruption.

"I can explain it to you," she said. "He has been relieved of his duties by Bund International. He did not reveal to me until now his dismissal."

"He was fired?" I said. "When? Who?"

She started to explain, but I sensed Li-Li didn't understand it, either. Light didn't always filter to the bottom of our pool.

"It is very unjust," she said eventually. "He had hoped at dinner he could clarify the situation for you."

"Clarify?" I said.

"It is a poor choice for Bund to ignore Mr. Hu and do work with this mayor," Li-Li said. "It is not my place to say so, but perhaps you should tell this information to your boss."

I should have offered her my sympathy, asked what Mr. Hu's dismissal meant for her own job. But I didn't. I had every desire to avoid deeper involvement. The turning of tomorrow morning, for me, was the tying of a knot.

"I'm sorry," I said, "please understand that my concerns right now are very specific. I need to locate Leo. Or I need to speak to Mr. Lightborn. Any help you or Mr. Hu might give . . ."

I wandered to a quiet mezzanine conference room. Its cavernous space was several degrees cooler than the lobby. I felt extra-sensitized to these tiny variations in the thermostat.

"Do you require your briefcase now?" she said.

I'd forgotten, for a moment, that I'd left that money in Li-Li's hands. But Leo would have to show up personally if he wanted to lay his claim to the mayor's gift—let him open a Chinese bank account, or show the documents of a provincial Chinese mayor to US Customs. Let him explain it to a congressional ethics committee.

"Keep it until morning," I said.

What I really meant was, run away with it, Li-Li. Go build yourself a hut on the most beautiful mountainside. Contemplate the stream water and the play of fog and light as morning wanes to afternoon and never for any reason let a person talk you back down to this world.

I WANTED ANONYMITY and air, and I ducked into a taxi and asked the middle-aged driver to take me back to the riverfront.

"You want lady?" he said.

"No," I said.

"I can show you girls. You have money?"

I told him I had a wife in the United States.

"I have wife, too," he said. "And now I drive taxi."

I wasn't up to humoring him.

"Do you see big acrobat show?" he said. "Very beautiful women. Bend every way. A lucky man marries these girls."

His English was good, but he ran out of conversation when we hit four snaking lanes of traffic.

I slipped out of the car and into the crowd at the promenade along the Huangpu River, filled with Chinese tourists and a few Germans, from the sound of it. All the Chinese tour groups wore bright flimsy baseball caps that couldn't hold a shape. A young couple in red hats staggered in front of me with wonder in their faces. They might have been even more confused by the city than I was, bused in from some distant interior province where all the hills still had names. The boy handed me his heavy camera, and I tried to frame him alongside his girlfriend's shining face, with the looming hypodermic needle of the Oriental Pearl Tower behind them. They looked so happy in the viewfinder. The camera needed a hard push and made a loud click. We exchanged vigorous bowing nods as they backed away.

The dark walkway reinforced the presence of the buildings on either side of the river. In a long arched row to my right ran the colonial architecture built by the British and French back when Shanghai was either the Paris of the East or the Whore of the Orient. Across the river, Pudong's instant skyscrapers towered out of wet, sinking sand, a whole new city plugged into a substrate primed for liquefaction the minute the earth rumbled. You could mistake the Huangpu for the river of time itself, I guess—the ever-flowing present that divides past and future.

As the muddy water deformed the lights of the Bund and Pudong towers, I found it almost too easy to come detached from the life I had been living—it wasn't so solid, or so constant. I felt several years of effort go limp in my hands. Leo's disappearance lifted a veil. I heard an oceanic rushing through my ears. I felt the shape of my head for its skeletal parts, poked at the jawbone that would outlast me. The rushing would not stop. I thought of the morning my father died, and how brown the park grass had looked, and how I had never stopped seeing the dead patches among the green. I thought of taking Alex to dinner in Venice one night, and how she worried she'd spoiled it just by asking me to talk about my job, what I stayed in it for, what I expected. I'd acted like she was the naive one—the way she'd talked about compromise while holding a champagne glass and a steak knife.

Standing at the railing, I was bumped and pushed by the crowd. One of these bumps was more forceful than the others and squeezed me up against a vertical bar. I stopped ignoring it when it didn't relent. Someone pulled my wrist hard to my side, and I thought I was being robbed. My wallet, full of the mayor's money, was in my front pants pocket, but the man behind me—I assumed it was a man—didn't reach for it. The hands on my wrists weren't brutish—the fingers felt thin, the palm tapered rather than meaty. I'd only thrown two solid punches in my life, both late-night, low-probability American haymakers, and each time I had a clear idea why I was doing it. I didn't hit the man grabbing me because nothing was clear. He let go. I turned and gathered his features up into a face at close range. It was the police captain from Kaifeng.

"I like your return to Kaifeng," he said. He had a hard, hoarse voice, heavy with drink and maybe more besides. "Where is Mr. Hu? It is necessary."

I assumed he'd tracked me to the hotel. He looked like he hadn't slept in days.

"I fly to Hong Kong tonight," I said as fast as I could settle on a story. "Please tell the mayor that I am very sorry."

I added the apology in his language, as though it gave me credibility.

"You speak Mandarin," he said. "You hid what you understand." He gripped my bicep, not tightly, as though posing me for a picture.

"I didn't hide it," I said. "I don't speak it."

"You understand," the captain said, squeezing. He came close to my face. "Where is Mr. Hu? There are matters we arrange."

I wondered why that word—"arrange"—like we were planning a birthday party. We attracted little attention along the walkway. One or two travelers in flattened baseball caps glanced as they ambled past, but they never left their herded groups.

"Now. Now. Now. Now," he said. Each one rose in urgency. He was smaller than I was and not in uniform. His empty right hand, at his side, kept attracting my attention. A gun would have been clarifying, at least.

He pulled me forward, and we walked that way, his hand creeping up to my armpit, and though his body shook, his grip on my arm remained firm. At the road, he settled me into his front passenger seat. I stared ahead into the yellow illumination of the last century's buildings. As a fog rolled in, they weren't even buildings anymore, just light and shadow. He looked like he'd been pulled from a freezing river. He leaned forward against the steering wheel, and I thought he might pass out.

"I can't go with you," I said. "You must realize that. You can explain to the mayor . . ."

"The mayor," he said, "is dead."

He said it to me again—"dead," in English—and I found it even harder to parse. He didn't say murdered, but then again, he might be holding "murder" in reserve, for when we'd crossed back into the city of his jurisdiction. He held the horn down with one hand and with the other reached into his pocket for cigarettes. The horn stopped blowing only long enough for him to light up. We stopped at a freeway entrance, behind an accident. Cars moving the opposite direction puttered in rain-slicked congestion. I needed to open the door and step out. If the captain reacted at the pace of the substances in his system, then maybe by the time he unfolded himself from the car, I'd be on the other side of the road. He was pale, staring off toward the river. I felt an impulse that I was in the right—his authority wasn't divine, he was a drunk in khaki pants whose boss was fighting a long quarrel with a man who wasn't me. I waited until his cigarette had burned a quarter of the way down its stem and threw open the door and left it open. I was behind the trunk before he noticed. He looked at me astonished, as though I'd been the one who'd dragged him from his quiet devastation and into a roaring car.

I weaved through stopped traffic, ducking low. The captain left his car in the middle of the road, and a dozen horns sounded. A panel van tried to slide around him and nearly crushed him into a taxi. Drivers rolled down their windows to curse me in a language I didn't speak, and others pantomimed their anger behind their windshields.

I made it to the sidewalk and ran toward a herd of tour buses, end to end like a line of elephants. A few young Chinese men hustled a group of Westerners onto a double-parked bus. The driver screamed at the guides. I stood near the end of the line, and the hurrying guide asked for my ticket. When I said I didn't have one, he looked exasperated and gave me another from his pocket. I walked to the back of the bus and slouched under the tinted window. When I looked over the rim, I saw the Kaifeng captain running back and forth. He waved his hands in the air, more to himself than like he was signaling. He threw his head back, stared at the sky. I could see, even as we were pulling away, that he was convulsing. He wept as I had never seen a man weep. His face looked twice its size for his wide eyes and open mouth.

THE BUS DROPPED us in a hotel complex, and the guides nipped at us like sheep dogs, hurrying our unwieldy group into a third-floor theater. The lights went down, and I felt safely shrouded. I wiped sweat and dirt from the back of my neck and finally took a normal breath.

It was an acrobatics show. The troupe built a precarious structure of chairs the shape of a house of cards. The littlest girl was catapulted from a seesaw, end over end, where she landed in the top seat. In the last act, a couple fell in love, and we were asked to believe that their love, not the cables linked under their clothing, made them light enough to soar through the air.

When the lights came up, I didn't want to be the first one out of the theater. Most of the crowd mingled around the lead actress, and I played the part of one more of her admirers, standing in the clump waiting for her autograph. I spent so much time scanning the distance that I paid no attention to what was near. I looked up to find I'd been pushed to the front of the pack, face-to-face with the lovely acrobat. I sifted through a few Mandarin phrases and was about to attempt one when a handler thrust me aside and summoned the person behind me.

The audience leaked out every exit, and I followed them into the street hoping to retain my part in this dying group. Most waddled to a hotel adjoining the theater. I walked to the street and turned in the direction the crowd was thickest. My hands in my pockets felt the ridges of my keys, and I kept my eyes cast down. Men and women became their shoes. I wanted to vanish into them, like I was made of coins, and every person passing could take a handful, stash me jingling into a pocket, toss me away for luck, disperse me into every corner of the city, until I was spent and gone.

I SCROLLED TO Li-Li's number in my temporary phone. She answered on the first ring.

"Li-Li?"

I heard a gasp and mumble, then a bump like the phone had been dropped to a hard surface.

"Can you talk?" I said. "Things are desperate."

I heard a tinny voice I didn't understand, and then a new person came onto the phone, speaking English.

"I am Li-Li's friend," she said. "She says she is very happy you call."

"Please put her on," I said. "It's very serious."

"She wants to know will you still call her from America."

"Could you ask her where I could meet her?"

"She won't stop thinking of you."

"Please put her on the phone."

"She has shame to speak with you. She is without comfort in her English, and you do not understand her Chinese, she says."

"Who are you?" I said. "Her English is excellent."

"You know her bar?" she said. "Tell the driver Sanlitun Lu. She says she goes to meet you now."

"Tell her I'm very sorry, I have to go." I hung up. I realized I'd called the wrong Li-Li. The other Li-Li didn't answer her phone.

I DUMPED MYSELF in a chair in the lobby of a Ritz Carlton. Two Chinese men behind me ordered Johnny Walker Red, and so I did, too.

I waited for my thoughts to still. Only when my hands became unsteady did I realize how hard I must have been clenching them. I glared blankly at the lobby lights. I steeled myself to go over Polk's head, notify the embassy that our trip had fallen to pieces. I wanted to blow the whole thing up. I wouldn't deal with a wayward Chinese police officer alone.

I had another Johnny Walker, even though I didn't like the watered-down taste of the first one. I was afraid when I called the embassy I would stammer or not make sense. We'd given them the basic notice that Leo would be in country, but our meetings had been arranged either through Bund or Lightborn, which precluded the usual consular intercessors.

When the whiskey took hold, I finally made the call. I spoke with a woman who was prepared to help me with a lost passport or medical injury. I began to unspool the disastrous story of our trip, and as I pictured her face on the other end of the line, I lost my thread. I imagined myself as her, listening, and then as her superior, listening, and then it was the superior to that superior that I was telling the tale to. I was telling it again and again, until the telling was televised and I was exposed and ashamed—this trip was a mess from its inception out to the far horizon, before the mayor's money, before Leo had disappeared, and long before a party official was dead. What an ethics committee might say, or the grand jury might hear, was entirely correct: I could not *not* have known.

I sat with the phone to my ear, the line clicking. I'd shrunk until I was two inches tall. I apologized and hung up the phone.

I tossed out my pockets until I held two numbers from the King of Mesh. I began dialing again. I was consumed by the disoriented belief that my circumstances had become so unreal that I wasn't accountable to anyone anymore. I wasn't even accountable to myself. I didn't call the King of Mesh, because I never wanted to see him again, but I called the number on the other card he'd given me. I didn't want to be alone. I spoke to a woman. Not for the first time it occurred to me: you will live all your life in thrall to your evasions, hurtling toward desires that can never be satisfied.

SHE COULD HAVE been someone's translator, a concierge. For tonight, she was my company, my solace. I singled her out from the scan she gave the lobby. She could walk in and out of this hotel a hundred times, and the men whose eyes gnawed into her would have forgotten her by the time the next pretty girl walked by.

I flashed two fingers at her. She came and sat: petite, expectedly; black hair, above the shoulders, cut in a flip popular in America in the last decade but just reaching China now. Pencil skirt, pin-tucked blouse, very little makeup. She wore glasses, but when she took them off the lenses didn't magnify or shrink the ice cubes in my drink. She asked me which room was mine, and I sat stupidly silent. She asked if I wanted another drink.

"Could we go somewhere else?" I said. Anxiety put me in perpetual motion.

"I will call for the car," she said.

We went outside to wait. An early mist had turned to rain. A car pulled around, and I wasn't sure if the man at the wheel was just a driver or a bodyguard, too. He was big enough to knock me senseless if he needed to, but for now he was just handling the car.

"Xintiandi," she said to the driver.

"You will like it," she said, looking me over. "All the Americans like it."

I saw what she meant when the car let us out—Xintiandi was an outdoor shopping mall, distinct from its American cousins only by its patina of history: worn cobblestones, narrow alleyways. We took an outdoor table at a beer garden, under trees strangled in coils of lights.

"How long for your China visit?" she asked. She spun her beer until foam crawled up the glass. I watched beyond her head, behind the fountain. I looked into the next cafe and up at second-story windows.

"I'm supposed to leave in the morning," I said. "But I don't know. Maybe I'll die here."

In the ambient light of the coiled trees, her face was expectant, chin turned up, eyes squeezed open.

"Why did you come?" she asked.

"Actually, I'm a little lost about that myself."

"You don't know why you come to China?"

"Not strictly speaking, no."

She watched a passing woman who looked to be shivering. She looked down to the woman's high heels, and then below the heels to the uneven cobblestones.

"Are you from Shanghai?" I asked.

"I do not know anyone from Shanghai. Not one person."

"So where then?"

"Henan Province," she said. "You will not know it."

"I've been to Kaifeng," I said.

"It is all poor," she shrugged. "You have to leave. Some time I would like to go to Paris. For now, Shanghai."

"People say Shanghai is the Paris of the East," I said.

"I don't know why anyone says that. This is not Paris. How is it like Paris?"

"It's not, really," I said. "Not at all, actually."

Nothing would slow my heartbeat, but Xintiandi clamored in a way that made our conversation feel very private. I heard a jazz band trying to render Miles Davis. If I sat at this table long enough, listening to chattering groups, I could probably learn six languages. The face of the police captain appeared in every third person who passed, and I shuddered each time, but the image always dissolved into the features of a different man.

"You want to hear a story?" I asked her.

"What is the story about?"

"That's what I'll tell you, but I'm asking first if you want to hear it."

"I can listen," she said.

She must know better than anyone the private side of public men, I thought. She might even have some counsel, or wisdom. I told her a story of improbable cities, exquisite dinners—corruption and disappearance.

"I want you to be honest," I said when I was done. "What should the assistant do?"

She let me sit quietly.

"I don't know," she sighed.

"I thought you might have some ideas," I said. I realized how stupid it was to pay this woman for her affections and then spend my time trying to discern the truth of her feelings.

"My idea is I don't think you are this person you say you are," she said.

"Why would you doubt that?"

"I talk to liars all day," she said. "Are you married?"

"No," I said.

"I don't believe that, either," she said.

"Well, it doesn't matter. Let's say I made it all up," I said. "Why does the congressman disappear? What happens to the assistant?"

"I think the official is very corrupt," she said. "His assistant is, too."

"And so what happens to them?"

"They kill themselves from shame," she said. "The official jumps from a building. The assistant drowns himself."

"That's the end?" I said.

"That's the end."

"That's a sad fucking story," I said.

"I have more thoughts."

"Tell me."

"You don't like to hear the truth."

"Maybe not," I said.

She'd been right that I did like Xintiandi. The upmarket stores were still busy and blandly prosperous. It felt familiar—the wealthy familiarity of the cosmopolitan no-place—at a moment when any quantity of contentment seemed so out of reach that even the most bloodless form of consumer activity was desperately desirable. I left cash for our bill, and we walked down an empty lane where stone walls rose around us on each side.

Eventually, as though she'd been thinking everything over, she said: "In your story, the truth is nothing happens."

"Nothing happens to who?" I said. Offering her my story had hurt more than it helped, made my confinement and poor choices feel more, not less, real.

"You see this in Shanghai," she continued, "once in a long time some person goes to jail for their lies. But it is not so common. And nobody very important. Or look at the man in my home province stealing children from the Zhengzhou train station. He took them to work in his factory. He beat the children and did not pay any money. When he is caught, he says to consider his situation. Running a factory is hard work, he says. He explains he is not so bad, that he did not murder anyone. For me, I would like people to be more honorable. They were this way in the past. In the old China, people take responsibility."

"And kill themselves?" I said.

"Sometimes," she said.

She took my hand, and I aligned my steps with this girl in the pencil skirt, without even knowing her name. Rain and mist returned, and revolved, one coming after the other. She led me through neighboring alleys of some of the oldest remaining sections of the city, a few gray stone houses with faded red roofs and bent lanes where narrow corridors cut to the width of my shoulders. She always knew which way to turn, like following the lines on her own familiar palm. I was too tired to believe I could ward off any harm coming to me. My thoughts were those of an escaped convict: if what was before me was the prospect of capture and long suffering, then tonight I would abuse my last few steps of freedom.

• • •

WE RETURNED TO the Ritz Carlton. I wanted a room unknown to my hosts, or the police captain, and I paid the full rate out of my jacket stash of the mayor's money. Upstairs, I paid her—she wouldn't shut the door until I did. She asked what I wanted. I couldn't tell her what I was thinking. She paced the room running her hands on the raised fleur-de-lis wallpaper. I smelled lavender. I told her I wanted to shower, and she said she would come with me. She took off her shoes. She smiled when she discovered the radiant heating in the marble floor.

"Lights on or off?" she said.

"Off," I said.

Water from the rain-head shower instantly steamed the glass. As her body emerged out of the darkness around it, I felt her slight pearing, her nails bitten ragged, her cold hands. Everything was a surprise: Her shoulders were almost broad, like she was a swimmer, and her flat smile hid sharp teeth. Her wet skin was smooth as stream stones. Under the shower spray, in the dark, I thought she was right about everything she'd said—the assistant is guilty, too, and he drowns himself from shame.

III.

LATE THAT NIGHT, discomfited by Polk's silence, I took my phone into the bathroom and called his house. A housekeeper told me he'd been taken to the hospital with breathing trouble. I phoned the hospital and pretended to be his brother. A nurse said he was on a respirator. I stumbled back to bed, and for the rest of the night, in scattered minutes of dozing next to the girl, I dreamed of the dead. They came like snow flurries, whipping in flakes and piling up around me. There was a cancer multiplying at the male root of the family line, from my father and his father. With the insomnia, it was my inheritance: all of us impotent before death.

The morning brought rain, and I braced myself against the sheets, trying to clear away my dreams. She was gone, though I didn't remember her leaving. Between last night and this morning, I'd already lost some of the contours of her face, but when I closed my eyes I could still feel her motion, the impression of her hands on my breastbone, like she'd pressed them into wet concrete. She'd bitten me once on my chest, hard. I'd held her face and gently asked her to stop.

The flat sheet had bunched to the bottom of the mattress, and I climbed out of bed, stepping over pillows on the floor. The ballistics of their dispersion told the story of our night's movements, but also suggested something more aggressive than the quiet reality of our brief coupling. She'd left behind a damp towel the room was too humid to let dry. I shouldn't have done it, and I already missed her.

Out my hotel window the sun came up over half-formed Shanghai towers. Cranes stretched high above jackhammers, and great engines came alive to move the earth. A copy of the state-run English paper thumped onto my doormat, and I paged through it to see if I'd find Leo's picture, if there was talk of mayoral corruption, American interlopers, abuses of power. I wanted to know if a man had really died. And I wondered if a state paper would tell me any of it—if there was news, and if the censors would let it stay news. After some desperate flipping, I found a short article announcing the elevation of a new mayor in the city of Kaifeng. It was a buried little piece, likely boring to everyone but me. The man promised to make Kaifeng "a model for central China and a new global-class city." No mention was made of his predecessor. Full of tight muscles and mysterious hurts, my heart raced too fast at images cast up behind my eyelids.

In ninety-six hours, I'd run through four pairs of black socks and three cities. The snowstorm of the dead, which fell all through my dreams last night, gave me very little confidence in this rising day. My best hope was that Leo was waiting for me at the airport and that no one else was.

AT PUDONG AIRPORT, a security officer wearing a blue button-up shirt and a red armband walked his circuit, and I froze on the opposite side of a "Departures" board. I ducked into the airport bookstore. Leo had two hours to arrive.

I hid in back among the books in English. The novels were limited to a single shelf, the beast fables of eighth grade: *Watership Down*,

Jonathan Livingston Seagull, Animal Farm. Animal Farm baffled me. The only part I could remember was the final scene: the pigs in the house getting drunk while the rest of the pitiable animals looked in through the windows. I bought a copy.

At a noodle counter, I held the book in front of my face and kept out of sight of the foot traffic in the terminal. I'd paid a messenger to bring my bags from the Hua-Ting hotel, and the more time that passed, the more I could begin to believe the Kaifeng police captain didn't know the details of our departure, that if Leo arrived we could leave the country without further incident. The counter girl wore a hospital mask, and I ordered noodles with "nugget of fish." I had to say it three times before I could make my voice loud enough for her to hear. When my food arrived, the noodles were dead and the fish boiled to golf balls.

At the other end of the counter, I saw a wan-skinned young man whose unshaven, squinting look was like staring at my own reflection. His head seemed inclined in my direction.

"Hua Ting Hotel," he called out. "Last night."

I flinched and put my feet on the floor, ready to leap up and run. He limped over and settled on a stool next to mine.

"The King of Mesh," I said.

Relief was slow to hit my synapses.

"You look like shit," I told him.

"You're fucking telling me," he said.

"You smell like soap and gin," I said. "And the soap just barely."

"I got Shanghaied last night," he said. He paused for a laugh I didn't give him. "But I've got twelve hours to Los Angeles and a handful of pills."

"You're flying commercial?"

"You have any idea what I'd have to do to get a private plane into China?"

"No," I said. "I really don't."

"So get this, I had this driver last night," he said. "He took us to this club—me and a couple buddies. You know what traffic is like. We're just sitting there, and I'm getting pissed and it's like, fucking do something, man, we're going to be here all night."

He paused.

"You waiting for someone?" he asked.

I'm waiting for everyone, I wanted to say. I'm in the waiting profession. I looked beyond his stubble to scan the faces in the terminal.

"So my driver, he cuts out of our lane and starts heading right into oncoming traffic. It was some real James Bond shit," he said. He held out his hands with the palms together and then opened them like he was swimming a breaststroke. "We were going literally 150 miles an hour."

"Literally," I said.

"We were drinking this wolfberry alcohol," he said. "Wolfberry. I always think they're making this stuff up. They said it was good for stamina."

"You running a marathon?"

"I was fucking a marathon," he said.

"Jesus, you're a scumbag," I said. It didn't make him angry. He leaned in close.

"I had these two girls, and we got this private room, sort of in this dome thing at the top of the club." His voice crumbled with something that closely resembled emotion: "Whole thing was beautiful. No one gives a shit about anything here. I mean, these girls, up on the roof. I've got my dick. I've got all Shanghai. Do you see what I'm saying?"

"Simple pleasures," I said.

I wondered anymore if there was any difference between me and him—a couple young white guys in suits. His puffy face mirrored mine. You could read his bespoke tailoring, against my off-the-rack blend of inferior textiles, and figure out he was much richer. But you had to talk to him to hear how the things of most use to him—women and money—were useful only if everyone knew just how many, and how much, he had piled up. I needed to be different from him and needed it more after the smell of sweat and lavender this morning in my hotel linens; I had a bite mark from the girl last night, right above my heart. Some of the jagged circle her teeth had made was already bruised over. It hadn't bled, but it felt like she bit down into muscle tissue, and now it hurt anytime my torso clenched. It hurt to have a fucking heartbeat.

"So you're headed home?" he said.

"Actually, I just like the food out here."

"Where's your congressman?" He looked mean saying it, and happy to be.

"Busy."

"I was hoping to meet the guy."

I looked back into my book and thought of children's stories where a little boy actually disappears into the pages.

"You want me to leave you alone?" he asked.

"It's nothing personal."

"You're really deep in this shit, huh?" he said, as though the clouds finally parted in his understanding.

"What's that?"

"You're shaking worse than I am. And I'm still drunk on no sleep."

My eyes began to water. I'd never had much respect for business sense—a nose for money, I thought, could help you smell a deal, but left the rest of your senses dead to the world. My instinct had put me off him, but what good are instincts if we don't live in the same jungle that gave them to us?

"Should I call you a doctor?" he said. He reached out and felt the pulse in my neck, a gesture that made me realize I must look on the verge of fainting. "What kind of stuff are you into?"

I could see my reflection in the patent leather of his shoes, and that was about how I felt, like my face was wrapped around his foot. For the first time that morning, I remembered all the mayor's cash was in Li-Li's hands. I wondered what she would do with it—if it would be something good, if good was even possible, given its provenance. I tried to steady my voice, but I had nothing to say. The King of Mesh looked me up and down.

"Feels like I'm talking to a ghost," he said.

The final call for his flight came over the PA. He came in close to me and put his hands on my shoulders.

"Look at me, friend," he said. "You listening? I've been in sticky shit myself. Dead ends and no good options. You don't want to be the guy. You know the guy?"

"What guy?" I said weakly.

"The one who's left holding the bag," he said.

I exhaled long, and my head tingled, and I couldn't think. I was sure I could bang my fists on the floor and nobody would hear a sound. So maybe he was right that I was somehow disembodied.

WHEN THE KING of Mesh was gone, I held my hands up under my jacket sleeves and looked hopefully toward every middle-aged Western man with a Leo-like slouch. Travelers splayed across chairs, legs tucked over armrests, too tired to care about their public conduct. Nearby, two girls ran a Jack Daniels promotion, handing out pamphlets like advocates of a religion: their communion vessels bottles of whiskey; their heaven a poster-board scene of a Las Vegas night.

There was no transport, I didn't think, that could take me back to the first time I used my congressional ID to skip the tour group line and walk unescorted into the Capitol Building. I had lingered in the old Supreme Court chamber where Jefferson was sworn in. I'd strained my neck at a rotunda fresco, *The Apotheosis of Washington*, our first president on a seat in the clouds where Christ would ordinarily be. I'd stood at the center of the city, marked by a star, where all of

DC's avenues converged. I remember calling my father to tell him about it, and I remember that he was dead six weeks later.

An attendant announced our flight. The world was reduced to a hollow buzzing. Near my departure gate. I stood in the thick crowd, close enough to scan every face as people boarded. Still no Leo. It felt impossible to stay and impossible to go. I stalled until the last echoes of the boarding summons, until there were no more passengers left.

I woke to full alertness when two public security officers appeared. They spoke intently with two clerks, the nearsighted foursome now handling a sheaf of papers, now scanning one computer screen. The PA chimed, and "Luke Slade" was called in a dead tone. My name was repeated again, and my ears rang with admonitions. I felt suddenly broken by every ambition that had brought me to China, by every compromised instinct to run to pleasure and avoid pain, even where pain brought knowledge and pleasure pulled a hood over the eyes. I'd become one of those shrouded hermits at the bottom corner of an immense scroll painting, the figure you have to strain to pick out against the sheer volume of the mountain. If those hermits ever had any reaction to the hardships they were about to endure, they were too goddamn small for anyone to see it. The public security men stood still, as though waiting for me to throw myself at their patient feet.

ONE YEAR EARLIER

VENICE

At THE DOCKS outside Marco Polo Airport, Alex and I were impatient and excitable, and it felt impossible to wait half an hour for the next groaning vaporetto, so we jumped instead into a handsome water taxi of polished, golden wood. We couldn't help notice more gold in our ferryman's hair. He powered through the shallow channel, quickly passing one of the lumbering water buses. Tucked into the back of our speeding craft, we watched our pilot standing up to the wind, the front end of our boat erect and out of the water. We were the fast and clever creatures who had won the waters from the monsters of the old lagoon.

Our boat bounced off a wake—this is what it must be like, I thought, to be two less-limited people. The driver had a tan without splotch or burn and a ruffled white shirt undone three buttons from the top. I teased Alex for how she watched him. The boat spun hard left. We knocked into each other. I have to say again how she looked, laughing so hard with her hair in her mouth, not just beautiful but unselfconscious, at ease with herself and with me. Everything was in precise counterpoint to the hours of plane flights. Flight—think of it, at thirty thousand feet, at five hundred miles an hour—it should be a miracle, and yet we had drained it of all magic. It was our expensive little boat that felt like the miracle.

We came around the cemetery island. Alex whistled us past, and I hushed because I couldn't whistle at all. Her hand flew past my face to point at two of St. Mark's gray bulbs appearing through the haze, like they had just been sketched there a moment ago. The triangle top of the campanile stood beside them, pointing up at her own pointing finger. I thought, right then, everything would work out—Alex and me. I thought that my own life, even with the still-recent sadness of my father's death, might still end up a lucky thing.

We looped under the fish tail of the far bits of the island—a city that had been dropped from the sky, shattered into a hundred pieces, and bridged carefully back together again. Lido was south, the barrier island protecting us from the open water of the Adriatic, and we sped through the middle channel between San Giorgio Maggiore and the Doge's Palace, shining and slightly pink. Palladio's church suffered in a full body cast, its scaffolding reminding us that even paradise required maintenance.

We motored past the launch in front of Harry's Bar, west of where the vaporetto shoved travelers out at San Marco, and turned up the mouth of the Grand Canal. We took a smaller inlet, and the driver weaved into a dock fronting a hotel. He took Alex by her forearms and steadied her up. I didn't want to get out of the boat.

I paid him out of my wallet, though I felt I had crossed over from ordinary life and should be paying, by otherworldly custom, with the coins left in my mouth at death. A couple thirty years older than us waited to board our boat. They managed to come across as both elegant and drunk, the lady with a gold brooch swaying from top-shelf gin. The ferryman sped off, leaving Alex and me looking down into the wake with our hearts broken—broken because we could never have back those moments of first arrival, no matter how perfect that it had happened and that we were here.

• • •

LIGHTBORN'S PALAZZO OCCUPIED the west end of a square reachable only by a tight sidewinding passage where the walls narrowed in like a dead end—Alex and I couldn't pass side by side. And yet once through, a full campo appeared with a crumbling church on one side and two fat tabbies stalking each other in the shade of a cistern. We saw an old man, a few inches over five feet, in a buttoned vest and a tie. He hailed and shuffle-stepped toward us. He introduced himself as Lightborn's caretaker, Pierpaolo.

Pierpaolo shook with some kind of palsy. He tried to take Alex's suitcase. She let him only after she saw it might be taken as a comment on his infirmity if she refused. It pained me to watch him weighted by our belongings.

The old man showed us inside, and the boom of Lightborn's iron door shutting behind us was an echo I would hear in my mind long after. Our steps bounced up through the stone vault of the entryway. Settling us into a second-floor suite, Pierpaolo informed us that Leo and Lightborn, who I knew to be traveling by private jet, had stopped to golf at St. Andrews and would now arrive the next day. When the caretaker left, I fell happily into one of the wobbling lacquered chairs. Above me, in a cloudy, angel-filled fresco, fat naked babies swarmed Jesus around a giant cross. I took a moment to stare at the flowing industry of the fresco—everyone around Christ always seems so busy.

I heard Alex batting around in the bedroom, squeaking open the windows. I thought I heard a gasp, and I got up to find her. She seemed to have somehow left the room. I looked for her means of escape. Finally, I saw that what I had taken to be a full-length window was in fact a door, slightly ajar. I found Alex on a terrace, one hand on the stone balustrade and the other covering her mouth. We had come in the back entrance of the palazzo, unaware that its real frontage was the Grand Canal. I think she heard my footsteps, but she didn't look up until I stood behind her.

She was crying—not just welled up, but really crying. Maybe it was travel stress or exhaustion, the lifted weight of her job and the shock of her boss's death. Or maybe it was just the unanticipated appearance of this postcard waterway. We watched the regatta—sturdy boats filled with trash and construction cement; police watercraft speeding past the moored skiffs of vegetable sellers; elegant gondolas filled with honeymooners. I remember being more impressed than I believed I could be, happy that my familiarity with the image had not blunted the aura of Venice in its much-seen crumble and sink. It's all so beautiful, Alex kept saying, and I said I thought so, too.

She turned to me and said, "It makes me feel like I've wasted my whole life."

WE SHOWERED TOGETHER, and the flight cramps washed out. Alex's thin hair clumped into thick ropes. It seemed possible that I had never actually been awake. That I'd been—what's the Yeats line?—a tattered coat hanging on a stick. Alex and I turned the thought over, of our wasted young lives. Our DC days, the brain at half-mast. The interminable pleadings of constituents. Meandering hearings productive of nothing but suicidal ideation. Our bodies held up less by spine than by caffeine. A nice day was a brief lunch stolen together in the basement cafeteria.

"My boss lived his whole life that way," Alex said. In front of the mirror, she tugged her hair out. "And it's over now. And for what?"

I couldn't imagine being Leo, either—being even that successful—so if that success seemed hollow, then better to give up the ghost now.

Rinsed clean, we walked the Riva degli Schiavoni until it was dark. We wandered into the Piazza San Marco and paid outrageously for drinks at Florian's and listened to a band run through the American songbook. No matter, because we were inventing new lives. I was staggered into a fresh awareness and determined not to lose it. I cast

Luke out—invited the ghosts that crept from all the buildings to linger around us in place of our own familiars.

So when I said to myself later that Armand Lightborn was responsible for three of the best days of my life, this was what I meant—fifteen-euro glasses of prosecco and "New York, New York" bouncing between the ransacked decoration of the Byzantine church and Napoleon's old administrative buildings. I owed it all to Lightborn—Alex close, her arm linked into mine above the elbow, and what was really a baffling happiness, not just the absence of stress or foreboding or boredom, but a solid feeling of elation all by itself.

When the cafe closed, we lingered in the all-but-empty piazzetta with the clock tower behind us ringing midnight. Even the pigeons had gone to bed. The last people on the Riva were scruffy immigrant rose sellers and sad-eyed men near the Bridge of Sighs selling stolen or imitation Italian handbags. Something of an almost religious dimension radiated off of Alex, in her dreamy smile, like she had suddenly found it possible to reclaim her lapsed faith in a stupid world.

STRONG CAPPUCCINOS, WITH patterns in the foam, washed out our midmorning drowsiness. Alex and I drank them standing at a polished tin counter in a cafe catty-corner to Lightborn's palazzo. That day, Alex discovered she liked pistachio gelato, the Guggenheim mansion, the view from Dorsoduro across the Giudecca Canal. She preferred most things Gothic to most things Baroque and loved nearly any Byzantine mosaic with radiant gold tints and extensive halos. I liked whatever she liked. I especially liked her, and the feeling she gave me that this life of ours could be touching and vivid. We went back to our rooms after a day-long wander and tore our clothes to shreds without bothering to close the windows.

Leo and Lightborn descended that evening like an expected storm. I tried to lock myself down for it, determined not to let Leo ruin this feeling. They laughed their way into the palazzo, with Leo hanging off Lightborn's elbow. Plenty of people clutched at Lightborn that way, like they were mobbing him around home plate, and though it didn't speak well of my boss that he was among them, I tried to remember that in other ways it was Lightborn who seemed to require it. Not all of us need to be so admired. I wanted to believe we could live compelling lives with our unknown names, and be satisfied with the love of a handful of intimates. The respect of others would not add any number to your days, and what comfort a powerful reputation might give on long, difficult nights must be easily matched by the fear that success simply gave you more to lose. I felt there was just as much subservience in Lightborn's need for admiration as there was in the sycophant who offered it.

"Not bad, huh? Not bad," Leo said, squeezing my arm at the elbow.

"A revelation," I said. Lightborn was now behind him, speaking Italian without pause to Pierpaolo. I couldn't say if his Italian was good, but it sounded forceful and made me credit him with full command.

"Mr. Lightborn, you're a Renaissance man," I said when he approached us. And it was true—because he was cruel and kingly and deserved a public beheading. And yet, after last night, I was willing to love him, too.

He shook my hand, slapped my back. He kissed Alex on the cheek, and she stiffened. He barely knew us, but his effusion was calculated to disguise that. And then he was gone, off to his rooms, calling back to us that we'd meet on the terrace for drinks. So how, I thought, do you get a fix on a man like that, one so accustomed to public display? You had only his few light remarks to work from, his generosity that was overawing and yet cost him nothing when compared to his vast stores of wealth.

"Alex, can I steal Luke for a second?" Leo said. I'd nearly forgotten he was next to me. I looked at Alex and then to pallid Leo, with his brutish bag-eyes, and wanted him to notice how he intruded. She excused herself to change for dinner, floating away like one of the pink-cheeked, hair-tossing girls in the ceiling frescoes.

"How are you kids?" he asked. "How is she?"

"She's managing," I said. I wondered if Alex could be passed off as someone even remotely in mourning.

"It's so tragic for her," Leo said.

"I should probably go check on her," I said. "She doesn't want to be alone."

"Of course," Leo said. His eyes asked: Who will be consumed by grief when I'm gone? His hanging face said his tally of mourners was coming up short.

WE GATHERED FOR an aperitif on the terrace—Campari spritz, canalside above the green water.

Lighborn was a southpaw, drink in his right hand so he could gesture and emphasize with his left. It occurred to me he fought that way, too, on the sinister side, keeping everyone out of balance. We had just worked with him on an issue you would think had nothing to do with him: labor laws in the Marianas Islands, a US protectorate exempt from the federal minimum wage but still able to use the "Made in the USA" seal. Lightborn was right there in the background lobbying to hold back a proposed extension of the minimum wage to the island's garment workers. Many staffers speculated that Lightborn's next move would be some huge building project that would benefit from poaching the cheap labor. No plan of that sort had yet appeared, but that was just the point. His thinking ran far ahead, to purely conjectural things. It seemed he'd never be stuck or run out of rope.

"Ten years," he said when Alex asked how long he'd owned his "palazzo." I watched to see if she could say the word without laughing.

"Is it a hassle?" Leo asked.

"Worth it so far," Lightborn said. "Even the headaches."

"And those are?" Leo said.

"The tourists. Most of the summer. Carnevale. And of course nothing works for long—not the pipes, not the showers."

We sat up listening to him until the sun dimmed out somewhere over Mestre. A substantial portion of what I knew about Lightborn's history came from a *Vanity Fair* article, which wasn't a profile, exactly, because he hadn't cooperated. It detailed the early family fortune, how his father had years ago bought a small hotel and replicated it into a national chain before selling it for millions. Armand was the only son. He went to Choate, where he left quietly, and suspiciously, before turning up at a baseball academy, having discovered the power in his left arm. Division I recruit, college career ended by blown ligaments. There were whispers of drug-related arrests (paperwork mysteriously lost), but the more substantial rumors surrounded Armand's career-making land deal with a Wyoming mining company that underwent layers of convoluted title transfers no one could make heads or tails of except to say that Lightborn had managed—perhaps fairly, perhaps not—to evade tens of millions in legal culpability for an open pit still leaching ore into surrounding lakes. Responsibility for the cleanup would have sunk him before he even began. When the magazine piece was published, Lightborn vigorously denied everything, even prosaic matters of public record. He wrote a letter to the editor in retort: "There are so many errors in the litany of falsehoods in your recent article on my private life that it seems silly to try to correct them. Most are too egregiously fabricated to bother denying. I cannot, however, let one fact go uncorrected: My college ERA was 1.13 and not, as stated, 1.33. Yours, A.L."

Three drinks before dinner had me sailing, and it was only by pinching myself that I kept from sinking into a catnap. Lightborn and Leo had dinner plans at Armand's "regular" spot, the Hotel Danieli, but Lightborn said he would call in a reservation at a great little place he sometimes dropped in on. He sketched me the directions, off of Campo

Santa Maria Formosa. Had Lightborn next promised me the moon and stars, that he would fetch them down for me and let me pet them like docile cats, I would have believed him entirely. Alex took my hand in hers. We had barely let go of each other since we arrived. It reminded me that on regular days we spent too much time circling around each other, sharing the same space without really being together. We each had phones that rang with our bosses' plumbing emergencies at three a.m. Why didn't the boss call the plumber first? Because that was our job. I lurched with Alex from crisis to crisis, and what got lost was just sitting next to her, as we were now, with a drink, touching. We left for dinner, and the shining stars were covered in a soft, pleasing fur.

WHEN WE ARRIVED at Enoiteca Mascareta, there was a placard on a corner table with my name on it. From behind the raucous bar up front, the owner appeared, a chinless man with a crashing wave of gray hair. He opened a bottle of champagne for us with a sword. I saw a twitch in Alex's smile.

"Let's play Vegas oddsmakers," she said. "Do you want the over or the under on Lightborn's implosion?"

"Tell me what you mean by implosion," I said.

"Federal agents," she said. "His offices at dawn."

"What's the line?"

"A year," she said.

"Is this a fair bet?" I said. "Or insider trading?"

"I'm taking the under."

"What'd you hear?"

"Nothing proprietary," she said. "All public record."

"I would have bet the over anyway," I said. "I'm sure Lightborn will be with us awhile. I'd put a billion dollars on it."

"Good," she said. "You can pay me in his seized assets."

"Shake on it," I said. We did.

"Here's my other question," Alex said. "Why does everyone like him?"

"You don't?"

"No, I'm not saying that," she said. She posed her hands palms up, weighing. "But don't you think you shouldn't?"

"What's he been convicted of, exactly?"

"That's a Beltway line," Alex said. "I was hoping you had something better."

She picked up a large serrated steak knife and tossed it hand to hand by the butt. The bartender stared, and the owner cocked his head. She was making everyone nervous. I reached out and flattened her hands on the table.

"You can't see a black hole, either," she said. "You figure it out by what's around it."

"Guilt by association," I said. "That's not really fair, is it? He's been pretty good to us."

She must have taken this to include her champagne, because she put it down faster than if it had drowned flies in it.

"I'm not saying he isn't a swell guy in some social capacity." Her eyebrows went up at "swell." "I'm talking about the rest of what he does."

"What he does is called capitalism."

"You think leading Leo around on a leash is capitalism?" she said. "What good is that Marianas Islands vote doing Leo?"

"That's principle," I said. "Leo doesn't believe in minimum wage, period."

"And meanwhile Lightborn's fucking his wife."

"That's a rumor," I said.

"You saw it yourself," she said.

"No," I said. "Technically, I saw them talking at a party."

"So Lightborn doesn't worry you?" she said.

"You want me to cancel our entrees?" I said. "Pack tonight?"

The owner, with his big eyes and hams for hands, set an overflowing plate of meats and cheeses down in front of us. Alex had a quick exchange with him in her guidebook Italian. When she turned back to me, the focus of her indignation had shifted.

"This is your decision," she said. "Tell me you see that."

"Yours, too."

"I've left," Alex said. "I'm leaving."

"So that makes you better?" I said. "You're in the clear?"

"I'm just saying it gives me a fresh start," she said. "A clean slate."

"Your boss died," I said. "That's a real ethical awakening."

"This is what worries me: you're always trying to smooth things over," she said. "And with Leo? With Lightborn? They'll use that—you never want to make a scene."

"So how about let's not have one here," I said.

She stabbed a toothpick at the plate and came up with a paper-thin sheet of meat.

"What's this?" she said, holding it up. It was white-marbled and pepper-studded.

"It's speck, I think."

"What's speck?"

"Pig," I said.

She wrapped it around a triangle of collapsing cheese.

"You say clean slate," I said, after a long silence. "But you know that's not how life is. There's no such thing."

WHEN THE MEAL was done, she got up to use the restroom, and when she returned I told her I had settled the bill. But of course there was no bill. We took a long silent walk back through Campo Santa Maria Formosa and beyond, drifting without definite aim. The Rialto Bridge appeared without being looked for, and we crossed it and wound past the closing shops south of the fish market. I lived a continual surprise, never more so than when, immeasurably lost, we came a few steps apart out of a sotoportego and paid half a euro to have a traghetto take us across the Grand Canal. I tried to pick out Lightborn's terrace. Alex linked her arm through mine and kissed my neck.

"I'm sorry," she whispered.

"You don't have anything to be sorry about," I said.

"I didn't mean to sound like I was accusing you of something," she said. "Or like I've been better."

"Forget it," I said.

"But did I ruin it?"

"You didn't ruin anything," I said.

"I want more for us, that's what it is," she said. "I mean, I want more from us."

She skimmed her hand in the water, but I didn't respond. I sneaked my arm around her hip and tugged her nearer. I couldn't pretend it was right, to be in Venice with her under these circumstances, but I was asking her to look at Venice and not who'd brought us. The soft splash of the long pole in the water and the gentle rocking of the black boat was pure hypnosis. You could squint the world medieval on the canal by night. Clusters of fondaco buildings, trefoil arches. The lagoon had done what no city wall ever could, providing a thousand years of immunity from Ostrogoths and Visigoths, and now from Fiats and Peugeots.

"I know you feel done with DC," I said.

She pulled her hand from the water and shook it off.

"If I move to New York . . ." she said. "The train is an easy ride. You always say you get work done on trains."

"I do," I said.

"So," she said.

She pressed her hands together between her knees.

Whenever she'd talked about New York City and nonprofit work, I was sure she idealized it for seeming the very opposite of the world she took congressional business to represent. I couldn't personally see how New York City was the right place to escape feeling strangled by money and power, but I understood that she wanted "more." I wanted more, too—I just couldn't say what "more" was. I was grasping at a language for fulfillment that I didn't actually possess. We were coming to the pier.

"But what are you going to think of me for staying?" I said.

We swayed into the dock, and I helped her out, careful not to slip on the mossy bottom stairs. She never answered my question. The thought of her leaving focused my attention in a melancholy way, but I wondered, too, whether it was Venice itself that made me painfully aware of a disjuncture between where we were and the world beyond the lagoon. It was like I could reach out, hold time, feel its wriggling mass, and feel it blowing and blowing away.

LIGHTBORN AND LEO came crashing in late that night, their drink-roughened voices and mismeasured footsteps echoing up the stairs. By the next morning, Leo was pouting, and Lightborn's palazzo was hardly big enough to contain it. I wanted nothing more than to get out from under Leo's emotional weather and back into the city.

We were trying to slip out when Lightborn caught us in the kitchen. He stood before us sleepy-eyed in a terrycloth robe embroidered with a cursive "AL." A demitasse espresso cup in his hand was stamped with the same design. He asked our plans, and we admitted to not having any.

"Take the boat," he suggested.

My dumb response: "We don't have a boat."

Lightborn leaned back on the kitchen island, under a Murano glass chandelier, and laughed hard enough to make the glass tinkle.

"I meant take mine," he said. "Keep it for the day. You'll be gone tomorrow, right? You have to see the islands at dusk. It's too perfect. Don't skip Mazzorbo. No one talks about it, but on the back side of the island there's a crumbling church that I think is the ne plus ultra of crumbling churches."

I followed Alex's eyes looking him over, and it was like we spoke telepathically of what we were seeing—his few gray chest hairs poking out from the robe, and his body showing all the care and labor of other hands. The hair cut well, and often enough that it didn't look messy even when messed. The rounded pectoral definition from some Brazilian personal trainer. The cared-for skin, smelling far off not just of today's regimen but of thousands of consecutive days of that same attention.

"Can I get you anything before you go?" he said. "Macchiato?"

Alex said yes like she made them every morning, and it seemed to please Lightborn to see us so pleased.

THE BOATMAN RAN us out on the lagoon and docked us at Burano. We picked up provisions for a picnic and walked across a small wooden bridge to Mazzorbo, where a group of schoolchildren ran around in the little churchyard. We spread out on a patch of ground between the water and the crumbling church, watching the kids and drinking cold Peroni from the can.

"There's nothing we have to do today," I said. The rarity of it astounded me.

"Did you hear them arguing last night?" Alex said.

"Who?"

"They were smoking cigars out on the terrace. I could hear it through our window," she said. "Leo was furious about something."

I watched two kids squat and pick flowers.

"Sometimes a cigar is just a cigar," I said.

"Then why aren't they speaking this morning?"

"Fucking Christ," I said. "Is this really what we want to talk about?"

"Don't you?" she said.

"No," I said. I meant not, at any rate, today, or right this minute.

"Armand was saying, 'It's foolish, Leo. It's desperate,'" Alex said.

She did an impression, dropping to a stern baritone. "Leo apparently didn't see it that way."

"Leo has this power to ruin what seems unruinable," I said.

She pulled her shoes off and leaned herself back in the grass on her elbows, staring up at the sky.

"They'll sink the whole island they're so full of themselves," she said.

That's when I realized she could take them lightly because she viewed them at a distance. Last night, she spoke of leaving, and this was leaving's tone—Leo and Lightborn already figures of a shabby past, not quite real to her. I swallowed my own responses, and before I could think of a way to turn the conversation back to our escaping Venice moment, she moved over and kissed me. I tried to collect through her lips some of her limpid ease. I would have been ecstatic for her if I hadn't felt like I belonged entirely to the life she was so happy to be leaving behind.

WE WENT OUT to Torcello to see the church before it closed. Loneliness crept over me with the afternoon shadows. Torcello was an odd, unsettled place, grown over with thick rushes and blooming aster. The Norman church, a thousand years old, was at the far end of the island, and to get there we took a cobblestone path alongside an unruffled canal, past perhaps a dozen houses and three empty hotels. It looked for a minute like we'd have the church to ourselves. But soon the grounds were inhabited with breathless visitors in shorts and sunburns. The illusion of our own private island was nothing more than arriving a few minutes ahead of the latest vaporetto.

We climbed the campanile, and at the top Alex wouldn't get near the edge. We started to talk about what was ahead for our relationship. I can't remember how, precisely. I looked out to marshlands and puny uninhabited islands, and I'd begun to feel angry at the thought of her leaving, so I pretended, meanly, that we could dispassionately reason this out. I talked like we were not two people in an emotional tangle as much as two logicians. So she would move to New York City, I said. I couldn't. My father had used his name to land me this job, and anyway Leo was a pathway for me, a ladder. I wanted Alex to protest, to console me, to tell me I should abandon all that and go with her. She didn't. She let me go on. And so I said a weekend thing wouldn't work, that the proof was overwhelming. Long-distance relationships should be settled science by now, as impossible as cold fusion or the sun rotating around the Earth. All I wanted was for her to disagree. We came out of the campanile, and I needed to hear her say it would hurt her to leave me behind.

"What you're saying makes sense," she said.

She should have said I was crazy and that reason, in these matters, was the wrong tool entirely. I wanted to hear how much she loved me, though I was too small to say the same to her.

"It doesn't have to be difficult," she said. "We'll still see each other sometimes. Or we won't."

"It's that simple," I said.

"Easy," she said. And that's when I told her I didn't think people often enough discussed these sorts of breakups, where good feelings were retained by both parties and hands went unwrung over the fate of it all. Fate isn't cruel, I said—it would be better if it was. It's just inconvenience dressed up in mysticism.

"I'm glad we can talk about it like adults," she said.

So that was it. What I'd entered meanly and weakly, hoping for a love-ratifying fight, I blundered out of having accomplished a dissolution between us that I didn't really want.

BACK AT THE palazzo, I passed Leo's door with light steps and heard some kind of snuffling noise. The old door didn't fully shut to the frame, and I pressed my eye to the slit. Leo was flat on his back, cold compress on his forehead. His eyes were wide open as he no doubt cast blame as far from himself as it would go, up through the palace walls, through the pink Venetian sky, his swarming curses landing at the feet of God, who had thwarted his ambitions.

Pierpaolo, shuffling off to his room, caught me peeking. He asked skeptically if there was anything I needed.

"Did Mr. Lightborn go out?" I asked.

"To take a late dinner," Pierpaolo said.

He padded off in his slippers.

I returned to my room and sagged onto the bed next to Alex. Her bags were already packed for the morning. I tried to kiss her head, but she pulled away.

THE RIVA ON an April night was just brisk enough for a suit coat, and other than the occasional banging of a wheeled suitcase over the cobblestones, there was no sound but boats rocking into the piers. Yellow lights hung crooked from the lamps under a waning quarter moon. A spotlight shone back onto the frontage of the Hotel Danieli as waiters on a high terrace packed away outdoor tables. I considered stopping but didn't have the nerve. Near the Bridge of Sighs, I declined to purchase any of the handbags offered by three chatty Senegalese men.

"Girlfriend?" one asked, holding a purse out to me.

I demurred, and he smiled like he knew just what code I was speaking. He opened a handbag at his feet, full of small plastic baggies of nicely clustered green buds. I wasn't going to smoke anything tonight, but I felt it was polite to ask how much the marijuana was selling for. He gave me some prices that seemed wildly inflated, and I continued on my way.

When I passed the Hotel Danieli again, I buttoned my jacket and walked into the lobby like I belonged there. The bar was to the left. Near the piano, in red-tinted light, was Lightborn, the southpaw, tipping his drink alone. He was as still as I'd ever seen him, for once not gesturing big pictures in the air with that powerful left hand. I hesitated to approach him. Lounging under frescoes in his palazzo struck me as fairly impersonal compared to cozying up to him in a private moment. I thought how infrequently he must be in public alone. Any party where you found him these last and most successful years of his life, the ballroom would be filled with people he knew, or people who wanted to know him.

I took one of the tables that spilled out to the hotel lobby, a good distance from him. Were he to see me and wave, or nod, but make no further movement, then I would sit, and we would drink, together and alone, and I would walk back to his palazzo, and that would be the final word on the questions I had about why Leo was so angry. A server offered me a menu, which read "Dandolo's Piano Bar." I asked him who Dandolo was, and he happily recounted the story of a captain who bashed his brains out on the mast of his ship after losing a vicious battle with rival Genoa.

Lightborn's eyes followed a bottle-blonde woman who threaded the lobby. My table sat in the arc of his gaze. When she'd passed, he turned to look at me again. His face clouded, accompanied by a barely there slump of his shoulders. He came and joined me, like he didn't have the capacity not to make pleasantries, even as it drained him.

"The server was just filling me in on Mr. Dandolo," I said.

Lightborn rolled out a long, tough sigh. "Leo put you up to this?"

"I'm off duty," I said.

He sat and leaned his elbows onto his knees. "You know, he could be rich, and he could be happy, if he'd stick to representing dirt farmers. Be content to be a big man in a small place."

"You're wrong about that," I said. "He'll never be happy. Even if he gets what he thinks he wants."

Lightborn turned his eyes to the piano player who'd just begun.

"I don't want him pestering me with this presidential campaign shit again," Lightborn said. "I'm not throwing money down the drain for that, and neither is anyone else."

"He needs to be let down easy," I said. "That's always the way with him. He needs his care and feeding."

"You're a poor son of a bitch to put up with it," Lightborn sighed. "Look, I told him this, but maybe you can really convince him, yes?"

"I'll do what I can," I said.

"He has to drop the fantasyland presidential shit and focus on something actually in his control," Lightborn said. "I've got a project in mind for your district, something actually within his purview. Really promising stuff with some contacts in China I'd like him to meet. We could run a trip through my foundation, sometime next year. There'd be money in it for him, no question. So will you reason with him?"

We finished our drinks, and he ordered something I'd never heard of—a Negroni, two of them, in fact.

I know now that retrospect will sometimes show you what mattered all along, in defiance of where your attention initially landed. There are moments in our lives that are only released to us in the fullness of time—conversations occluded or half-understood, paths you follow without having noticed where the road forked. I only mean, and without defense, that the conversation I had with Lightborn was quickly swamped in my mind—that by the next morning, after too many drinks, it was something indistinct, and by the next week, it was still more distant, and nothing I wanted to think about. Then came a year of days, of showers and shaves, of insomniac nights mourning my father and Alex moving away. I filled my head with chaff—with rejiggering Leo's breakfast fundraisers and drafting his honorary resolutions to be read into the House record and staying late to research laws he would never sponsor. Over all that time, Lightborn's talk—scoffing at Leo's presidential dreams, but replacing them with the promise of a district project and Chinese money—was transubstantiated, in my obliging memory, into its scruffy but common counterparts. Bribery became business. By the time I was on the flight to China, the schedule looked perfunctory to me, a mere junket, barely related to Venice at all except that it was still Lightborn's money underwriting the trip. Leo's presidential ambitions might still exist in his heart, but they were an office joke—the exploratory committee merely Polk's act of appeasement. A district project was nothing Leo ever spoke about, and so my recollection that Lightborn had once referred to a mutually enriching scheme was cast largely into oblivion. Largely, I say, rather than entirely. Because this is how complicity works: You know and you think you don't. You believe what is most convenient to you. I was surprised, in Kaifeng, to be handed money, but that only proves how easily innocence can be manufactured—that if you need it enough, a feeling can survive the absence of a quality, the way flowers will still look in bloom for a time even when cut from their roots.

The Negronis arrived, and we clinked glasses. I loved the bitterness, and the punch. What I later remembered with shame, I experienced that night with pride—a rich man had welcomed me as an equal into the world of his private pleasure.

MANY DRINKS LATER, I sat next to Lightborn at the lagoon's edge, on a pier where we were protected from view by an enormous docked boat. I inhaled deeply, imagining the smoke curling through the pockets of my lungs then rushing back out. I pictured God exhaling the entire world.

"The African sold us some powerful shit," Lightborn said.

The marijuana had been my idea. I felt it in my legs, which sacked out numb underneath me, and in my head, which began to tingle.

"The Moor was right," he said.

"The who?"

"The Moor of Venice!"

He tried to focus, but he was somewhere out in the heavens.

"Can you promise me something?" I said.

Lightborn looked at me, pulling a serious face.

"Hey," I said. "Ground control to Major Tom."

He choked out a laugh.

"Ah, fuck yourself," I said. I got up and walked back along the Riva. Lightborn followed, singing. "'Sitting in a tin can . . . Far above the world . . .'"

Every congressmen I could think of had one of two things guaranteed in the broom closet: a scumbag businessman or a crazy preacher. They were corrupted of flesh or corrupted of spirit, and often they were both. I don't know what further clarification I was searching for.

Lightborn caught up to me. "You seem pretty miserable. This about you and that girl?"

"Leave her alone," I said.

"Don't hold on too tight," he said. "Those ones leave if you hold them too tight."

"She's leaving anyway," I said. I cupped my hand and trained the lighter on the tip of the paper. "This is the last of it."

"Save some of that," he said.

"No more for you," I said.

He snatched the joint out of my hand.

"Listen to me," I said. "If you fuck Leo over, you're fucking me over, too." I put two fingers in his chest. He grabbed them like they were the barrel of a gun. Maybe Leo wasn't any better than Lightborn as a person—quite possibly he was worse. But Leo was still the weaker party.

"The world is a rock," Lightborn said. "Leo wants to lift it. So what? We all want something. If she's all done with you, I want your pretty girlfriend."

I threw a wild punch at him, more desire than direction. I thought about that impulse for years afterward. I only clipped him, and his swing in return was one of those flailing haymakers with a low success rate, but it caught me broadly under the chin. His momentum carried him down with me. I got up first, and he sprawled out laughing like it wasn't clear to him how he'd fallen.

A group of Frenchmen, dragging their wives behind them, helped get Lightborn up. Back on his feet, he took an old-time boxing stance, fists swaying in large, rough circles. I ignored him, and he grabbed one of the French women and twirled her like they were dancing. To the men's credit, no one else swung at him. I hadn't walked far when Lightborn ran up and wrestled my neck under his arm.

Whenever I remembered the swing I took at him, foremost in my mind was that I could not hurt him. Worse, he considered it a joke that I'd tried.

"You're not much of a puncher," he said, holding me in a headlock. "But you're a hell of a guy. Did I hurt you? Did you chip a tooth?"

I SLEPT AS close to Alex as I could get. She kept wrestling away, telling me I was making her hot.

She had us in line early at St. Mark's. We hadn't yet been inside. I still felt smoke in my lungs and eyes, which lent the saintly faces in the mosaics a hallucinatory reality. The undulating flagstones beneath my feet felt less like a floor than like my own uneven way of walking. Alex spoke more words to the guards than she did to me. I had already begun to think of her as an absence. Leaving the church, four bronze horses—looted in the siege of Constantinople—soared brightly over the piazza. I had the feeling that after she moved, I would go visit and we would try to make it work. We would probably sleep together, and it would be a little bit sad and beside the point, but we would do it anyway.

SHANGHAI

I.

HAD MY head on a swivel, skittering down a long corridor through Pudong Airport watching for faces I thought took me in too long. I drifted behind three generations of a family pushing an overburdened luggage cart. The placid grandfather looked like he'd lived eighty hard years, but he shuffled through the check-in crowd like he was meditating in a garden—hands clasped behind his back, face screwed up in concentration. The midforties father, with a face like a turtle and the short arms and neck to match, gave me a squinty look. I felt his gaze bend my spine. I ran into a restroom.

I called Li-Li from a toilet stall, where my worn leather shoes put the first scuffs in a new-laid floor. She knew from my voice I had trouble.

"Perhaps you should go to interview," she said, when I'd explained. "Public security can then correct the mistake."

Her tone wasn't confident, and I took "interview" as a fantastic underselling.

"Go alone?" I said.

"It is worse to wait," she said.

"I want a hotel," I said. "But this needs to be private."

A catch in her voice told me she was trying to conceal her rising panic.

"A hotel will want your passport," she said eventually.

"Maybe you could check in with your name?" I whispered.

I hung on her answer.

"You still cannot contact your boss?" she asked.

I SHIELDED MY face with my hand and kept pace with the streaming crowd, sorting the word "EXIT" out of all the indecipherable ideograms above my head. Two drivers approached me, neither of whom stood near a licensed taxi. I gave the less aggressive man my fare to the hotel Li-Li had named. He held one arm crooked, and it looked painful, possibly broken. He finished his cigarette and had trouble lighting another. This wincing man with the tight buzz cut and bent arm called himself Driver Wei. I hunched below the rim of the window and dialed my phone as he swept me through the city. His car was like a broom dusting pedestrians from its path.

The hospital staff put me through to Polk's room.

"I never heard from you," I said.

His voice was hoarse. His vitals sounded weak. I cupped my hand over my mouth to keep the driver from overhearing.

"I'm sorry, Polk," I said. "Maybe I haven't said that before. I'm sorry about what's happened to you. And you've kept going. I don't know how."

"Okay," he said, barely audible. "Okay, okay."

In traffic in front of the car, a man had strapped an office desk to his motorbike. As he sped, the desk swayed like the pole carried by a tightrope walker.

"I've got calls out," Polk said. "Lightborn's . . . I don't know. I haven't got him yet."

"What about anyone else?" I said.

I heard metallic clanging, like falling pans.

"It's not a missing-child alert I can just post on the freeway." He was banging something in his room. "The idea is not to make an international fucking incident out of this."

"I'm just going to say this," I said. "I took some money."

"I can't hear you. Talk louder."

"I was offered money for Leo," I said, "and I took it."

"Are you crying?" he said.

I cleared my throat.

"There were police waiting for us at the airport," I said.

Polk was silent a long time. The car wound off the freeway into Shanghai proper. A few old men, walking at the pace of another era, shuffled at midday through the streets in their silk pajamas.

"You took money?" Polk said. "Why did you take money? Who in the fuck told you to take money?"

"They offered it," I said.

"This conversation isn't real, is it? I'm already dead. I'm dead, and you're a demon."

"I didn't know," I said.

"Fuck yourself with 'I didn't know.' You just took it? How stupid are you?"

"What do I do?"

He started to yell, and I wondered what strength the yelling sucked out of him. "Give it back. To whoever gave it to you."

"I can't," I said.

"Can't what? Give the goddamn money back. We don't want it."

"He's dead," I said.

"Who's dead?"

"The guy who gave it to me," I said.

"Are you recording this?" Polk said. "Are you wearing a wire? Jesus Christ, Luke. You know what? Don't say anything else. Not another goddamn word. I'm innocent, and I'm going to stay that way."

"Yeah, you're as innocent as I am," I said.

"What are you trying to do to me?" Polk said. "Do you think dying isn't hard enough?"

With his haze, and my circumstances, our conversation oscillated between unforgiving and dissociated. I heard my voice come out so plaintive, so lost. The same sound as when I'd heard my father was gone, and no one could explain it the way I wanted to hear it, in terms of restoration or reversibility.

"I'd feel safer if we brought the embassy in on this," I said.

"Understand this," Polk said, "if you blow Leo up, if you attract any attention at all to whatever you've fucked up, then I will bury you so deep in shit the Feds will be blaming you for the Kennedy assassination."

"Can you imagine what I'm facing here?" I said. "Chinese police?" I couldn't imagine it myself. The King of Mesh told me I was a ghost, and Polk must have sensed an absence in me, too. His severity felt designed to shock me back to life.

"You will not earn my sympathy," Polk said. "I wouldn't care if you were in jail in China forever, except that it would fuck Leo up to have to explain you."

I leaned my head out the car window for air. A group of besotted men in coats and ties banged out of a restaurant, laughing and shouting after some eternal "*Gan bei!*" lunch.

"Can you pull yourself together?" Polk said. "Can you stay out of sight? Anything? Give me time to try to unfuck you. Are you okay with that?"

"I'm not okay," I said. "Nothing is okay."

Polk hung up. I'd slouched so far down the seatbelt was slicing my neck. We arrived at the hotel, and Driver Wei didn't let me go without formally presenting a business card. It felt strange to have such courtesies remain, even under summons.

· · ·

THE HOTEL LOBBY was on the fifty-third floor, and the rooms extended forty floors above that, one of the tallest buildings in the city, with a square hole carved out of its towering peak so that from a distance it looked like a giant bottle opener.

Li-Li met me with no expression outside the downward slope of her finely plucked eyebrows. She wore a black, form-fitting pantsuit, which showed that her form was a straight line, and a pair of wire-frame glasses I hadn't seen before. We were quiet in one another's public company. She handed me the mayor's briefcase and walked in short steps to the check-in counter.

The room we were shown to was nicer than every apartment I'd ever lived in—ironed white linens, hardwood floors with no dust. It had a picture window overlooking the Huangpu River, where beaten ships floated out to sea. The view gave me vertigo, and all at once I felt part of a centuries-long line of misbegotten travelers to China—men who'd moored in unfamiliar ports or rattled overland by caravan into Silk Road cities thousands of miles from home. Li-Li hooked her thumbs into her pants pockets and shifted her feet. She kept her own counsel, her demeanor more like an old man who'd been through a war than someone young with any faith in the future. A double curtain—one sheer and white, and a thicker blackout one behind—hung on two tracks controlled by an electrical switch. It felt like a test—to flip the switch would be to succumb entirely to paranoia. No one could honestly be watching us, at this height, from some perch in a nearby office tower.

"Could you call Mr. Hu?" I asked. "Could he help me with the police?"

She was a thin carving, her arms hanging straight. I laid the briefcase on the bed, and her eyes fell over it for a long moment. She didn't respond.

"What about the Bund executives I met in Beijing?" I said. "I have their cards. I have a hundred names."

"You met partners," Li-Li said.

"Charles, right? My first night here. Wasn't he a vice president? Somebody with connections . . ." I trailed off.

"Bund does many related ventures," Li-Li said. She seemed distracted. "Charles's official title is with another group."

A hotel porter slipped through the door with my luggage. He was all of sixteen with a floppy haircut and a narrow, severe face. He put my suitcase on a folding rack, and I noticed a red stripe around its zipper that I didn't think I had seen before—such a disconcerting feeling, to have the material of your own life come into view as though you've never laid eyes on it.

"I will sometimes travel for Mr. Hu as a note keeper or translator," Li-Li said. "Such as when I met you in Beijing. It is really only his business I know, not these other men."

I wanted her to be quiet while the porter stood near. I hoped he understood nothing more than a few sentences of hotel English.

"So who is Bund?" I said when I'd latched the door. I heard anger dispersed through my voice, none of which I meant to direct at Li-Li.

"There are me and Mr. Hu in a small office in central Shanghai," she said.

"That's it?" I said. Beyond her, my eyes fixed, I could see the clock of the Customs House, rendered miniature by distance, but couldn't read the time figured by its hands.

"No," Li-Li said. She tightened. "There is in addition the biggest Bund headquarters, outside the city. Nearer to Suzhou than to Shanghai. Mr. Hu would go there one to two days each week. I stay in Shanghai to answer phones."

The building listed in gusts of wind. Footsteps outside tapped along the corridor. The porter's face sprung to mind, the suspicious intelligence in it. I toed the floor, trying not to squeak it, and pushed my eye up to the peephole. An attendant came into my fish-eyed sight, lifted a spent tray of tureens and tea up from the baseboards, dropped cutlery into a bin, and went clattering back down the hall.

"Could you take me there?" I said, turning back to Li-Li. "To the Suzhou office?"

"I am no help," Li-Li said. "I have never gone to that place."

"It's the only help I can think of," I said. "Unless Mr. Hu is able to assist us?"

The "us" felt speculative, a weak plea. She put her hands to her face and squeezed. As the blood ran out, I saw the faint white line of a scar I hadn't noticed before. Even that's not right: I must have noticed but forgotten.

She exhaled and told me she'd had a migraine last night, flashing lights and holes in her vision. She'd silenced her painful phone. When she finally checked her messages, Mr. Hu had called a dozen times. His ranting took her several listens to decipher.

"Mr. Hu recites old poetry when he is most upset," Li-Li said. "Does your boss do this?"

"Poetry?"

"Mr. Hu likes Qu Yuan," she said. "You have heard of him?"

"No."

"A very old poet," she said. She'd dismissed the ramble of Mr. Hu, attaching himself like a barnacle to ancient history, as mere drunken grief. But now she believed differently.

"Since then, I cannot reach him," she said. "He was very distressed. Now I hear of your circumstances, and I must say I have extra worry for him."

I leaned my forehead on the window until the height made my kness weak. In every new hotel high-rise, these windows didn't crack open at all, for whose benefit I was never sure. There's nothing more unnerving than the suggestion that it's only institutional foresight that's keeping you from suicide. Finally, I understood the full shape of her hesitation: My hurry was to genuflect to the occupiers of Bund's corner offices, men she didn't know except by hard reputation. These were executives whom she had no reason to trust, no standing to beg from. Undoubtedly, they weren't charitable souls, more likely petty tycoons who leafleted poor neighborhoods with eviction notices and forced underlings into acts of oral sex in the office stairwells. But if they could lift this curse of suspicion from my forehead, if they could help roust or recover Leo, then I would push their failings to the distant edges of my consciousness.

I reached for Li-Li's hand, which was slick and soft. I hung too long on her delicate fingers. I can't really say I would show a similar generosity of spirit in her place, that I would let myself linger in the hands of the accused. I indicated the mayor's briefcase on the bed.

"Did you open this?" I asked.

"No," she stammered. "I would not do that."

I grabbed the case by its handle and turned out its contents. The pile of bills, thumping to the floor, brought an upwelling of heartache. Li-Li looked stricken by the lumped cash.

"Mr. Hu and I were there just before the mayor died," I said. "Maybe you're right and the police just want to talk. But it's suicide to go plead without some better guarantee than my stupid name can provide. You understand? I'm guilty enough."

Li-Li bent down, stacking the money back into the case. I heard the refrain in my voice: me and me and me. She registered that one brick of bills was missing.

"Is that why your boss is here?" she said. She wouldn't look at me. "For this money? From a man like that?"

"This?" I said. I touched the lock on the briefcase. "It can't be the whole reason."

"Why not?" she said.

"Because it isn't enough, and there are easier ways," I said.

"How much is it?" she said.

"I didn't want my hands on it."

"Except for what you took." She erupted. "You make me hide stolen money. You want me to take you to Suzhou. And still you will tell me that you do not know anything about anything."

I was shaking hard, somewhere deep, deep down, but the energy seemed to expend itself before it reached my body's surface. It left me numb.

"What if you take this?" I said. I lifted two bundles of bills. "For your trouble?"

She took this like a fumbling come-on. She shook her head and crossed her arms. I pushed the bundles onto her, trying to make her hold them. A look bloomed on her face that I believed was her mind bending toward an unthought-of possibility.

"You could start your business," I said. "Skin cream, right? The expensive stuff. Those pretty little bottles."

She bounced the bills in her hands like she was guessing their weight.

"Maybe the Suzhou men will speak to you," she said. "But how can I know the future of this?"

She set the packets on the bed. She split up the rest of the money, placing as many bundles as would fit into the room's safe, and then tucking the briefcase, with what money remained, into the closet. She handed me three packets. She kept nothing for herself.

"I cannot tell you what other men you will meet along the way," she said. "But money always is a help. Only never let anyone know all you have."

I CALLED DRIVER Wei, and he returned. We pushed across the river to the Puxi side of Shanghai, where young kids fought to cross streets in high traffic and pretty, pale girls held umbrellas in dry weather to shade them from the sun.

Li-Li looked past me to the far gray Shanghai sky, with its hazy filtered sun, the small shine not occluded by pollution. Or she was looking at nothing, and her eyes were unfocused. I fiddled with the button for the windows. I felt a need to explain myself to her in some more profound way, and I did something even I was startled by—I reached out, took her under the chin, turned her eyes toward me. I did it lightly, but it unnerved her. I dropped my hand, and there was a long silence.

"Perhaps for you there is sensitivity," Li-Li said eventually. "Public security will know that if there is a chance of international attention, they must act more carefully. It is for others that there is no sensitivity."

She delivered the last line into the floor mats. I worried about us being overheard but soon was certain we could have screamed and it wouldn't have attracted the absent mind of speeding Wei. It must be difficult to drive with one good arm. I'd never tried it.

Leaving the city, the buildings were lower to the ground, tracts of sprawling retail wilderness. Bamboo scaffolding enshrouded a five-story building, and workmen dangled on precarious ropes. Driver Wei stopped at a light, pulled the handbrake, and leaned his head out the window as far as he could manage, looking for where the traffic ended. He put his eyes back on the road with a grunt and spat to show he was dissatisfied with the answer.

"This will be a long drive to Suzhou," Li-Li said. She pumped her leg so hard it rattled the window. "The whole city is getting empty for Golden Week holiday. Everyone goes home."

"You're not going?"

She rubbed her hand across her neck, hard enough to leave a red swath on her skin.

"My father always would say to me that because I am ugly I had to work harder," Li-Li said.

"That's an awful thing to say."

"But I am not pretty," she said. "He is right."

She drew a line along her jaw all the way up to her ear. The scar was only prominent when she smiled, which maybe explained why she so rarely did. She looked up at Wei, who took a sharp corner one-handed.

"My father was driving," she said.

"It isn't very noticeable," I said. Now that I had seen the scar, I couldn't see anything else.

"I don't care to be pretty or not," she said.

Her lips disappeared into a line.

"You know that Mr. Hu always wanted to drive me home at night," she said. "He said it was because he kept me working so long. In the beginning, I was happy for him to take me in his car. He has bought a Mercedes for which he is very proud. Many nights were so late—to drive me over to Pudong New Area where I live, it took much less time." She paused. "But soon he would get out of the Mercedes. He walks to the door. He asks to stay. He wants to have a whiskey."

"Do you drink whiskey?" I said.

"He gave it to me for a present," Li-Li said. "I thought it was a strange gift. And then I understood. Mr. Hu is one of the world's loneliest people, in my opinion. I have thought so ever since we went to the desert. He cannot survive his loneliness."

"He was always like that?"

"The desert was the worst," she said. "But he always had trouble. He was always hurt."

She sailed quietly across her thoughts.

"Mr. Hu is Shanghainese," she said. "You know what that means?"

"No," I said.

"There's a dialect. They speak it to one another when they want to say something more private. I only know a little part. He says he wants to teach it to me because it would help in our business. He would come inside for whiskey and stay very late to practice conversations. It got me so tired, and he would still be so angry if I was late to work," she said. "He was worse and worse."

The tires hummed beneath us, and Driver Wei elbowed the horn like it was necessary to our propulsion—the yellow line separating us from oncoming traffic was only a suggestion to him, and the cars in front of us an insult.

"Mr. Hu slapped me once when I fell asleep at my desk," Li-Li said. "I forgot to remind him about a meeting. Very important. He was not there, and he lost face. I cried so much I didn't think he would ever do it again. And he came to my apartment even that night."

"You live alone?" I said. I wanted her to keep talking. Mr. Hu felt like the key to something.

"I live with another girl. She's more shy than me. We are both indoor girls," she said. "I would ask her to get up in the night if she hears Mr. Hu. She would come into the kitchen to make tea. Sometimes that could help him to leave."

"I have a guess," I said. "Mr. Hu is married?"

She closed her eyes. When she opened them, they'd grown wet.

"He has a very nice wife," Li-Li said. "I know he did not think I was pretty. I thought it was safe not to be pretty. Sometimes I was only sleeping for three hours on a night. His wife would call his phone. He would say he was still in the office. He is a very sad man."

"Did you say 'bad' or 'sad'?" I said.

It was clear, even as I asked, that she was telling me this not to condemn Mr. Hu, but to convey her attachment, her sympathy. I hated how well I understood that restraint, stopping short where we would have been justified in ruining the people above us. I sometimes thought we endured their cruelty because we wanted to advance above it, even to change it. It occurred to me now that in tolerating their cruelty we were also learning how to become cruel ourselves.

"I know what he did with other girls," she said. "He would tell me."

"Why would he tell you that?"

"To compare me," she said. "To the karaoke girls. To the barbershop girls."

She was deep red, digging her nails into her palms.

"He would always say how I was better," Li-Li said. "Because they treat clients like dogs, but that I cared for him like a man."

She looked small and very thin, boyish, but grave beyond what children can imagine. If she was angry at the whole world, then I thought she had every right to be: a small girl with a jawline scar; most visible emotion a blush; not ever pretty and treated even worse for that. I didn't get the sense she had ever spoken of her entanglement with Mr. Hu at such length. Perhaps she believed instinctively in that story of Lot's wife, the danger in looking back over your shoulder. It's only a modern idea that it can heal your traumas to turn around and face them. The much older notion is that the look will dry you out, take all your life away, until you're no person anymore but a column of salt.

We drove down a wide street with a median, through business parks surrounded by ten-foot hedges. I thought Polk might call at any moment, and yet I had the feeling that Li-Li was saying the most important things I might hear. Her boss was broken and selfish and whoring, but you don't dwell on those failings in a eulogy, and she seemed to believe he was gone.

She turned to me. "I wanted to explain to you that the girl was Mr. Hu's idea. It is how the men do business."

"What girl?" I said.

"He thinks everyone is like him," Li-Li said.

I was distracted by her tear-swollen face. I didn't understand what girl she was referring to.

"He worried he offended you, but you never said anything about it," she said. "You should see Mr. Hu when the girl called him. She was so angry. She said she would scream it to all of Beijing if we did not pay her three times the agreement."

I went searching for it. Finally there, in my mind, was the girl standing in my hotel room in Beijing in a too-short skirt.

"That girl looked so young," I said.

"Mr. Hu was very confused," Li-Li said. "He would not believe it. She said you chased her under the bed. I listened on the phone, and I did not want to laugh. I was not confused like he was. I knew what it meant. It showed me you were good."

We stilled at an intersection, and I watched part of a neon sign burn out on a building across the street. I should have explained that I'd been sure that girl was searching my room on the police captain's behalf. The whole story depressed me—not just that a girl I'd mistaken for a ransacking snoop was some "gift" from one of my hosts, but that Li-Li seemed to trust me, even admire or like me, based on an act that was no indication at all of my character.

DRIVER WEI BROKE up our conversation by shouting back at Li-Li. We circled a set of fences, once, then twice.

"Is he lost?" I asked.

We rolled along a forlorn patch of paved road that ended abruptly at a compound. I couldn't see any buildings beyond the fences and thin shrubs.

"He says this is it," Li-Li said.

"Where?"

"He says we are wasting our time," she said.

Wei slowed the car, and I jumped out before it stopped. Rain fell. A steady wind rattled the cyclone fencing. Li-Li joined me, and we splashed through mud around the perimeter looking for the entrance. The shadows changed at every angle, cloud cover sifting broken sunlight.

I pushed open a gate and saw what might have once been a construction site. I didn't see any evidence that work had been done in months, or longer. Heavy equipment was absent, the Mandarin signage had blown off what might have once been the foreman's trailer. No windows were in those conjectural buildings, and rain swirled through the open framing and rushed out the other side.

"What is this?" I said. "Is this right?"

Li-Li checked the address and placed calls to Bund's titular heads, never connecting with anything but a switchboard. She was dour but suggested, tentatively, that perhaps Mr. Hu worked elsewhere on his days out of Shanghai. There must exist a real office, she said, where he'd done real work.

I waved her explanations away and started to trace a different logic out of the shadows. Bund International was a name, nothing more—an act of collusion between Lightborn and all the government officials of his acquaintance who had public money to funnel to questionable construction. Embezzle, skim, divide the spoils. A win-win situation.

"Bund is a shell," I said to Li-Li. "A fiction."

She looked like she'd seen a ghost, and that was just it: she'd been employed by spirits who'd bid her to push their paper.

I left Li-Li pecking at her phone, dialing number after number, and I walked through the steel-framed room of what should have been an entryway. Under these naked girders was a more complete view of Lightborn, in all his complexities: He'd shepherded Leo to China under the auspices of a company that didn't meaningfully exist, in order to tour the congressman through a few show projects that featured Bund's name, but were more likely an impenetrable agglomeration of fraudulent partnerships that served only to enrich Lightborn and his government patrons. With Leo's help, Lightborn intended to open an American market to his Chinese partners, land a deal of real size and scale in our district, and continue the process of vacuuming up public money for his private enrichment.

I'd been party to all manner of congressional business—fundraising, junkets, meals—in which Leo was willing to cheat and shade the truth. But I was sure now that when it came to Bund, Leo only thought he would profit from the deal, when in fact he was Lightborn's dupe. I wondered if this was what Mr. Hu had been trying to convey to me at dinner—that Bund was a game, a parasite—and his anger at being fired, or his conscience, would have turned him whistle-blower on the whole enterprise if I'd allowed it. Instead, I'd left him in the restaurant and run off in search of my boss.

I leaned back on Bund International's fence, because in this whole Suzhou headquarters, I couldn't touch anything else. It was a ghost town that had never been a town, and so I suppose that meant it had no real ghosts, only trails of money that had floated above the physical ground. A thousand years ago, a holy man, the wild Bodhidharma, who must have felt as overwhelmed by the circumstances of his world as I now did mine, climbed up Mount Song and sat in a cave for nine years meditating. What puzzles me is that he eventually got up and left—that after nine years of contemplation, something became clear enough that he could get to his feet and venture back outside. It seemed to me that staring into shadows only resulted in more shadow-staring.

The unfinished buildings spit out a sulphurous, rotten-egg smell of low-grade drywall.

II.

THE LATE AFTERNOON came brightly clouded, with a lower atmo-
sphere glare of factory smoke. Wei blasted us toward the city at
axle-rattling speed. I was not only no closer to finding Leo, but even
more poorly situated for defending myself from any inquiry of the Chinese police regarding Kaifeng's mayor—his money or his death.

"You look weak," Li-Li said.

"Me?" I thought she was the one who looked sick. Driver Wei gritted
his teeth over his arm each time the car jarred a pothole. Li-Li insisted
he stop the car. We needed air, if nothing else.

We tried to collect ourselves, standing in front of a drab apartment
block fronted by a row of food stalls. The nearest vendor roasted duck
heads on a grill that was welded onto the back of his bicycle. Li-Li made
me sit on the curb, and she wandered off with Wei.

When she returned, she sat next to me and handed over a small plate
of crusted tofu and said it would give me strength. I picked at it and
the chili sauce alongside. She sat near enough to eat from the same
plate. People stared at me, and I tried not to notice. Down the lane,
Wei examined a sliver of charred meat on a stick up close under his

eye. The woman who'd sold Wei the meat wore a dirty white apron, and the man next to her was in a tatty white T-shirt. His eyes were rheumy. Power lines, phone lines, and cable lines crisscrossed in a firm mesh above my head—I could be called to rapture in heaven and I'd still be electrocuted or strangled on the way up. Li-Li and I sat lost in brambles of thought.

"I'm a burden to you," I said.

I took her long silence as agreement.

"What about the train?" Li-Li said finally. "I could show you."

"Where am I going?" I asked.

"To Guangzhou. Maybe sneak to Hong Kong?" she said. "It could be easier to fly from there."

I didn't really see how it would work. I could press on—run hundreds more miles, try to slip off the bottom of China like I was sneaking out its unlatched back door. But my constriction wasn't strictly geographical. No Leo, no Hu, no Bund—to approach any of them, like pools of water on the desert highway, was to see them evaporate. If I could have vanished now with them, I would have done so, but instead I seemed condemned to high visibility.

"Polk says he's working on it," I said. I was talking as much to myself as to her. "Polk says. Polk says. But what does he know? He's drugged up and half dead."

"Poke?" she said. She stuck a finger out.

"Never mind," I said.

Three stacks of caged fowl stunk next to me, confined so that none of the birds could turn around. A rabbit sat in its cage, so grossly fat its haunches pushed through the bars. I could almost reach a finger out to him, but I thought he would bite it, placid as he looked.

"Do you know if Mr. Lightborn ever got to Shanghai?" I asked.

"I never could discover," Li-Li said. "No one I could speak to knows."

I felt like I was holding my head out in front of me, squeezing my temples with all my strength. Wei was deep in conversation with the man with the rheumy eyes. Together they tested Wei's forearm, opining on his pains, and the unkind sidelong glances that came with pauses in their conversation seemed always to be directed at me. Li-Li retreated back into herself.

I felt swallowed by the noise of the city. Mountains of earth were excavated every minute, and sky-sucking towers altered the whistle of Shanghai's wind. Grandparents walked and clapped for their exercise. Bashful girls giggled and leaned on their surly boyfriends, who were uninterested in anything but the sheen of their motorcycles. A febrile, high-toned argument between two old men attracted an onlooking crowd, and the crowd grew rife with voices. If you were born in Shanghai, and were over sixty and sentient, then recorded in your mind, perhaps imprinted on your body, was a half century worth of ideological murder, utopian promise, and bad faith. And yet for me to extract even an eyedropper's worth of truth about this city took laborious work. The nearest passerby was a harrowingly dull, medium-build man in golf attire, his pants belted higher than his belly button. I felt so lost. I wished I understood him.

"What would you call those girls in English?" Li-Li said. "The kind my boss sent to you?"

"Girls?" It was my first glimpse of the conversation she'd been having with herself.

"You know the girls I mean."

"I don't," I said.

"What's the correct word to use?" she said. "I do not want to use an impolite expression."

Once I understood the family of words she was searching for, none seemed particularly polite. I couldn't immediately bring myself to pronounce any of them to her.

"I am not a little child," she said.

"I know that," I said. Bent double with her elbows on her knees, her shirt hung down, letting scarce light hit her flat, skeletal chest.

She was so skinny you could see the flares of contoured bone along her breastplate.

"You do not know how many times I have to see those girls," Li-Li said. "How many times to wait for them. I give them directions from parts of the city they do not know. Talk about their lives and their mental troubles."

She expelled all her breath in a long sigh, which turned into a cough when she inhaled the hanging exhaust in the city air.

"Still I call them, and I have to arrange," she said. "The men go to dinner, the men go to massage. The men go to a banquet, and the men go to karaoke. The important visitors from everywhere need to be entertained. Government men. Business associates. For all of them, 'entertained' is girls. The girls are poor and they fall in love with money. They get money and they want more money. One girl says she would rather be crying in a man's BMW than laughing on his bicycle. Other girls, their stories I cannot talk about. The places they come from. What has happened to them."

It was a destitute evening as the sun sank. I nodded at what Li-Li said but had nothing to add. The man in golf attire refused the grilled oysters and chose shrimp rinsed at the curb in tap water. He gnawed them effortfully and spat the shells on the ground. Li-Li asked me for paper. I reached my sweating hands under my pant legs to wipe them on my socks and then gave her my notebook.

"I know the girls Mr. Lightborn will use," she said. She wrote down an address from out of her phone. "The girl he likes calls herself 'Rose.' If he is in Shanghai, you can find out from her." Li-Li pointed at the corner of the notebook and added: "I will tell her you will come speak to her. She is not a good person."

The way she said the last phrase made me realize we were parting ways: she warned me now about Rose because she could not do it later. She looked miserable, but there was no reason for her to look otherwise.

"I have concern for you," she said. She'd seen the look of abandonment spreading on my face. "But what other help I can do? I am no one."

"I shouldn't have asked so much from you," I said. "It's selfish. It's not right."

She hailed a taxi. It added to my guilt that her situation was as without promise as mine. The taxi seats were covered in white fabric that looked like bedsheets. My hands were shaking.

"Perhaps I will call you from Tunxi?" she said.

"From where?"

"Home," she said, not looking at me.

Earlier, she'd made it sound like she wasn't going away for the holiday—or I'd just assumed.

"To Anhui Province the trip takes overnight," she said. "The trains fill to every corner. It is a very unpleasant obligation."

She said something else I didn't hear. The driver grumbled through the passenger window.

"If you do not find Mr. Lightborn . . ." She broke off.

"It's okay, Li-Li," I said.

I thought of her winding farther and farther away from me on a slow provincial train. It filled me with panic I tried to conceal. I held out my hand for hers, but before I'd thought much about it, I grasped her into a hug. Maybe this confused her, but she responded by clawing back into me, her small fingers like pincers.

"I would prefer not to go," she offered.

"Thank you," I said. "I know that about you."

She pulled away.

"You do not know it," she said. "And you do not know why."

She kneaded her hands and stared into them.

"I think you are a person who is very . . ." she said. I watched her mouth move, rejecting phrases, swallowing words, like she was trying to get beyond business English and into a more fraught and shaded usage. "A person who is very agreeable to me," she said finally.

I met her dark eyes. Her hair had come unstuck from its pins.

"I hope I can see you again," I said.

She took off her glasses to wipe her eyes.

"Maybe in better conditions." She smiled thinly.

"It'd be hard to find worse ones," I said.

I kissed her on the forehead. I wondered where she would find herself, a month from now, a year from now—whether still pushing back against Shanghai, or unemployed and evicted, back home in Anhui Province, living with her father. I wouldn't know. Also unknown to me: her last name, her apartment address, what extra codes I needed, if I left the country, to dial her mobile phone. Or if I didn't leave, or couldn't, whose custody she would find me in when she returned—if I was in Shanghai, would she know? And if she knew, would she find me, or could she? Nobody knew the answers to these things. Behind her departing taxi, a street sweeper scraped down the street squealing a song like an ice-cream truck. The tune was "Happy Birthday."

Driver Wei circled back into a Shanghai I recognized, past vendors saddled with baskets of cherries and lychees, up Hengshan Road into the corridors of the old French Concession, with gracious trees and wrought-iron balconies.

"You are fellating with her, but she has no smell," Wei said, trying to find my face in his rearview mirror.

"Excuse me?" I asked. His smile was ugly and sincere, and he spoke the line again. I picked the sentence apart, repronouncing every word to myself until I had molded the taffy of his syllables into a comment that seemed to me more reasonable: You are *flirting* with her, but she has no *smile*. I assumed he was referring to Li-Li.

"You like no smell?" he said.

"Smile," I said.

"Smile," he repeated.

"Yes, I like her," I said.

"Very not special face," he said. He waved his good hand like he was shooing flies. He dragged a finger up his cheek, and I understood him to be speaking of Li-Li's scar.

"You're going to make me angry, Wei," I said.

We passed a stubble of British-themed bars, empty but for a few paunchy white men with shaven heads. Wei looked at the address in his lap and then threw my notebook back at me. He caught me unaware, and the book spun into my chest.

We came to a halt at the edge of an estate. Above a high iron fence grown over with ivy poked the top of a mansard roof and a row of dormer windows. Some colonial-era banking magnate would make an appropriate ghost of the house—Western adventuring, dancing courtesans. Maybe the new owners still detected an ancient poppy incense in their walls. The commotion coming through the ivy, barely dampened, sounded like the voices of a hundred people.

"Here is the other girl place," Wei said. He indicated not the estate building, but a grim alleyway alongside it. "You go take girl with more special face."

He held out the hand on his bad arm and gently curled his fingers. He tripled the fee we had agreed upon earlier. I thought some allowance should be made for his suffering, for the medical expense of his twisted arm. But as I counted out what he asked for, I watched his scowling face and thought of Li-Li. I slapped the cash hard into his hand. He doubled over and held his elbow like it would detach if he didn't hang on. He remained that way long enough for me to feel I'd really hurt him, then got back into his car and nearly crashed as he jerked without signaling into the fast lane of Hengshan Road.

The estate housed a nightclub in its garden—a band, two bars, an open-air dance floor. People inside were enjoying themselves on this clear, high-mooned evening of mild spring weather. It was an entirely expatriate crowd, incomprehensible Finns and fast-talking French, and

I even heard a few phrases of regional American English—a real Texan. The Chinese had all gone home to their families and entrusted the city to the care of its foreign population. I wished my evening took me that way, into a carefree embrace. Calm winds from the west blew out to sea, toward California, my side of the Pacific.

A few minutes of melancholy shuffling brought me to a crook in the alleyway and a bar where two girls in the neon entry beckoned for my attention. They jumped from their perches to take each of my arms. The one to my left dressed the part of a schoolgirl. She wasn't quite that young, I didn't think, but she must have found it in her monetary interest to blur the line between adult and child. Saddled with the attentions of the schoolgirl, I was pawed, too, by her friend, who was exactly as attractive as she needed to be for a clientele of drunks. She had a puckered, slightly misshapen face, with her nose and eyes scrunched together and a painted-on dress that didn't hide what was either a corset or a girdle underneath. I took a guess about how old they were—eighteen for the schoolgirl, maybe younger for the vamp. Neither looked Chinese—not Han, anyway—and it wasn't Mandarin they spoke to one another. The girls had well-lotioned skin the color of polished teak. I showed them the address in my book, but they pulled me toward the neon doorway. I shrugged them off and caught a delivery boy on a bike. He looked at my book. His hands zigged and zagged miming several turns down the alley. He made it seem very far.

I walked the delivery boy's way until I found a long lane, too narrow for a car to enter. Ground-floor industry spilled onto the tiny pathway. A bike repairman glowered at me, greasy and reattaching a fallen chain, and then turned his unhappiness back to his splatter of scrap parts and rusty tools. The hunkered woman sweeping the street with a brush of twigs looked at me with no kindness, as did four men playing cards and drinking yellow rice wine. Three-quarters of the way down the lane, I found the building, a three-story apartment with two lit windows. The bottom floor was a closed scrap shop showcasing a miscellany of bolts and canisters behind barred windows. The second floor housed a whole family—grandparents, parents, and kids alternating at the window, calling past me to their neighbors. It was the top room I was interested in, lit by a star-shaped paper lantern. I climbed a rusty staircase, bolted to the side of the building like a fire escape. With every step, it squealed like it might fall. The sound echoed between the buildings. My tongue felt swollen to the roof of my mouth.

Before I reached the top of the stairs, a woman opened the door. She watched me climbing loudly toward her. She wore a canary-yellow dress belted with a white sash. Her straight hair was long and dark, and she had coddled pale skin and heavily made-up almond eyes.

"You're Rose?" I said. I introduced myself.

She didn't shadow my movements with suspicion or even show much curiosity. Rose lived in a single room, with a barred-in balcony off the kitchen and a translucent beige curtain separating the front half of the apartment from the bedroom. I scanned the full square footage and felt an instant affinity with her priorities. She could box up and be on the run inside ten minutes and not have left anything behind.

We sat at a plastic folding table next to her single-burner range. Rose put on water for tea.

"You look like a man I know," she said. Her English was halting but nicely enunciated.

"Who?" I asked.

"He's American," she said. "He looks like you."

"Like me how?"

"Like an American," she said, "like all of you."

I could only guess her idea of the American look. I assumed she meant some wide-eyed aspect that money and naïveté paints on your face.

She poured our tea to steep and lit a cigarette. I thought she was perfect for her profession: she'd made herself over into an idealized construction of Chinese femininity. I waited for signs her stage-managed beauty would wear at the edges. But even her cigarette smoke didn't want to leave her and instead rolled off slowly like a fog. She didn't hurry me, but I felt her time would prove expensive, that not a minute could be had for free.

I put my elbows on the table, cupped my tea.

"You and Li-Li?" she said. "Old friends?"

"Not old," I said.

"She speaks very little," she said.

"I admire that," I said.

"My feeling about her . . ." Rose said, then she stopped. "It is not important. She is your friend. We are different people."

"There's been a series of misunderstandings," I said, "and now it would help me to speak to Mr. Lightborn."

"She says Mr. Lightborn is your boss," Rose said, "but he is not a boss you can call?"

She looked more amused than anything else. She might never have had a pimple or turned her face down for anything more sour than a lemon.

"I work for him indirectly," I said, which felt true enough. "It's a complicated business."

I watched her take a hard-boiled egg from a bowl on the table and break off the brown shell. She tore the white open and, with a spoon, scraped the powdery yolk into a glass of milk. I tried to explain my situation a different way, but she stopped me.

"What you say is good enough," Rose said. "I do not care about this, not one way or the other way."

She drank her egg and milk and noticed me watching.

"For my skin," she said. And her skin was flawless, glowing glass.

"Has Mr. Lightborn contacted you?" I asked.

She hesitated.

"Tonight there is a small party," she said.

The moment this fell from her lips, I felt the confirmation alone as a victory—Lightborn collected from uncertainties into a local space and time.

"We settle business," she said quickly.

"Tell me," I said.

"For my risk?"

"Okay, the business," I said.

At the part that mattered to her—the money—she was like a diamond jeweler, teasing out what I might have to spend so she could push past it. She didn't want Chinese currency: she asked for five thousand American dollars. If she was paid to be discreet about her clients, that seemed to mean her discretion had a price on one end, and so breaking it had a price, too.

I didn't care about negotiating. She wasn't even surprised I produced the amount in immediate cash from suit and pants pockets.

Once she'd counted, she asked me to stand up. She fingered my sweat-through suit coat and complained we didn't have time to find me another.

"This jacket does not even fit you," she said. "Your masseuse can be blind, but not your tailor."

She yanked at my wrinkled, dirty tie.

"Clean up," she said. She pointed behind the sheer curtain that separated the bedroom from the kitchen. "Try your best."

I went into her bathroom and wet down my hair. I tried to rub a stain from my shirt and dragged a wet finger across my eyebrows. When I emerged, she ran her hands over my shoulders and down my sleeves.

"No better," she said.

I said I was sorry, though I wasn't sure what I was apologizing for. She dashed my tea into the sink and turned out the lamp and lantern. We glowed in ashen light from the street.

"We can have a little bit more time," she said, "if you would desire."

She tucked her chin toward the spill of her dress. She nestled close to me, the first time our skin touched. She rested her head on my shoulder, and when I found my voice, I was answering directly into the half-moon of her ear.

"I'm under so much pressure," I said. She reached her hand into my pants pocket, and I don't know if she was expecting my wallet or expecting to feel the rest of me, but what she got was the rest of me. She might not know how much more money I had, but she was groping for the cord she thought might lead her to it.

"You would not?" she said. "Are you that kind of man?"

I took her to mean abstaining, as against the kind of man I actually was. She made sure to push against me, so that I felt her body through her dress.

"I'm looking for my way back home," I said, "and I don't think you're the way."

"You make me sad," she said.

"I'm sure you'll get over it, Rose."

"You make me cry," she said.

She drew her hand from my pocket and steadied her body against mine. Maybe there'd be satisfaction in stealing a moment with a woman Lightborn had singled out this evening for his. But I'd been down that path before. Sleeping with Theresa had given me no power over Leo; it only made me feel wounded and strangely more beholden to both of them.

"I don't understand why you will pay so much to go see a man," Rose said, "and nothing to have a woman."

I was grateful to feel a phone call shaking my pocket. The number on the screen came up long and jumbled, and I thought finally it was Polk, his call routed through local satellite towers. Rose let me out onto her back balcony for a modicum of privacy.

"Luke Slade?" the voice said.

"Speaking."

"Now you listen to me," he said. "My name is George Szczepanski, okay? That's S-Z-C-Z-E-panski. Got it? Now I've voted for Congressman Fillmore in the last four elections. I've written checks when I could afford to, and it just burns me up that you people aren't listening."

"I'm sorry?" I mumbled. "This is a bad time."

"It's my time! I pay your salary! So you tell me how the congressman expects me to make a living if he's not going to enforce the law on the Mexicans?"

"Call our office and ask for Glenn," I said.

"That boy told me to talk to you," he said. "Now you people are just jerking me around. I'm telling you I can see the Mexicans from my porch."

I hung up on him. Rose's balcony gave out on an eyeful of concrete wall. She had a potted ficus, wrinkly brown—if it were human, you would hear it wheezing. We left her apartment, and the men playing cards were still in the lane, siphoning out their plastic gallon of yellow wine in wincing gulps. Two old men squatted nearby, selling medicinal herbs. They didn't pay us any attention, talking with one another above the traffic noise in warm Shanghai air that smelled like fireworks.

III.

THE ONLY INDICATION of the party at the Shanghai Fortune Yacht Club were two men, fierce as the painted statues that guard imperial tombs, who stood at either side of a distant pier. My body was in messy revolt, head swaying and feet heavy as we approached the docked boat. The guards greeted us. Actually, they greeted Rose, looking past me to any place her skin escaped her dress. Certainly my eyes were large and searching, my face flushed. What they said I found indecipherable, but soon they were no longer imposing, only chatty. They let us aboard. Rose and I parted, strangers again.

The yacht filled slowly with guests and then pulled into the river. Faster boats cut past us, churning up wakes of phosphorescent water. Shanghai teemed on either side of me, its lights green and blue and yellow. In less urgent circumstances, I might have enjoyed this without reservation, watching the city like it was being staged for just the fifty of us.

I scanned the top deck for Lightborn. A group of Chinese men stood at the prow, clustered together like speakers on a dais, and a handful of Americans ringed them in a respectful halo. I took my search inside,

where boisterous guests crowded together in a walnut-paneled barroom. I saw no faces I recognized among the Americans, but I also did
my best to keep my gaze level with their loosened ties. I held my breath
and ground my teeth, trying to find the still calm of a temple Buddha.
Within a quarter hour, I'd been marked with an indelible dye that said I
must be some assistant, and the men present stopped paying me much
notice. I had no problem, myself, spotting the other assistants onboard.
Most of them stayed closely tethered to their bosses, as though they
shared an oxygen tank. I breathed in my small measure of safety: the
yacht, at least, was no place I'd be harried by public security. Two men
shambled up a set of stairs from belowdecks, but neither was Armand
Lightborn.

I wandered to the aft deck and sat on a bench next to a storage bin
for life vests that hid me from sight of the partygoers. On shore, tiny
heads bobbed in front of the old banks and colonial-era hotels on the
Bund. When so much else had been destroyed, it was hard to imagine
those buildings had been left to stand—monuments to markets backed
by gunboats, towers of Western money on Chinese land.

The hour grew later, and the city lights cast prisms across every
break in the water. I paced to a window and watched the party inside.
The men in suits became looser and sadder in pantomime. I pitied their
assistants, stranded on the late-night cruise, knowing the alarm doesn't
come any later in the morning just because the boss kept you out into
the small hours the night before.

What I would say to Lightborn, if I encountered him, was still something of a mystery to me. He might extract me from China, he might
know already what had become of Leo, but I wanted him to look at me,
too. For what I had done—for Venice, for Kaifeng, for all my silent years
preceding them—I had been made, and would be made, to suffer. And
I felt he simply needed to be made aware—that it should be brought to
bear on Lightborn's consciousness that out here on the margins there
were men like me, however distant in the etiolations of his schemes,

who were taken in, who might be at fault, but who suffered for those faults while no harm had come to him.

A group of Americans trudged out to my end of the ship. They took no notice of me. Three dark-suited men joined them, Chinese and exuding an official demeanor. I'd had my education. These were the sort of men who let praise for the masses fall from their lips, while the papers for personally enriching private ventures were packed into their briefcases. Most saw no contradiction in this behavior and would quote you what Chairman Mao liked to say: "Fish don't survive in pure water." Each official was soon joined by an early-twenties female with the irregular proportions of an underwear model. The girls were flower-stalk tall and equally slim, with an unmistakable sexual air whose most lasting impression was nevertheless fragile and unhealthy. I thought of cut orchids. I thought of wax museums. Rose had claimed not to know much about this party, except what she could guess from the other girls who'd been requested. Most were Russian, milky blonde, a species pre-ferred, she said, by the Communist Party elite.

I was so fixated on this tableau that I didn't notice someone had sidled up next to me. I felt a hand on my shoulder. He could have snagged my wallet if he'd wanted to start easy in a career of petty theft.

"You recognize that guy over there?" the man said.

"Which?" I said.

"White guy. Leather face." He pointed to a lonely man who'd come out to lean on the railing and was now gazing at Shanghai in utter con-fusion. The man's body wasn't built for a suit, with a gut and big shoul-ders and legs as massive around, each one, as my chest. I didn't find him familiar, though I could be convinced I had seen him before.

"Sorry, I'm Robbie," the guy next to me said. "Assistant to Mr. Lightborn."

I'd never spoken with Robbie. But rage is what I felt—an easy trans-ference, my burdens all his fault, just for him saying Lightborn's name. I told him he must be brand-new.

"Last guy only lasted three hours," Robbie said.

"Quit in three hours?"

"Fired in three hours."

"You must be the one not returning any of Lightborn's calls," I said.

"You're not the first person to say that tonight," he said. He shook his phone at me like a rattle. "You wouldn't believe the last few days."

I stared into the river's green, chemical trash, collecting myself.

"So that guy used to play pro baseball," Robbie said, pointing again at the thick man near the railing who was now throwing ice cubes at sea birds. I took a second look and realized I knew who he was, once I had him in the right frame. He'd pitched a perfect game. He'd won two hundred more. He used to hunt African game with a crossbow in the off-season.

"What's he doing here?" I asked.

"Some investment group wants our help building a stadium in China. They brought him over as a rep," Robbie said. "Baseball's got huge potential, I think. I mean, what's the competition, Ping-Pong?"

Robbie had a gap in his teeth that faintly whistled when he spoke. Underneath our small talk, I rehearsed an entirely different conversation.

"You ever play baseball?" Robbie asked.

"Not past Little League," I said.

"You know, Mr. Lightborn could have gone pro."

"He likes to say that," I said. "So why the fuck didn't he?"

"How about rotator cuff," Robbie said. "How about tendinitis. How about ligaments. Every piece of conceivable shit." He flexed his left arm at me, then uncurled it to about a quarter of the normal range of motion. "You know that's the furthest he can stretch it now without pain?"

"I guess his talent was cursed," I said.

Robbie was distracted by a squawking gull the ballplayer had pinged with ice. As long as I held my tongue, a conjectural evening took shape before me. We were two assistants on a night cruise, talking about bad luck. We could listen to the ballplayer tell stories about road trips and loose women. We could raid the bar and bust open scotch older than I was. At the end of the night, barely under my own power, I could leave in good company, arms draped over my compatriots' shoulders, Lightborn bouncing into his waiting car to be expensively fondled by every petal of Rose's flower.

"You know who Leo Fillmore is?" I asked.

Robbie cocked his head like it was a name he neither wanted, nor expected, to hear.

"You know about this?" he said.

"I know that I work for him," I said.

Robbie rocked back on his heels. His aspect turned dark and joyless, and he twisted his head to check our distance from the other guests on board. I followed along with his eyes, watching a young man in sunglasses carry drinks to the triptych of Chinese ministers.

"Where've you guys been?" I said.

"I'm not going to tell you any shit like that," Robbie said. He was drinking bourbon over ice. He crunched the ice with his teeth.

I took the wind in my face, diesel engine smoke from barges and ferryboats. It was a lovely night in spite of my feelings that I might sink under its weight. I started to sway, and soon I couldn't stop. It was a nauseous fit. I felt like I might collapse. Something had broken, talking to Robbie, in my ability to just stand and bear up. A police boat shot by us with discombobulated officers holding their hats to their heads.

"Are you drunk?" Robbie said. "Is something wrong with you?"

"I'll take it up with your boss when he has a minute," I said.

"He won't have one for you," Robbie said. He was trying to sound so mean and yet sounded so uncertain that I almost pitied him. For once, I caught myself looking at the two dim stars in the city's sky.

"I bet Polk has called you thirty-five times," I said.

"Yeah?" Robbie said. "Well, maybe he can wait his turn. We're still trying to triage your boss trying to fuck us."

He got the tough line out, but then his voice lost its edge. It would take him a few years' practice to grow expert at his bullying. His knuckles were white where he gripped his glass.

"The police didn't pick you up, too?" he said.

"Leo and I got separated," I said. "What police?"

"Am I interrupting?" a deep voice asked. Robbie's attention was divided by the ballplayer, who pushed in between us.

"No," Robbie said at the same moment that I said, "Yes."

I turned to Robbie: "Who has him? Who found him?"

"I don't even know why Mr. Lightborn owes him the help," Robbie said.

"You're going to have to be clear with me, Robbie," I said. "Because I don't have any fucking idea what you're talking about."

He gave me a look of disbelief, like I was trying to con him.

"If you assholes intended to set your own meetings, there's no reason for Mr. Lightborn to foot the bill," he said.

I tried to constitute the terms on which Lightborn would feel he was the betrayed party on this China excursion. I knew Leo had ambitions unending, bottomless wants, so perhaps that was my answer: if there was a district project he could steer to a bidder, why would he settle for Bund's first offer?

"Can we go somewhere and talk?" I asked Robbie.

"Do you know how far this is above your head?" Robbie said.

"Everyone here's so fucking serious," the ballplayer said. "Jesus Christ."

"We're just bullshitting," Robbie said. He pointed at me. "This is one more guy begging for a favor he doesn't deserve."

He gave the ballplayer his full attention. "Can I get you anything? What are you drinking? Shots? You tell me."

Robbie boxed me out with his shoulder, stepping in close to this poor, bored ballplayer who'd just come to get drunk for free with pretty girls. Robbie didn't pay me anymore attention as I slunk off, and why should he? This was Lightborn's boat, with Lightborn's guests. I was a deckhand.

I ENTERED THE paneled barroom, determined to speak with Lightborn. Rose stood next to a swaying Russian girl in a black dress, pulling the girl's hands away from her drinks. Each time, the girl shrieked. The Russian turned to me, smiled crookedly, and, in passable English, pointed at the skittish bartender and said he was putting cheap liquor in nice bottles and watering down what he poured. The boy shrank behind the bar, and he probably was watering the drinks, and he probably was pouring her the cheap stuff, but only because the girl was a mess. Rose dragged the Russian to the bathroom. They were gone so long that I went to see if I might help. I found Rose holding the girl's hair back out of her face as the Russian knelt emptying her stomach. I asked if I should bring water, but Rose waved me off.

I sidled through the galley kitchen. An aquarium of lobsters with banded claws crowded roughly on top of one another. Eels with oily black skins waited to die in their own gloomy tank. I interrupted two men examining a wine rack that covered one wall. I excused myself and left them to their whispered admiration.

At the far end of a hallway, I found a staircase. That Leo might be running a scheme of his own, that he wasn't merely a drunk loosed in foreign territory, was easy to integrate into what I knew of him. What I didn't know—what only Lightborn, as yet, seemed to know—was how exactly Leo's ambitions had gone awry, in what limbo he'd been left. I thought of Mr. Hu's stories of the bad ends of corruption—the bullet in the back of the state minister's head. I suspected if Lightborn were willing to help fix Leo's mess, it wouldn't at all be for Leo's sake—it would be because a missing American congressmen was a dangerous kind of attention. I climbed toward an open door at the top of the spiral stairs, stepping softly toward the sound of low voices.

On the stateroom bed, I saw Lightborn, seated. He wore an oxford cloth shirt with half the buttons undone. I hadn't spoken with him since Venice. Standing above him were two Chinese men. I mounted another step to get a better look. Lightborn was slumped down like he was maybe a foot shorter than he actually was. His shoulders were two fallen slopes. His belly was maybe the worst, a bonobo-like protrusion created by the odd angle of his slouch. The Chinese men had their backs to me, and they rattled on at Lightborn, working their grievances up to a violent pitch. They talked over one another, increasingly emphatic, hands choppy and wild, their words mostly in English but still difficult for me to make out. Lightborn started to stand up, as though to defend himself, and one of the men put a hand to Lightborn's chest and shoved him back onto the bed. I tried to back up and slipped down two stairs, catching myself on the railing. Lightborn lifted his head just enough to glimpse me staring at him.

One of the Chinese men, following Lightborn's eyes, turned and looked down at me. I saw pomade and cufflinks and shined shoes. His eyes were watery from the open cognac sitting on the sideboard. He'd taken his suit jacket off, and his belt divided his belly into two loaves. His partner struggled with the plastic wrapper around a pack of cigarettes. It slipped unopened from his hands, and he crushed the pack under his heel. The man with the divided belly shouted at me, and his partner with the crushed cigarettes joined in, but louder. He rushed to slam the door, but before it closed, I had one last look at Armand, the bagginess in his face. I spent a vertiginous second lost in his soupy eyes. I saw ladders of men ascending above Lightborn, men who had the standing to argue with him, to lay their hands on him, and I imagined men incomprehensibly more powerful than even those men, who surveyed the rest of us from the height of some Babel tower that could not be crushed. I heard the door latch, and I stood listening for another moment. There was no more conversational noise, only a shuffle of footsteps. Distantly from the deck, I could hear a cacophony of Russian and English and Chinese, and I thought it could be the roar of six more arguments, but perhaps it was one vast celebration.

BACK IN THE barroom, Rose had straightened her bright yellow dress, and she smelled like a fashion magazine filled with competing perfume cards. The Russian girl smelled like stomach acid and slept on the bar. Rose shook her awake, and together we dragged her to a love seat. The girl's body unfurled like a carpet. The bartender kept apologizing, like this was his fault, or we were the people to whom he owed explanations. Rose fidgeted like she was afraid to appear too familiar with me.

After awhile, Robbie came inside. He glanced at Rose and the unconscious Russian.

"I'm supposed to say it's safest for you to stay out of sight and we'll contact you in the morning," Robbie said in a monotone. He asked for the name of my hotel.

"That's it?" I said.

"Fluid situation," he said.

"Is Leo okay?" I said. "Tell me that much."

"He isn't dead," Robbie said.

He waited for me to press him for more.

"Enjoy this now," I said. "You'll be me someday."

Robbie had been instructed to tell me exactly what I did not believe— that if I could just pass one more night alone, then tomorrow would dawn with infinite promise. I was being sent off with the hope that Lightborn wasn't so bullied or distracted by that universe of his connections, so incomprehensible to me, that Leo would be attended to while I'd be forgotten. I hoped that one day Robbie's children would have to carpool out to an upstate prison on Sundays to visit him.

"Do you ever read Chinese poetry?" Rose said suddenly. She stared at the men on deck with a faraway look, but she was talking to Robbie.

"What the fuck does that have to do with anything?" he said.

He shook his head at us both and took a bottle of cognac from behind the bar. He spread his fingers and stuck them like tentacles into four short glasses. On deck were the ballplayer and ebullient officials of whatever sort and the painted ladies in their company. I watched Lightborn join them. From a distance, I could detect no turmoil in his manner. He was somehow smiling. I didn't see either of the men he'd been speaking with. He threw his pitching arm around the ballplayer. Rose looked contemplatively from the shallow-breathing Russian girl to the clustered men. She told me she'd remembered some lines of Li Bai she once memorized in school:

> Empty a wine-cup to end grief, and grief remains grief.
> You never get what you want in this life, so why not
> shake your hair loose on a boat at play in dawn light?

She left me and joined the party. I watched Lightborn kiss her neck.

We came banging into a pier somewhere near Suzhou Creek and the teepee form of the Monument to the People's Heroes. I don't know where the rest of the night took Lightborn and the ministers, or the ministers above those ministers, but as I walked off the boat, I'd never felt more envious, or more small, or so overfilled by hatred.

IV.

RETURNING TO MY hotel late that night, two clerks halted me in the dim lobby. One took the lead, wringing his hands. He asked if I was Mr. Slade. A pair of public security officers appeared from the darkness behind him, looking brutish but bored. The older officer stepped forward and spoke almost into my ear: "Please you will come with us. For tea."

"Should we sit?" I said. I pointed at an arrangement of lobby chairs, empty of guests at this late hour.

"Sensitive matter," the officer said.

He brought his arm out mechanically and rested it on my shoulder. He seemed to move several seconds behind his thoughts. He led me forward, and in a clipped voice I asked everything I could think to—what this was about, and where I was being taken. The clerks fled, in search of any other task they might perform.

An Indian businessman wheeled his suitcase out of the elevator and glanced at the officers leading me. The officers openly stared the man down, like they wanted to empty his suitcase and turn out his pockets. The businessman ignored their attention and offered me a pinched smile. I guessed from his impassive expression that he assumed my guilt, as you do when the police have a drunk corralled outside a bar. What was terrifying to me must have looked respectable and without violence to any passersby.

In the elevator, the officers talked haltingly to each other—the younger asked questions, and the older grunted short answers. I guessed he was the higher ranked, if he had the power to be unfriendly. In the guts of the building, we passed a service laundry the size of a bowling alley. The damp was cave-like, as were the echoes. After walking longer than it seemed possible without exhausting the building's foundation, the officers dumped me into a room with a table and four chairs. A single row of puzzling interior windows near the ceiling was covered over with white paper. I could see the shadows of feet walking on the floor above me. From the way the ceiling rattled, I thought we must be beneath the laundry room we had passed some time back.

"You say 'Luke Slade' is your name, but we have different reports," the grunting officer said. He sat across the short table from me.

"Just Luke Slade," I said.

"No other names?"

"I only need one."

"Other identities?" the second called out, standing at the door. "Something for undercover."

The grunting man had sweat running down his jagged sideburns.

"You are fluent in Chinese, this is correct?"

"No," I said.

"Our report is that you speak the language as a native."

"That's a mistake," I said.

"This is also in the report," he responded. "That you will pretend you do not understand what you in fact understand."

I stared at his brass shirt buttons and thought how close "uniformed" was to "uninformed." A hiss of steam pushed in from the hall, and a third official entered. He wore a charcoal gray business suit with a Savile Row fit. He took a post in the corner, observing for a long time as the officers rotated stiffly in and out of the chair in front of me, asking who was I, and why was I here, who did I work for, and where had I been? The suited man looked distracted and never spoke until he summoned the officers out of the room.

I had plenty of restless time to wonder about the blueprint of the building and how far I was from an exit. I watched shadows pass above me, behind the covered windows, dragging longer shadows behind them.

Soon a teenage boy with red cheeks and wide eyes entered and addressed me in English. He would translate. Behind him, finally, was a face I recognized.

"Running and running," the Kaifeng captain said.

He remained as washed out and pale as when I'd last encountered him on the waterfront.

"I would like to call my embassy," I said.

"You are going to give this statement," the captain said through the translator. "The most simple is to admit everything."

"Give me a paper and pen and I'll write everything just as I've told it to the others," I said.

"I have your statement here."

He handed me a Mandarin script, notarized with three square, red stamps.

"If you translate this into English, I can read it," I said.

The translator relayed this, and the captain waved me off like a horsefly.

"Sign it, and you can make formal request for copy," he said.

"I think it's reasonable to ask what my statement says." I played attorney, as though I had rights. "I need to confirm that no mistakes or distortions have entered your official record."

"You are still playing tricks," he said.

"How is that a trick?" I asked.

"It isn't important what you think you know," the captain said, and here he couldn't resist a wide smile. "It's important that we know. And we know what you claim you do not know."

I looked to the translator and pointed at the statement: "Will you tell me what it says?"

I felt my whole life concentrated in my lower back, my slumped posture, like I'd never again sit up straight.

"You have stolen money from the people of Henan Province." The captain began to shout, only to have the translator relay everything quietly. "That is the already certain criminal act."

I flinched, and he puffed bigger.

"There are fifty public security who have not been paid wages in two months," he said. "There are village cash reserves that are now all gone. 'Community project' money has gone to where? People taken from homes to build for new business. Nothing is built, and those people do not get new homes. Where does the people's money go to?"

He cocked himself on the table's edge.

"To you," he said.

My peripheral vision caught a bat flying across the room, a spread wing that was actually the captain's open palm. He struck my face hard enough that I think he hurt himself. It was scalding water through my sinuses. I braced for more, but the captain was called out of the room by the man in the suit.

My dress shirt itched and stunk with sweat. I took it off and sat in the undershirt, yellow at the armpits. If I didn't dissolve into panic, it was only because I'd long ago succumbed. I might have been bodily confined to a basement room by Chinese authorities, but in truth I was embarked on some other journey—plunging into a valley I'd found in myself. It felt much like the desert valley where I was born. I asked myself who I was, and I could find nothing to map of a topography so featureless. I was fits and starts of a person, not a whole or a good one. For years I'd flowed along, a dirty stream, and let pass in silence events I told myself I had no power to change. I could say that in this room, under interrogation, I discovered my fatalism—but it was a fatalism enlivened by no religious spirit, no conviction of an order beyond the visible. It was a dry valley in the heart and soul.

It might have been morning. The charcoal-suited man appeared and greeted me in uninflected English. He was maybe forty, with a lean face that looked more Central Asian than Han. He latched the door behind him, sniffed the air, lit a cigarette, offered me one I declined, and tried out three chairs to find the most comfortable. He asked if I had eaten and introduced himself by an English name: Albert. He said he was the officer in charge of foreign visitors to Shanghai.

"I have listened now to this man from Kaifeng," he said. "At this time, you should tell me your story."

I thanked him. Albert struck me as vastly more educated than the Kaifeng captain and like a man who needed me to recognize that distinction.

"First let us establish: Did you meet this captain in Kaifeng, as he says?" Albert asked.

"I was sent to Kaifeng," I paused. "I'm here at the invitation of Bund International. Have you heard of it?"

He looked at me as though I'd just told him the order of the seasons.

"You know about the mayor?" Albert asked.

"The man from Kaifeng . . ." I said.

"His name is Zhang," Albert said. He said the name like it was funny to him.

"Zhang told me the mayor of Kaifeng was dead," I said. "But he seemed not . . ." I searched for the appropriate words, "entirely believable."

"The death is sensitive. An open matter. That's the report as I have it," Albert said, as though he was sorry to hear it. He continued: "But

LAST DAYS IN SHANGHAI

you admit it was you in Kaifeng. It was not your boss the congressman who attended? Many have reported contact with an American official."

"I went in his place," I said. "Some of the guests may have been confused."

"Or misled," he said.

I let his assertion stand without protest. The table between us was empty, but Albert looked at it like he was reading from a file.

"What's 'Shoes'?" he asked.

"Mr. Hu?" I said. "He's a project manager for Bund."

"I have never heard anyone called 'Shoes,'" he said.

I tried to put the facts in order, at least those at my disposal. "We left the mayor's house very late. Everyone had been drinking. I flew to Beijing in the morning. They were Bund meetings. Armand Lightborn? Have you heard of him? That's all that happened."

"It's not all that happened," Albert said, drawing out the last word. "There was a briefcase."

"It was given to me as a gift," I said.

"And somewhere you possess this briefcase?"

I thought I should be direct with Albert.

"Yes," I said.

"And you say this is where your involvement with the Kaifeng mayor ends," he said. "How was the mayor when you last saw him?"

"Drunk," I said. "But still standing."

"Captain Zhang is certain that not only have you taken money, but you have a part in the sudden death," Albert said. He stood and paced to the wall.

"I can't even imagine how," I said.

"You don't need to imagine," he said. "The man is dead."

"Not because of me," I said. "I promise you that."

"I have no opinion of your promises. I have no ideas about you as a man," he said. "I do not have special information that tells me your private capabilities."

My heartbeat reached into my throat, but my voice was caught at my tonsils. I'd adjusted to the room's smell of smoke and mold, but I stopped breathing long enough that the stench became new again. I placed my head between my knees and stayed that way until Albert hoisted me up, disapproving.

"You say you are no killer," Albert said. "I have a man who insists otherwise. You see the situation I am in. Who would you like me to believe?"

"Me," I said when I realized he expected an answer. "Believe me."

He surveyed the room like a scientist taking air-quality samples or cataloging indigenous life-forms.

"Your error is that this is not a question of belief," Albert said. "I can see you are very tired."

"When you talk to Mr. Lightborn . . ." I said, "or to Mr. Hu . . ."

Albert held up his hands.

"I am here to speak with you only," Albert said. "My recommendation is that you untie yourself from concern for Mr. Hu."

"Have you talked to him?"

Albert took this placidly, not interested in answering.

"I have only one problem for this late evening," Albert said. "I would like to send five people home satisfied that there is justice. Myself. The man from Kaifeng. These two officers he has pled his case to. And you. Therefore: How might all five of these men agree?"

For all his philosophical distance, he had a predator's footwork. He stalked me in logical circles and left me speechless.

"Some cause exists for the death of the mayor," he continued. "My duty is to determine if the cause requires you to accompany our visitor back to Henan Province. There are 'many edges to the sword.' Is that your expression?"

"Close enough," I said.

"Now you can 'play your part,'" Albert said. He leaned on his English idioms, slowing down their enunciation. "How is it the mayor of Kaifeng has died? Who were his enemies? Who were his rivals?"

"I barely knew the man," I said. "Maybe he had a stroke. A heart attack."

Albert weighed these. "This is your educated opinion, having observed the man and his health?"

"I'm not a doctor," I said.

"Very good, very good," Albert said. His way was to make me feel hopeful and then stupid. "You are lacking this expertise. Let us establish that speculation is uninteresting to me. I am not asking for ignorance or guess. But now you have offered your 'point of view,' so let us consider it. If what you say is correct—a stroke, a heart attack—then there is nothing more for you and me to accomplish. The mayor died at his time."

"Middle-aged men," I said, and here I spoke from experience, "hard jobs, bad diets, excessive drinking, no exercise, no sleep. They die for all sorts of reasons. No one has to murder them. They're as fragile as hamsters."

"The case that can be made, of course, is whether he was pushed along that course," Albert said. "Arrived at his death more quickly than expected."

"He wasn't pushed by me," I said.

"Here again you are talking about your word only," Albert said. His eyes wrinkled. "And I cannot establish justice simply based on your word."

"What else do you want?"

Albert didn't like this question.

"We must establish the truth," Albert said. "I am asking you to participate in the truth." He touched two fingers to his temple. "The men who were loyal to this mayor in Henan Province will have testimony of perhaps a dozen men. Every one will swear to the local judge what evils you have committed."

"What about a coroner's report?" I said. "That should tell you everything."

"Is a coroner a lifelong position?" Albert asked. "Who holds a coroner's salary in his hand? Who protects the coroner's side business? And who will feed a coroner's family if he loses his position?"

I exhaled, unable to answer.

"The medical records your accusers will possess will look favorably upon their version of events. Is that much understandable to you?" Albert said. "Now, if you are interested in establishing your version of events, one that is more true for you, then perhaps your truth can counteract theirs."

"Maybe he drank himself to death," I said.

A look of frustration passed over his face.

"You are still in search of the irrefutable answer to how this man has died," Albert said. "But only the dead man's ghost knows it. For our purposes, no cause is irrefutable. This situation is contested by men with loyalties. Please understand: You were in close proximity to an unfortunate event. You are a foreigner and, worse, an American. So they will have a suspicion of you that will never be disproven. It can only, if you will take the appropriate measures, be disputed."

The paper over the high windows had begun to come unstuck at the corners. It let in a small light from the room above.

"How can I prove to you I'm innocent?" I said. "You won't take my word. You're saying the medical reports will be tainted."

"It is a hard problem, I do not disagree," Albert said. "This man Zhang believes that someone has introduced a poison. In all probability this was in the late evening when the mayor was too compromised by baijiu to pay attention to its taste or early effects. Now, we know the mayor has had two late guests—this man who will call himself 'Mr. Shoes' and also you."

He pulled a grave face, but there remained in his features a soft afterimage of empathy. This brief moment of compassion was so unexpected that it made me aware of a space Albert had been trying to leave open for me since the moment he'd entered the room. I felt like I'd come out of a long tunnel. He was not talking about fair adjudication of the accusations against me. We were talking about exchange.

"The truth isn't with that man waiting to take me to his province," I said.

"It's not even with us here," Albert said.

I tried to pick up his elliptical way of speaking. Albert would never entrap himself, never be caught saying what he wanted outright. I took up the paper that had fallen from the window. I held it in front of him.

"There are some people who can construct a beautiful bird from a flat piece of paper," I said.

Albert looked at me as though I was an unpromising student who'd suddenly decided to apply himself. He smiled, his muscles for it unpracticed.

"What was nothing becomes something," I said. I folded a loose airplane and placed it on the table.

"A paper truth," Albert said.

"I understand that a fair investigation of the accusations against me would be a great expense," I said. "But I'm a person who believes in the truth." I fixed my eyes on Albert's. "And I'll pay whatever it costs to discover it."

"The price could be very high," Albert said. He picked up the plane and floated it across the room.

"The mayor's briefcase has papers that should be examined by a professional," I said. "I have the case in my room. I think you are the appropriate man to take possession of this evidence."

Albert was too wary to believe promises until he saw them realized, but I'd apparently interested him enough that he rose and invited me to follow. What had happened to the mayor had irremediably happened—but the tale belonged now to the highest-bidding tellers.

· · ·

WE FILED BACK into the industrial guts of the hotel. Captain Zhang waited, drinking unfiltered tea and spitting out the dark green leaves that stuck to his lips. Albert called over the two arresting officers and spoke to them in Mandarin. Zhang looked to Albert and then to me. He must have noted the easy manner between us. He began to protest, and when the Shanghai officers approached him, he smashed his teacup against the far wall.

Albert tore a sheaf of paper from Zhang's hands—my "confession"—and waved it in the air.

"He insists you are a thief and a spy," Albert laughed. "A foreign assassin."

The light went out behind Zhang's eyes. They became small with rage. He addressed me with a haltingly pronounced English sentence: "The money is not for him. The money is for the people."

Zhang swung his fists in the air—it was peasant money, he said, stolen money. The Shanghai officers tried to placate him, but when he shoved the older one in the chest, the younger closed in and bent Zhang's arms behind his back. A wincing Zhang protested another minute, but he was soon reduced to hurt silence and looked resigned to my release. The young officer let him go, and Zhang shook his body loose to quell the pain.

With his newfound freedom, Zhang cocked his welterweight arm and hit me in the eye socket. He punched me at least twice more, and someone was shrieking like a whipped dog, and that was me. Albert tried to lock Zhang's right arm, but with the next concentrated stroke of his left, Zhang hit me hard enough across the mouth that I twisted and fell onto my stomach. I crawled to the corridor wall. My nose and mouth had broken open with what I didn't at first recognize as blood because it tasted so sour. Captain Zhang was duck-walked out of sight, arms bent behind his neck.

• • •

HIGH UP IN my hotel room, six faint inches of dawn shone through a gap in the curtains. The ventilation system filled the room with a dry chemical air that left a prickly sensation in my throat. My steps landed off balance, and I couldn't find the switch for anything but the entryway light. The bed was an unmade lump in the dark.

Albert walked to the window and peeked out in private meditation at the first indigo of the rising sun. A cut leaked beneath my eye. I'd only ever been hit that hard by a steering wheel when I'd spun out once on a country road. I knelt in the dimness and searched the mayor's briefcase out of the closet.

Behind me, I heard Albert mumbling a low, soothing Mandarin, something he might address to a child or offer as a prayer. I didn't pay it much attention until I turned to see a figure huddled up in the bed. Albert had moved to its edge. I had to cross the room before I could see that he was speaking with a woman. She turned to me: blank face, sharp bangs, a body so light she barely dented the mattress, though she'd wildly mussed the sheets. I started to say Li-Li's name, in wonder. The first syllable fell out before I held up—I didn't want to identify her to Albert. I tried to disguise my voice as a groan. Albert tensed, ready to jump to his feet. He relaxed when I placed the briefcase gently onto his knees. I touched the heel of my hand to the open skin on my cheek and met Li-Li's half-opened eyes, trying to convey the hello I didn't voice.

Albert switched on the bedside lamp and bent up the shade. Unaccustomed to the new light, Li-Li looked away and smoothed a lick out of the back of her hair. He took an evidentiary approach to the money, fanning the packets near the bulb. I could see it now—provincial Zhang pleading his case to these big-city men and Albert concerned only with discovering if this money was a fable, contriving how he might gather it for himself.

He closed the briefcase and stood. Something almost joking entered his manner. It was nothing that I would have noticed in another person, only visible against the backdrop of his nightlong detachment.

"Many men spoke to say an American congressman is the honored guest at this banquet in Kaifeng," Albert said. "They have no doubt he attended. And yet, when I visit this congressman in his hotel, even when we drink tea for a long time, he will still claim he has never in his life visited Kaifeng. For two days this problem has occupied me."

As a kid, I'd once jumped off a small bridge into an irrigation canal—and what I remembered was there was a point where I thought I would hit the water, but instead I kept falling, and I didn't know when the water would come and I wished I hadn't jumped. Something like this feeling came over me as Albert spoke.

"Your boss insists on his innocence in that forceful manner in which liars always insist," he said. "I was sure that his presence in Kaifeng was a truth waiting to be confessed. But now I am humbled to find he did not tell me a lie, at least about this matter. You were in Kaifeng. You played the honored guest. I am very satisfied to discover the source of this error."

I put my hands on my face and pulled all my skin forward and felt the oil left behind on my palms.

"I find this an excellent lesson to reflect on," Albert said. "When you become too certain, you invite limitation in your thinking."

Li-Li went into the bathroom, and I heard the sink run. She came out with a wet washcloth and held it out for my face. I'm sure this was intended to be consoling. At the moment, it felt grotesque.

"Where's my boss now?" I asked. I didn't feel lucid. "Is he free to go?"

"Your travel must be immediate," he said. "But that is 'in other hands.'"

He asked that I pass on his greeting to two men from Bund International, but he didn't use Lightborn's name, and I didn't recognize the ones he did say. I wondered if he was referring to the stateroom men I'd seen bullying Armand. Albert left us, and the door puffed quietly shut.

I checked my cuts in the bathroom mirror. The bleeding would not be staunched, and my reflection showed me deep black panda eyes from no sleep. I faucet-washed blood from my twisted hair. My suit had relaxed its cheap fibers and hung off me like I was a skeleton.

"Is it okay?" Li-Li said. She spoke to me in the mirror, my back to her, but also face-to-face.

"Maybe," I said. Nothing in my situation felt like more than hope or supposition. I massaged the muscle between my neck and shoulder.

"Your boss has been with police?" she said.

"Misunderstanding," I said. "It seems to be my fault."

"Your fault?" she said. I explained that public security had kept my boss confined in his Shanghai hotel while they investigated the mayor's death in Kaifeng—a city Leo had never set foot in.

"Did I make you miss your train?" I asked.

"No," she said. "I arrived in enough time."

She told me a man had fallen onto the tracks before they could depart.

"People tried to pull him back," she said. "I do not think he wanted the help. I waited and I wondered why I am going at all."

"Was he okay?"

"I don't know," she said. "I left."

"The captain from Kaifeng is convinced someone poisoned the mayor," I said. "Do you think Mr. Hu could do something like that?"

She frowned. She said softly: "I do not know what anyone will do."

She left the bathroom, and I heard the bedsprings squeak. Her words echoed in my ears, and I thought Li-Li had discovered as good a principle to live by as any. I threw the bloody washcloth into the trash, soaked a new one with cold water, and raised it gingerly to my cheek. When I joined her, Li-Li was sitting on the bed, both nightstand lamps on, staring into the closet.

"You gave that man everything?" she said. "And you trust that is the end?"

"Not everything," I said.

I pointed at the safe. Her mouth fell open, and she covered it.

She spun the combination, pulled the remaining money out, and we surveyed it between us. Her tired eyes, like mine, widened at how much was left.

"What would you do with it?" I asked her.

"If it were mine?"

"It could be ours," I said.

"It does not belong to me," she said.

"It didn't belong to Albert," I said. "It didn't even belong to the mayor." She considered this for a very long time.

"What if you just imagined it?" I said. "Where would you want to go?" She looked reluctant to think this over, as though she might commit graft or fraud even in the hypothetical.

"It's pretty in Guilin," she said finally. "Do you know it?"

"I've heard the name."

"Or the Li River," she said. "If you want to see mountains and river."

"That sounds very beautiful."

"Or the south of China," she said. "I have never seen it."

"And farther," I said. "Tibet. Or Cambodia. Angkor Wat."

"I want to see pyramids," she said. A fan kicked on and began to cycle. She didn't raise her voice to speak above it. "And cities. Beautiful cities."

"Which?" I said.

We began to recline.

"Venice and Paris for me," she said. "Or New York City. I have never been."

"I love Venice," I said.

She wore a white, almost-sheer V-neck undershirt. Above the rim of her pants poked a band of red cotton underwear.

"I could show you California," I said. "The rest of it, and better this time. We could drive down to Mexico. All the way to La Paz."

We pulled up the pillows and adjusted them behind our necks. She was so careful when she spoke that she barely opened her mouth. She'd washed off her makeup, tied back her hair. She talked with her hands up near her face. Her pale moles grew visible in the light.

I remembered a game Alex and I used to play. The oval mole on her forearm was Venice, I would say, and that raised one on her neck was New York, and I ran my finger from one to the other, a route. All the marks on her skin became the dots of cities on a map. The brown circle on Alex's heel was Istanbul or Buenos Aires, depending on where she fantasized that night of going. She would kick her foot out, laughing. She played the game on me, too, though I had so many more spots to choose from, between any two cities, a thousand forgotten, freckled towns. We dreamed together. I thought it might last forever—as though close would always stay close, intimacy outlast its contingent circumstances.

Li-Li and I talked, near but never touching, about all the places there were to see, until she'd fallen asleep, and I was drifting, and there rose an aberrant daylight of Shanghai's full sun.

SHANGHAI

O N THE TARMAC, fifty yards off, I caught a figure at the top of the rollaway stairs—hard hair, sagging slacks, short-sleeved dress shirt. Leo, slumped. By the time I was aboard Lightborn's plane, Leo had vanished into one of the guest cabins. A towheaded attendant seated me. Her skin was pale as the fjords, and her face looked rested six months of the year in total northern darkness. I asked her for an orange juice with lots of ice. She brought the ice in a terrycloth towel and held it toward my swollen eye.

I'd left Li-Li curled next to the money, my good-bye no more than a shameful note. She'd been hardly asleep when I was summoned back to the narrow strait of my circumstances by Robbie's call and a car downstairs. For my quiet disappearance, I could offer Li-Li only this explanation: I did not want to know if she would, or would not, take what wasn't hers. I couldn't bear to see her refuse the money, as she no doubt should, and I didn't want to see her succumb—as I also hoped she might—to start a life closer to the one she'd dreamed of. It seemed to me anymore that there was no action that did not leave in its wake an abiding sense of regret.

After we leveled off, I pushed open the door to Leo's cabin and found him asleep. An alcohol fume filled the airless compartment. The space was small but held a twin bed and a fold-down desk with a leather chair. On the nightstand was a can of club soda, half of it poured into a high-ball glass. I stood at the foot of his bed until the sense of a foreign presence took hold of him. He woke and looked at me blankly, trying to discover where he was. I knew that confusion.

His face was busted-veined and red-gray like a bruised apple. His feet searched for the floor, and even when he planted them, he looked unsure it wasn't water beneath him. Every action of his body looked painful, as though he'd been stricken with a muscular disorder, but he was able to make a show of composure, a veteran of many pretended sobrieties. He reached out and patted my arm hard twice, under the shoulder. He'd come to China thinking he'd outsmart Lightborn, arrange his own meetings, and try to hunt up a little more money for himself to feed the presidential ambitions no one else believed in. And now he was leaving with nothing, and even Lightborn would cut him loose. I almost pitied the wreck of him, even as my tongue wanted to sling fire.

"Here we are," I said.

"Here we are," he said, tapping the floor. He massaged his legs like they were asleep. He didn't ask about my face.

"Sit," he said.

His voice was low, muffled further by the air-breathing turbine engines. His eyes searched the cabin like he was sweeping it for bugs. I settled into the chair, and we sat two feet apart. I had a hard time peeling his puffy face away to find any recognizable expression.

"Theresa's up at the lake house. I suppose we'll lay low a few days," Leo said. "Hope nothing catches in the wind."

He closed his eyes, pinched the bridge of his nose with his thumb and forefinger.

"You owe me an explanation," I said.

"Owe you?" Leo said.

"Yes," I said. "Me."

He wouldn't speak above a whisper. I don't know who he thought might be listening—the sparse population of the East China Sea was thirty thousand feet below. Perhaps he felt possessed of a seismographic sensitivity, already registering the distant rumble of federal prosecutors who might want to discover what his Chinese entanglements with Armand Lightborn amounted to.

"You look tired," Leo said.

"Try to imagine," I said, "why I wouldn't have slept in five days."

"We're going to do this civilly," Leo said.

He paused for this to register, like counting the seconds between lightning and thunder.

"Do what?"

"You're young, and you were basically family," he said. "After your behavior, this is special treatment."

"My behavior?" I said. My anger felt better than a warm bath. "My behavior?"

Leo looked out the window, our blue planet below for his eyes to traverse in a glance.

"All I did was exactly what I thought you would have wanted," I said. The low oxygen of the pressurized cabin made me feel short of breath.

"What I wanted?" Leo said. "You're worse than this fucking migraine." And then for one long complaint, he didn't care who overheard. Leo started to accuse me, at full volume in great detail, of lying, taking money, running around with whores. He shouted at me that I'd compromised him in ways beyond remedy. I had extensive practice at being berated by Leo, and I endured his yelling in foot-staring silence. Leo could froth himself up over minor annoyances like cold meals or lost keys, but as he dressed me down over my "behavior" in China, it occurred to me he'd finally encountered a situation that filled his anger to capacity.

"Trust me," he said, as he finished his rant. "I heard it all."

Leo pushed past me into the aisle. It seemed Lightborn or Chinese police had enumerated my sins for Leo, but I wasn't the only guilty party—I had accusations of my own. I followed him to a curtained-off section at the rear of the plane. He twisted around the liquor bottles until he found a label he liked.

"I won't even get into this with you," Leo said. "You're fired, if you didn't already guess that. But I'm just too worn out. I will say I'm disappointed. I never thought you were so weak."

My ears popped, a sting I felt down into my neck.

"Yeah, you were exemplary, Leo."

"You see? That's what's disconcerting," he said. "That you still blame me for your faults. I'm a sinner, Luke. But at least I know it. Your problem is you don't have the courage to be honest with yourself."

"You're unbelievable," I said.

Leo wanted the world to see him as a calm port, a reckless man grown wise. I saw him at sea, hoping these outbursts of faith and penitence would save him from sinking in the chop of his envies and failures.

"You left me stranded," I said.

"We're all fucking stranded." His voice rose. "But I would have met you in Shanghai if you hadn't gotten me picked up by the police instead."

Here I cut him off and began my own tirade. I felt like I was addressing a jury. I confessed to him that, yes, I'd participated in the banquet charade. But in my defense I was only in Kaifeng because of Leo, and he'd lied to me about our reasons for being in China at all. I told him how reckless he'd been, sending me to Kaifeng alone, and how stupid, chasing money to Shanghai and thinking he could run his scheme in secret. Even Polk had been unaware.

"What are we talking about, Luke?" he said. "Lightborn tell you all this?"

"You're delusional," I said, "If you think anyone was telling me anything. Polk's nearly dead, by the way—nearly dead and still concerned about protecting your reputation."

He ignored Polk's name. "You've got no right to hold yourself above me, Luke. Don't kid yourself."

"I'm on Lighborn's fucking jet," I said. "How much kidding myself do you think I have left?"

Bitterness stooped Leo's shoulders—it was a physical malady for him.

"Lightborn was going to fuck you," I said. "There is no Bund. It's a shell company."

"You think I don't know Lightborn's an asshole?" he said. "How stupid do you think I am? I wouldn't trust that guy to save me a seat while I went to the bathroom."

He repeated Lightborn's name under his breath, hateful. I wondered if that was the only possible outcome, when you'd admired someone for so long, shadowed and studied them so astutely. Maybe you couldn't help but grow to despise everything you'd imitated, your mimicry confronting you every day with evidence of your limitations. I watched Leo sulk in his skin. It was like watching a snake try to skid backward into the discarded husk of itself.

"I just want to say it now." I ached for some kind of dignity. "If people show up demanding that I talk about this, I'm going to talk."

Leo didn't flinch. "What would you have to discuss, Mr. Slade?"

"I'm not making a threat, Leo. But if you think that because you were a friend of my father, or any of that, that I'm just going to shut up if the FBI starts asking questions . . ."

"Oh, Luke," he said. His "oh" gave me chills, like our situation was all sewn up in his mind. "Give your father more credit. He understood this stuff better than you ever will."

I tried to ignore his insinuation. I didn't want to hear anything that would contradict the image of my father as I remembered him. Every morning since my father had died had been a day less new and just more compromised than the last. I needed to hold his memory apart and upright.

"You can do whatever it is you think you have to do," Leo continued. "But be sensible, Luke. What do you think all your escorts and dirty money make you look like on a witness stand? Or in the media? If you want to try to tell a convoluted money story about me and a bunch of foreign executives with unpronounceable names . . . well, I'm just asking: which story do you think people will be more interested to hear—mine or yours?"

I leaned back against the wall and felt the engines vibrating. I'd done so little I could defend. At least I felt in the right for finally being an enemy to him.

"Don't think cutting you loose gives me any joy. I've thought of you almost as a son," Leo said. "You know the first thing Theresa asked once she found out I was okay?"

I stood stupefied.

"You," Leo said. "She asked about you."

"Nice of her to be concerned." The words came out painfully. I was reaching out for a thread of self-possession, but I'd begun to lose hope of grasping it. "So what'd you tell her?"

"I told her the truth," he said. "The whole truth."

"You think she's telling you the whole truth?" I said. It was a pathetic way to try to hurt him. He brushed this off, too.

"You have to live with your own conscience, Luke," Leo said. "I live with mine. That's all there is to say."

"Fuck you," I said. "And fuck her."

Leo finished his stinking cup.

"It's true," he said. "She'll fuck anyone."

He chose his bottle and went back to his cabin, and I heard the door latch. We never spoke again that night—or any other night, either. My letter of resignation would arrive by certified mail. I'm certain it was Glenn who wrote it. The stated reason was "moral turpitude." Leo included return postage and a space for my signature: I put my name to it, every word.

NEW YORK CITY

I CAN STILL SEE Alex standing on the Manhattan Bridge the night I returned from China. It felt right, hung out over the East River, no land beneath us, suspended between two boroughs. The winds were fierce and she, always sensitive, was wrapped in a fitted trench coat. Trains screeched beside us on the rails, conductors at the helm finishing a day of running back and forth between Astoria and Bay Ridge, Coney Island and Yankee Stadium. Boat lights leaked over the East River. A salty wind kicked up, and with one gust I felt like I was right back in Shanghai, my arm bent up behind me while I stared at the Huangpu River.

The view from the bridge was spoiled some by a chain-link fence, high and curved inward, spot-welded onto the original waist-high railing. More fencing stood between the walkway and the subway tracks. The observation bays looking over the East River, like stations for patron saints in a church, had all been padlocked. Apparently, from the point of view of the municipal government, anyone who might pause, to look south to the Brooklyn Bridge and the Woolworth Building, or north to the white and blue lights of the Empire State Building—anyone who desired to take stock of the city, or of himself—would invariably come to a single and overwhelming conclusion: jump! What else could it mean that the earlier century had built these bays as spaces for contemplation, and we had added padlocks and "No Trespassing" signs?

We shared the bridge with a policeman on bike patrol and a Chinese woman carrying leeks and bok choy that poked out of an orange plastic bag. Two battered old drunks passed a can of Steel Reserve back and forth, leaning against the fence. The officer dismounted to move them along. Trains roared by, and we saw a hundred multiethnic mirrors of our own solemn faces looking out of the B and Q trains at nothing in particular.

Alex kept glancing at the broken capillaries on my face. She listened to my story—money, China, police—with her face turned toward the southern tip of the city. Her reaction struck me as deliberately stifled, perhaps from shock or confusion. But I'm sure I confirmed for her that if she ever had doubts about what she'd left behind in DC, she shouldn't. We mounted the middle hump of the bridge in silence. The full skyline grew downward out of the dark—the building tops visible first and then their foundations stretching out to touch the ground.

"You know, I got an invite from my old boss to some fundraiser thing tonight at the Waldorf," she said finally. "I wondered if you and Leo would be there."

"Your old boss is dead," I said.

"I meant the chief of staff."

"The one who had a thing for you?"

"He didn't have a thing for me."

"He must have invited every staffer to Antibes," I said.

I'd never been able to connect the hazy first time I came to meet Alex in New York with any other visit. There was a subway we took over a bridge without a name across a river I thought was the Hudson and later learned was not. We'd walked to a mysterious bar on some shrieking avenue in Brooklyn, where I sat with her trying to piece together what was going to become of us. I remembered the church across the street and its huge marquee: *Jesucristo Es El Señor*. Though I knew now that the train was the Q, the bridge the Manhattan, the river the East beneath us, which is really an estuary, and the street distant Fourth Avenue, I had still never been able to assimilate any of that later knowledge into my first picture of New York City, when it was so new and unknown to me. Now she lived with two other girls on the garden level of a poorly maintained townhouse just off the Brooklyn side of this bridge, in a makeshift bedroom where a folding screen was her only privacy. They were all giving up whatever they had to live here, no one sure yet who would bear it out and prosper and who would be just more fuel, burned up to realize other people's dreams.

"Can you take tomorrow off?" I asked. I had so much more to say.

"Can you?"

"I don't have a job," I said.

"So you're stuck in Baltimore," she offered. It was one of our old jokes—anything interminable, inconvenient, hopeless. An Amtrak train, stuck in Baltimore.

"I thought we'd go do something," I said.

"Don't expect me to absolve you of anything," Alex said. "It's not my place, and I don't want to."

Her disappointment was in the white of her eye, in her refusal to look at me. But I would rather see myself with her eyes than with my own compromised ones.

"I can be better," I said. "Does that count for something?"

"In horseshoes and hand grenades," she said.

"Come have a drink with me."

"Luke," she said. "I shouldn't."

I liked thinking Alex was still free, that she existed at the loose ends of the possible. I wasn't interested in hearing her contradict it.

"Is that where you work?" I asked, stabbing my finger out toward a hollow to the right of the Woolworth Building.

"No," she said. "You can't see it from here."

She started to give me a roundabout letdown.

"I don't need to hear about it, Alex," I said. "If you can't get a drink, then you can't."

"If it helps, I'm about to break it off," she said.

"How's he going to take it?"

"I've been avoiding it a month."

"So let's walk," I said. "We can sort each other out."

"I'm so tired," she said.

"I'm half dead."

"I'm not skipping every bar in the city until you find the one empty one you like," Alex said.

"The first place you like, that's where we'll go," I said. "Wasn't there a bar near that dumpling place?"

"I haven't been there forever," she said.

"I miss it," I said.

I hoped at least I could make her understand where I'd arrived, after China—what I intended.

"I'm starting over," I said.

She took this in silence. The downward slope of the bridge into Manhattan was dead of pedestrians, alive only with late construction spotlights. The black car-service Lincolns tapped their horns at every slowdown, and that night I remember thinking of them as the underworld ferrymen of the East River. We passed an apartment covered in graffiti, right above East Broadway, immigrant tenements jammed with delivery boys and dishwashers. Alex's phone rang, lost deep in her purse, and she had to stop and crouch down and use both hands to search it out of the bag's maw.

A skinny Chinese man inside a dimly lit apartment, ten floors up, eye level with me, clicked on a single-burner stove. Over the flame sat a huge black wok. He glared straight ahead from his open window, entirely still. He might have seen me return his stare. It was a strange night, lived in innocence of knowledge I would soon acquire. Because even by morning I knew about Mr. Hu. That much turned up when I went looking for news of our last days in Shanghai—news of Leo, or news of myself. Instead, I found this "disgraced project manager," as various reports put it, from "an international firm." Tabloid reporting: The man had bound his hands with red rope, filled his clothing with stones. A container ship called in the sighting. The police fished his waterlogged body from the Huangpu River. A note in poorly wrought calligraphy was pinned inside Mr. Hu's jacket, lines from a lament of Qu Yuan—*My heart was caught in a mesh that I could not disentangle; my thoughts were lost in a maze there was no way out of.*

Later, I would linger on the impression he left of a man at the end of his tether. I could hear all his cadences as those of someone who believes everything is finished for him, and not just finished, but squandered. And I came to believe it was true that Mr. Hu had killed his rival—only I didn't think he'd done it ambitiously, with hopes of prevailing, because Mr. Hu had already been discarded. Nor was it mere revenge, because so much of his rage seemed directed inward. He would have poisoned the mayor, I believed, simply for being the one who, in defeating him, had also shown him the emptiness of his own strivings. It was some part despair, some part nihilism. I imagined that after I'd left Mr. Hu at that riverfront restaurant in Shanghai, he'd ordered himself an extravagant meal—he'd already thrown the die and was only waiting for the croupier to read the numbers and collect his losses. We are shackled to dead men, all of us.

But that night with Alex, no word had yet reached me of his reported suicide—that night I had no reaction for Mr. Hu at all. I only watched a woman appear in the kitchen of a tenement apartment and yell at the man standing over his wok—her mouth wide open, arms flailing. He responded by pointing. Soon the woman came over to the window and followed his raised finger, which indicated either me, or something beyond me. I lifted my hand to wave at them both. They pulled the blind—as I would have done, had it not been me raising my hand to wave; as I would have done, had it been me in a city so far from home.

I turned back to Alex.

"This is a fresh start," I called to her. She returned the phone to her bag and began to hurry toward me. She had consternation in her face, about what, I didn't know—me, or the other man.

"A clean slate," I said.

I faced her and waited.

"There's no such thing," she said, and she made up the steps between us.

ACKNOWLEDGMENTS

I'm grateful to my agent, Henry Dunow, for his editorial acumen and steady bedside manner, and to Rolph Blythe, Nicole Antonio, Megan Fishmann, Kelly Winton and the whole Counterpoint team.

My own trips to China, and continued correspondence with people I met there, form the backbone of this book, but I owe a massive debt to the expert work of other writers. Particularly important to my understanding of contemporary China were *Oracle Bones*, by Peter Hessler, *Out of Mao's Shadow*, by Philip Pan, *Will the Boat Sink the Water?: The Life of China's Peasants* by Chen Guidi and Wu Chuntao, and *The Corpse Walker*, by Liao Yiwu. I have at certain points taken small liberties with a city geography or with the timing of certain news events.

The support of the Iowa Writers' Workshop (Sam, Connie, Deb, Jan: thank you!) and of Jeff and Vicki Edwards helped me bring this novel to a close. Thank you to my teachers there: Kate Christensen, Ethan Canin, Charles D'Ambrosio, Andrew Sean Greer, Marilynne Robinson. For a week each spring, Antonio and Carla Sersale open their exquisite Positano hotel to the Sirenland Writer's Conference, and I owe thanks to their hospitality and the community it fosters. Thank you to dear friends Dani Shapiro, Michael Maren, and Hannah Tinti for keeping that community alive.

To my indispensable mentors—the devious, blistering intelligence of Jim Shepard; the wisdom of Charles Baxter; the magic of Aimee Bender. Karen Russell—mind twin, insomniac—thank you for refusing sleep and for text messages a mile long.

Iowa friends who talked late into the night—Brian Booker, Jake Hooker, Sara Martin, Dina Nayeri, Jen Percy, Devika Rege, Jamie Watkins. And Jamie again, for a late, great read. Jake Hooker—who spent more than a decade in China, and received a Pulitzer Prize he never talks about for his journalistic efforts there—patiently read two drafts and answered my rudimentary questions over chicken tenders at the Bluebird Diner. Thank you for that time, Jake.

To Mom and Dad, Kiel and Liz, Mike Beard, Jim and Martha Thompson and, finally and gloriously, to Hazel June: I live on your love and support. The El Centro crew, the Frequency, the Shadows: Essential inspiration and more essential distraction.

This book would not exist—not in its present form and not in any form—without Nathan Ihara and Karen Thompson Walker. At my most stubborn low points it was your readings, your friendship, your insistence, your brilliance that made me keep working. Thank you for everything, Karen: Your wisdom, love, care, and our little girl.